For Robert Charles,

The Butcher's Daughter

Jane E James

First published in 2019 by Bloodhound Books

www.bloodhoundbooks.com

Print ISBN 978-1-912986-23-1

Also By Jane E James

The Crying Boy

Information Sourced from Wikipedia

Little Downey is a picturesque old fishing village situated at the southeast corner of Bride's Bay, Pembrokeshire, Wales. Here, you will find a shingle beach and a tiny untended cove. At low tide, the bay widens out to form a coastal walkway to more accessible family-friendly beaches. With a mainly older population of 1,300 and the nearest town thirteen miles away, the village is self-sufficient, boasting one pub, a post office-cum-grocery-store, a butcher's shop and slaughterhouse. It even has an asylum on its doorstep! Up until 1911, Little Downey was a popular holiday destination for families, but a spate of unexplained cliff-top suicides gave rise to its gruesome new nickname of Suicide Bay, which saw the former seaside resort go into decline.

The House By The Sea

Its pitched roof and gothic windows look down on the beach and Suicide Bay, where people come not to enjoy the view, but to deliberately step off the crumbling cliff edge and topple to their deaths—or at least that's what the regulars in Little Downey's only pub, The Black Bull, would have you believe. Perhaps it is this macabre history that gives the house by the sea its melancholy air, as if it yearns for happier times.

A nicotine-stained porch wraps itself around the half-timber, half-brick dwelling and the decking creaks with every tentative step. A child's swing, left to rust, sways eerily. You know without being told that nobody has sat in it for a long time. The stillness of the place is unsettling. Even the birds do not rest long on the dilapidated picket fence that zigzags its way around the overgrown plot. The spell is broken only when a rat scurries out of an old tin barbecue and takes off down the well-worn path to the shingle beach. So off you go, following the same trail of grey sand that *it* took. First, you must pass a derelict outdoor building whose whitewashed walls have turned a rotten-tooth yellow.

There are rusty bars at every small black window and nothing could persuade you to peer inside. Bad things happen to those who do. You do not know how you know this. You just do. So, you keep your eyes averted. Only when you are safely by do you notice that the sky is duller than it should be and when you arrive at the beach and look up, you can at last fully appreciate the dramatic hilltop location of the house. Now that there's a little more distance between it and you, the shadowy windows do not feel as menacing; until you see the silhouette of a woman with long black hair standing dangerously close to the cliff edge, looking down on you, and then you become paralysed with fear.

Chapter 1

Little Downey – Natalie

Sixteen Years Earlier

I was seven when my father took me to see the animals for the first time. Although I had been promised piglets and newborn lambs, the first animal I met was a grey pony with the kindest eyes I ever saw. Far kinder than my father's, whose were steely blue and insistent on me being the boy I was not. The pony had bits of straw stuck to its coat and stood in an outdoor pen with its head held low. It must have carried many children on its back because when I stroked its ears, it breathed on my fingers and looked for a treat in my pocket.

The sound of snorting and shuffling coming from inside the grey windowless building up ahead was all the encouragement I needed to go in search of more animals. For once, I did not object to my father's rough handling as he prodded me forward.

Together, we passed through double doors that clanged noisily even though there was no wind and I saw my father's shadow stretch onto the ground in front of us, turning him into even more of a giant than usual. Once inside, he instructed me to "wait" while he went off to take care of some business. This was not unusual nor entirely unexpected. I was used to being left on my own but I wasn't known for being particularly obedient, so it wasn't long before I wandered off, drawn to the sound of pigs squealing.

First, I had to conquer my fear of the shadows that crowded around me. The darkness had never been my friend, but I was not fond of sunshine either, preferring to remain indoors. As a result, my pale white skin and big black eyes made children younger than myself nervous. My classmates already thought me odd and were one of the reasons I hardly ever went to school. My father said I needed "curing" but I did not know what he meant by that; not yet anyway.

The grunting of the pigs made it sound like they were having fun, a game of tag perhaps, so I shuffled forward in my too-big wellington boots along a sloping wooden walkway with metal rails around it. It felt restrictive, as if there would not be room to turn around if I wanted to. A feeling I did not like. The smell of fresh animal dung reassured me I was getting closer. In the distance, I could hear the muffled whine of a saw and a cow frantically mooing; sounds that puzzled me because they did not seem to go together.

Then, from behind me, I heard the whinny of the pony. It sounded frightened. So, I stopped walking. Stopped breathing. Stopped feeling. By then I was as frightened as it was. If I did hear something else—a single shot perhaps—I have long since erased it from my memory. The silence afterwards was even more unbearable and it felt as if the blackness had pushed itself right into my face, like the clenched fist of a school bully, yet I refused to call out in fear. I had stopped wanting or needing anyone's help a long time ago. At seven, I already knew about suffering in a way that I shouldn't.

After a while, I became aware of a greasy burning smell that reminded me of the hot bacon rolls my mother used to hand out on Sunday mornings before church, her hair still in rollers. It was the kind of smell that made me want to cover my nose with my hand, but my boots noisily squelching in something sticky helped take my mind off it. When I eventually came up against a metal door that had spongy fist marks in it, I pushed it open and was greeted by a different smell—one I had no trouble identifying— my father's bed reeked of it. "Working men's sweat is something to be proud of," he would protest whenever he caught me wrinkling my nose up at it. I already knew not to believe a word he said.

The powerful overhead lighting made me feel dizzy after the dark but I could see enough to know that the inside of the building matched the outside—it was sterile and cold. Everywhere I looked, splashes of red, purple and green showed up against grey concrete and gleaming metal. All around me there was laughter as if the three adult men standing in front of me couldn't have witnessed anything funnier than a little girl's confusion on stumbling into their unfamiliar world. Judging by the expression on their faces, they took pleasure in it.

One of the men was known to me. Bob Black used to be a regular visitor to the house, always speaking more to my mother than my father, whispering things in her ear that made her blush. She never laughed when he was around, which was out of character.

Short and ordinary looking, with round spectacles that sometimes slipped to the end of his nose, I could tell by the way Bob stood with his hands on his hips that he was in charge. His surprisingly large hands were wrapped around a saw that had more teeth in it than I did. I was still waiting for two of mine to grow back. The missing ones had been thrown away. There was no point keeping them as there weren't any tooth fairies in Little Downey.

When I finally saw what the men in overalls wanted me to see—the head of a bullock sitting in a puddle of its own blood—I felt as if I had been punched in the face. The bullock's eyes were black, like mine, and seemed to call out for help as though it thought it was still alive, but I knew this to be impossible because the rest of it was dangling from a hind leg strung up on a heavy chain. Blood pumped out of two gashes cut into its massive chest and dripped into a concrete drainage area below.

Drip. Splat. Drip.

In a world of stainless steel, where sounds echoed and intensified, that is exactly how it sounded. A short drip followed by a louder more ominous splat and then another high-speed drip. I watched in horror as the river of blood found its way to an overfed plughole that belched greedily with every swallow.

My eyes darted back and forth between the headless carcass and the three men who were shouting "Beef coming" at the tops of their voices, and I finally understood why my father felt the need to remind me I was a butcher's daughter before allowing me to set foot in this place. Clearly, he had been afraid I would get upset and make a fool of him. Rather than face up to his latest betrayal, I watched spellbound as a line of bobbing black and white heads and swishing tails were herded single file through a gangway. These cows were much smaller than the dead bullock and appeared docile, as if used to being handled. Their swollen udders swayed from side to side, leaking milk and turning the air sour. Without knowing much about cows, living cows that is, I could tell these were "old gals". I could also tell that they did not want to die, because every one of them looked frightened. Yet they waited in an orderly line as the lead cow was loaded into a galvanized steel stun box; jumping only when the hiss of the pneumatic gate slid down in front of her.

All by itself, my thumb found its way into the deepest corner of my mouth as I watched the men advance on the cow. She was shaking as much as I was. In my head, I named her Daisy, knowing all along that this was not a good idea. I later found out my father was watching from a short distance away; waiting to see how I would react. To Father, this was just another one of his tests. But it was a moment that would irreversibly seal all our fates in a way he could not have anticipated.

Chapter 2

There was more laughter as each of the men took it in turns to try to kill a beast that plain refused to go down. I could tell by their sweaty red-faced excitement that this did not happen often but when it did it broke the monotony of their day. Daisy's distressed bellowing meant the rest of the herd were becoming increasingly anxious, pawing at the ground, defecating and rolling their eyes. This made the men nervous too, so they renewed their efforts to bring Daisy down. As they waited to see if they could stun her once and for all, she and I glanced at each other and I saw the terrified whites of her eyes acknowledge my existence. I sensed that the poor creature was disappointed with humans and felt she had every right to be. I knew such shame, I wet myself right there on the spot, not caring that my boots were splattered with my own urine.

With hands as big as shovels, Bob aimed a bolt gun at Daisy's head and this time it worked. The powerful crack made both me and Daisy jump, but the latter would never get up again. As soon as the side rail was released, her body slid out on its side, steam coming off it. Words like "beyond the farm gate" and "the killing floor" were not new to me but now that I had witnessed them for myself, they took on a sickening new significance.

Instead of waiting to see the next cow being loaded into the stun box, I ran out of the bloodied room, which stunk of freshly slaughtered meat and followed a gruesome conveyor belt being used to transport the wet bodies of unborn calves into a chilling room. There, I hid behind a tank overflowing with blood, while workers in white overalls and hairnets wrestled with the carcasses of butchered cows. When I was sure no one was looking, I ducked out back into an animal holding area, which reeked of ammonia and fear.

Everywhere I looked, pink-bottomed pigs lay on their branded sides, tongues lolling out of their elongated snouts. If I had not already witnessed the slaughtering of the cows, I would have assumed they were simply sleeping. Though dead, they were much nicer to look at than the angry pink-cheeked men who worked there.

One pig had managed to escape the massacre and was scrambling to get out of the pen. I did not try to reassure it that it would be all right, because that would have been a lie. And no matter what anyone else in Little Downey said, I wasn't a liar. Ignoring the pig's frantic squeals for help, because there was nothing I could do, I crept into an adjoining steam-filled room. Through a gap in the awful mist, I could see another pig, much cleaner than the one I had left behind, being whisked around in a huge metal machine containing boiling water. The same greasy burning smell from before was at its worst in there. The stench was unlike anything I had ever come across. A combination of boiling meat and burnt hair.

***

As if it happened only yesterday, I can see myself standing there—a little girl with black unbelieving eyes—watching in horror as the pig turned over in the broiling machine; cloudy eyes bulging and bloody hooves flaying. I was only seven, but there was no one to wipe away the blood smears from my own face; nobody to remove me from a place of bloodshed that no child should find themselves in. My mother did not come to rescue me that day or on any other because she had toppled to her death a few weeks before; becoming the latest victim of Suicide Bay's so-called cliff top suicides.

Despite losing my mother at such an early age *and* losing count of the number of times I'd been told to "toughen up", I think, looking back, I'd done a pretty good job of doing exactly that. My father expected a lot from me, girl or not, because one day I was going to inherit his butcher's business. At least that was what he was always saying. Until then, there was to be no crying, screaming or talking back—*Frank's Law* he called it. For once, I agreed with him, making up my mind not to cry. I was too young to know where such thoughts came from but after being tricked into visiting the slaughterhouse that day, I knew there was nothing he could do that would make me eat the flesh of an animal again. Not even if he slammed my head into a plate of raw meat, like he had the last time I stood up to him. Nor would I take over the butcher's shop as he expected me to. Butcher's daughter or not.

Chapter 3

Thornhaugh

'Then'

I wake up at Thornhaugh. Familiar. Menacing. Safe. Terrifying, Thornhaugh. No matter what I do, or where I go, it will not let go of its grasp on me. I wonder if perhaps after all this time, Thornhaugh *is,* and always will be, my real home. During World War II, US Intelligence Forces occupied the three-storey Tudor building and there are leftover relics to prove this—old typewriters that were once used in the CIA typing pool, whose keys are now eerily silent. Set in ten acres of woodland and made from traditional red brick, it has a sweeping drive with elaborate iron gates and has every appearance of being a country house hotel. Except it is not! The Thornhaugh of today is a mental institution.

When I hear Dr Moses' familiar tread outside the door, my heart sinks. Rather than think about how he is going to react when he sees the fresh cuts on my arms, I think about the terrible nightmare I had last night, where everyone I knew kept on insisting that my mother was dead but, in my heart, I did not believe them. I still don't, come to that. The dream was there on my pillow when I woke up and stayed with me all morning while my head was still clear and not yet blunted by medication. I have been warned, many times, that these nightmares are a hindrance to my getting better.

'And you do want to get better, don't you, Natalie?' Dr Moses will insist on knowing. His disappointment in me is obvious, but as my doctor, he understands that I sometimes slip into a world of blackness in order to escape the truth. That blackness can take various forms, including self-harming, but I don't think even he is aware of the extent of my problem. I am grateful that he finds time for special long-term patients like me though, because without the calming, gentle influence of that man, who is more uncle and protector than doctor, I doubt I would be considering returning home.

After my latest setback, I am surprised that he still thinks it is a good idea to send me away, but apparently that is his intention. I do not know how I feel about this. All I know is, the thought of returning to my father's house makes me want to cut some more. Hating what goes on inside my head, I remind myself of a mad dog I once saw on the beach who could not stop attacking the waves, despite never getting anywhere, and I wonder who else but me wakes on a glorious morning like this and immediately has such black thoughts. The answer comes to me on my next breath. My mother of course.

They say that daughters eventually turn into their mothers and I have good reason to believe this to be true in my case because my life has turned into a living nightmare, as my own mother's did. In the end, it was mental illness that destroyed her, and I worry the same thing will happen to me. "Everyone has to die sometime," she used to say, in that disarming, carefree way of hers that made it sound as if death didn't matter. And perhaps it doesn't. Because as I lie here, with my long black hair spilling out on the pillow, I imagine she is close by; that her hand is resting a few inches from mine. And why not? Her warm breath against my face feels as real as anything else I have experienced today.

The truth is, I am no longer sure what *is* real anymore. At times, a black cloud occupies my mind, fogging up the past. Sometimes, I remember with clarity everything that has happened to me; other times I am lost and confused, suspicious even of those I love. They accuse me of seeing only what I want to see but I see things no one in their right mind would *choose* to see. I try to explain that I feel as if I am a ghost, flitting in and out of people's lives, barely there at any one time, but no one listens; except when it's bad stuff, and then it gets written down and repeated back to me in a dramatic tone of voice, which makes me want to laugh aloud. *But I do not. Because that truly would be insane.*

They say the psychotic imaginings I sometimes experience can be caused by a sudden withdrawal of the medication they have prescribed for me, but I do not believe this. All I know is, on the days when I deliberately stop taking my pills, the world is a less confusing place. That's when hazy memories from the past, the kind they don't want me to remember, haunt me, until I start to think that I am not the mad one here. They are.

***

In the afternoon I am summoned to the library, where I have been warned not to touch the rare and irreplaceable books. I look out onto the landscaped lawns instead, which are surrounded by gravel walkways that do not lead anywhere, except back to Thornhaugh. A gardener, high up on a ladder, wrestles with the claustrophobic ivy that clings to the dark and shadowy east wing where I was kept against my will for endless winters, a pale white face pressed up against a long grey window.

As I watch patients meandering about the grounds, I realise belatedly that none of them are known to me. I have spent most of my childhood within these walls, thirteen years in fact, but I have made no effort to make friends, mainly because I always felt I was not like *them. Them,* is a word that can be used to describe either patients or staff; depending on whose side you are on. Now that I am finally leaving, I watch *them* with renewed interest. Nurses escort some but others sit alone on benches and pluck at their clothing. I get the feeling that if I came back tomorrow, they would still be there, doing exactly the same thing.

I should be happy because I am going home. But inside I am terrified. The same scared little girl I have always been. I dare not let on that I have my doubts, that I am not sure I am ready, otherwise...

Through the partially open door, I catch a glimpse of the grand staircase and gold leaf ceiling belonging to the main hall; a place of beauty that largely goes unnoticed here, blinded as we are by our own afflictions. Back when Thornhaugh was a wedding venue, brides used to have their pictures taken gracing the oak staircase and I find myself wondering if I will ever marry. I often daydream about slipping my arms into the cool silky folds of a wedding gown and having it fastened by my father's hands.

I am not allowed in the main parts of the house though and perhaps for that reason, I long to explore its forbidden rooms. Sitting here, in the old-fashioned library, in the smaller of the two leather armchairs, has me imagining I have gone back in time, to another life. I suppose this tendency to dip in and out of different worlds is why I have been kept under lock and key so long.

There is a flurry of excitement at the door as Dr Moses finally makes an appearance. Behind him, a blurring of white uniform, stockinged leg *and too much perfume*. In he comes, appearing stern and serious, shooing out the nurses and closing the door on their indignant faces. But as soon as we are alone, he smiles and takes his place in the chair opposite. A fatherly figure with a grey beard, he observes me kindly enough, but although I am a grown woman, I cannot meet his eye, because he is looking down on my bent head as if I am still an inconsequential child. Under such well-meant scrutiny, I feel like one.

'You think you're ready, Natalie?' Dr Moses appears doubtful.

I nod and look at my hands in my lap, resisting the urge to bite my fingernails but losing the battle to pinch and twist as hard as I can the skin between my thumb and forefinger. The pain calms me as no sedative can.

'Your family doesn't think so.'

At this, my head bounces up. The very mention of my father causes my face to sharpen.

'You're the doctor. What do you think?' I demand haughtily.

Dr Moses does not like to be challenged, not even by me, who he looks upon as his own daughter. However, like my real father, his disappointment is obvious. His eyes blink away from me and grow distant. Then, from underneath an elbow, he removes a Manila folder and places it on his lap. Always immaculately dressed, he wears a suit in a pale shade of grey that is the same colour as his eyes. In all my life, I have never seen him without a silk tie and cufflinks. I watch him flick through pages of typewritten notes and notice that the file has my name on. *Case notes – Natalie Powers,* it says, and my curiosity is piqued. The content must be particularly damning because Dr Moses appears deeply troubled.

'You always do that. Look at your notes when you don't know what to say,' I observe.

Dr Moses leans back in his chair and appraises me clinically. 'What if you start doing it again?'

'I won't.' I'm determined, because it is important that he believes me.

'The law says I can't keep you here against your will. But if you screw up, Natalie, you could end up being sectioned indefinitely.'

Chapter 4

Little Downey Beach

'Now'

The gulls can scream and taunt me all they like but I will not budge from my favourite rock, where I sit, looking out to sea. The outcrop is smooth and cold against my skin, like the blade of a knife. A feeling I like. But the sea betrays me; because it is calm, unlike how I feel. Glancing over my shoulder, I glare at the house by the sea, whose shadow I have never been able to escape. It figures in my life as a cruel older sister might. Even from here, my old home appears neglected and uncared for. *Home.* Did I really use that word, if only in my head? I know that if I stare long enough at its creepy windows, I will see the silhouette of a ghost staring back at me. My mother is always there, waiting, somewhere, in the distance.

The smaller gulls keep to the skies, I notice, but the larger more aggressive herring gulls hold their ground. Their screeching would send a chill up most people's spines. But not mine. The biggest of them dances on the spot and flaps its wings. It has my father's eyes. Small. Blue. Cold. The authoritative stance is similar too. I stretch out a hand, only for it to attack me with its beak. The red staining on the end of its bill immediately makes me think of blood. Glancing at my ghostly white legs which are crisscrossed with angry scars—a plethora of old and new cuts—I fight back the urge to dig in my nails and open them up.

Instead, I take the photograph out of my pocket and look for fresh clues in my mother's face, even though I have looked at this picture a thousand times before. *Why did you do it? Why did you have to go away?* These are the same questions I ask myself every day before fresh doubt sets in, like—*But what if she didn't do it? What if she didn't go away?* I try to look at her as if I am seeing her for the first time. *What do you see, Natalie?* I ask myself. I see that my mother has the same serious face and haunted eyes as me and is beautiful in an intense, dreamy sort of way. Her hair is long and black, like mine, but there is a lightness to her eyes that is absent in my own. People tell me I look just like her but I suspect they say this to be kind. Like me, she is painfully thin. I am twenty-three and I have still not filled out as I had hoped to. Odd that she should look so serious when I remember her being quite the opposite. On occasion, she was even able to make my father laugh, which was mostly unheard of back then. Zero chance now, I reckon. She often accused him of taking himself too seriously and I wonder if this is where I get my solemnity.

Thinking about my mother still makes me feel sad but sometimes I get angry too. There are times, like today, when I hate her more than I ever loved her. *How could she leave me at a time when I needed her most?* I sigh and hunch my shoulders, tired of the same old arguments that go on inside my head. Guilt haunts me though. I must be as bad as they say I am to have such thoughts about my own mother. As for my father...

It is time. I cannot put this off any longer.

I scoot a pebble into the sea and slip on my sandals, noticing that my toes have turned blue from dangling in the water too long. As I get to my feet, a breeze lifts the hair off my shoulders to partially cover my face. Through this blindfold, I can still see the distant rooftops of the village beckoning. Somewhere amongst them is my father's shop.

Chapter 5

Little Downey

An old-fashioned bell above the shop door announces my arrival long before I'm ready to enter, yet everyone's eyes are on me as soon as I step inside. Out of the corner of one eye, I see a blur of red, white and grey cuts of meat in a glass counter and standing behind it is a man I do not automatically recognise because he has aged dramatically. *Did you expect him not to have altered?* Even though he saws energetically through a carcass of beef, I can tell that his size and strength has diminished. I will myself not to feel good about this but at the same time I cannot help willing him to glance up. To notice me. He is aware of my presence, but deliberately keeps his eyes downcast, giving me time to get to know his face again. The nose is bigger than I remembered and redder than the steak mince in the window. The thinning hair is also new. For some reason, this cuts me to the core and I feel my eyes well up, even though I have warned myself against this. *Don't go all soft on him, Natalie.*

He might have changed but the shop has not. It is still dark and cluttered inside and the colourful bunting does little to jolly it. The jam pots with frilly covers have faded labels on them that are impossible to read, and over there, in the corner, is a rusted chest freezer whose lid used to catch. I wonder if it is still used to store game. An older boy, somebody who worked for my father, once shut me inside it, ignoring my screams to be let out. Inside there were dead animals. My skin crawls at the memory of their bodies lying next to me.

I turn my attention to the clean-shaven blond-haired assistant who has not taken his eyes off me since I entered the shop. Could this be the same boy who put me in the freezer *for a joke?* He is a few years older than me and looks more like a college graduate than a butcher's assistant but his striped apron and white-indoor hands indicate otherwise. He has a look of the village about him. The same eyes. Small. Blue. Cold. Like my father's. Luckily for me, I inherited my mother's beautiful brown eyes that are so dark as to appear black. Although he is staring at me open-mouthed, I decide there is something likeable about the young man's face, even if he does have Little Downey stamped all over him, just like the meat in the counter.

Nobody moves. Nobody says anything. It is almost as if time stood still the second I walked through the door. But I know, better than most, that time is not something to be thrown away. Haven't I promised myself not to waste another second of it.

'Father,' I say, taking a deep breath.

'Daughter.'

Behind me, there is a shocked intake of breath and I sense that multiple pairs of eyes are gawping at us. But my father bestows on me the most cursory of glances before resuming his hefty sawing. The eyes are as I remember and give nothing away.

Frank, my father, can hardly bring himself to speak. 'It's been a long time.'

My reply is also slow in coming. 'Thirteen years.'

***

Fighting back tears of rejection, I close the shop door behind me and almost trip over the butcher's bicycle propped up on the pavement outside. Each morning my father wheels it out, dusts off the sign that claims a tie which no longer exists— "Frank Powers & Daughter" and wheels it in again at night. I am surprised it has survived. My father disowned me years ago and judging by his reluctance to acknowledge me just now, continues to do so.

Not knowing what else to do, I make my way down the sloping hill towards the beach. The pavements are smooth, but hills go off in every direction, making walking difficult. Tucked away in a steep-sided valley adjacent to the coastline, there is no escaping Little Downey in the winter months when ice and snow make the roads impassable. Eight people are said to have disappeared during the severe winter of 1911 when the village was cut off from the rest of Wales. Although presumed dead, their bodies were never found.

I am not surprised when several villagers come out of their cottages to stare at me. Word soon gets around in a community of this size. One or two nod in recognition but mostly I am met with hostility. They have every right to be suspicious of me, but I am not immune to their reaction. These are my people, and many have known me since I was a girl.

Keeping my head down, I familiarise myself with the layout of the village and find nothing has changed. The pastel-coloured cottages still look as if they are about to tumble down the steep inclines they cling to. There are no new additions. Some of the cottages even have the same curtains hanging in the windows. Beyond the houses, rocky cliffs rise out of nowhere, 250 feet high. A stone's throw from the sea, the Pembrokeshire coastal path runs straight through the heart of the village, but visitors rarely come through here now. Outsiders are not welcome in Little Downey. Only those who are born here tend to end up staying.

To my left, up another hill, is Little Downey's only pub, a rustic seaside inn that overlooks the bay. It is an impressive building, painted white with glossy black woodwork. A few broken fishing boats, relics of times gone by, are docked side by side in a rocky cove beneath the pub, giving it a quaint air. I have never been inside the pub, but I know that this is where the likes of my father and his cronies go to talk shop. *Shop* being butchery, everyone's favourite subject in the domino corner of The Black Bull.

Feeling the hairs on the back of my neck prickle, I come to a standstill, certain that more prying eyes are on me. Sure enough, when I glance over my shoulder, I see that my father and his assistant have come out of the shop to see me off and I experience a strong sense of déjà vu, as if I have lived this moment many times before.

The two men are the same height but my father slouches with his hands in his apron pockets, his eyes hiding in the pavement, whereas the young man has his chin in the air and is staring boldly after me. I would give anything to know what they are saying.

Chapter 6

Little Downey – Frank

Frank rolls a set of keys around in his apron pocket until the metal feels warm against his fingers. As he watches his only daughter turn troubled eyes in his direction, the corner of his mouth twitches, as it sometimes does when he gets a whiff of bad meat.

He can feel today closing in around him like a dark cloud. And it is only going to get worse. All the same, there's nothing he'd like more than to cross the street and yell at everybody to go back inside.

What the hell do they think they are looking at? They should be minding their own business not poking their noses into his. He feels like kicking the hell out of the butcher's bike. Doesn't know why he bothered keeping it.

Frank Powers and Daughter be damned.

His young shop assistant, Daniel, who is no better than he should be, finally quits staring after Natalie and turns to frown at him. Frank wants to tell him that he is the boss and nobody gets to look at him that way, but he does not.

'Is she going to be trouble?' Daniel wants to know.

'I'll take care of my own. You worry about that delivery.' Frank grunts.

Chapter 7

Little Downey Beach – Natalie

I am a quarter of a mile from home, *there's that word again*, when I see the gypsies. They have set up camp on a patch of rough sandy grass, seeking shelter from the sun under the giant shadow of the cliff edge. They are far enough away not to be bothered by the incoming tide but close enough to enjoy the spoils of the beach. Every window belonging to the battered caravan is wide open, the metal door pinned back. Whoever is inside must be sweltering. From within, I can hear the whistle of a kettle getting louder as it prepares to scream. I close my eyes because I know exactly how this feels.

There are two deck chairs outside and a collection of tea towels hang from a makeshift washing line that barely moves in the stillness. An inflatable paddling pool, empty of water, sags in the heat—the air almost gone from it. Seagulls must already have been at the rubbish bags because a trail of litter spills onto the pebbled sand.

Parked up behind the caravan is a dusty old Mitsubishi Shogun with a flat rear tyre. I can only see half of it but I know its rusting chassis and damaged bodywork will not be tolerated long. It is an eyesore in an otherwise unspoilt location. Yet when I look up and see the house by the sea peering disapprovingly over the cliff edge, I find myself smiling. My father's house would throw stones down on the campsite if it could.

Raised among folk who refuse to have any truck with gypsies and who would have them run them out of town without any hesitation at all, I remember that my mother envied their unconventional lifestyle and thought their superstitions and fortune-telling were romantic. Because of this, I tend to think that they cannot *all* be bad.

As soon as I see him I change my mind.

He has his head buried in the 4x4's engine, which is why I did not spot him sooner. Had I known he was there I would have turned back and gone the other way but now that I *am* here I stand my ground. *This is your home. Not theirs,* my inner voice tells me.

Naked from the waist up and wearing torn jeans stained with engine oil, I watch the ponytail of hair, which is almost as black as my own, swing back and forth over his sun-harmed shoulders. He is thin and about the same height as me but the tattoos on his arms ripple over muscle, making the scantily clad women appear to dance over his perspiring skin. Even from here, I can tell that these tattooed women have voluptuous hourglass figures and I know a moment's jealousy because of it. Allowing my imagination to run away with me, I sense that the women are from the gypsy's past; that they are very much real and known to him. Perhaps because of this, I make up my mind he is not to be trusted.

He looks up and sees me at the same time his dogs do. The two lean lurcher types immediately bark a warning and circle me, warily sniffing my ankles. I do not move, not because I am scared, but because I am transfixed by the gypsy's different-coloured eyes, one is blue—the other brown. I have never seen eyes like this before. They are hypnotic. *Womaniser's eyes.* The warning comes from nowhere, but I heed it all the same; viewing him with even more suspicion than before.

'They won't hurt you.' Gesturing to the dogs, he speaks with a soft lilting Irish accent. The kind I could listen to all day. However, I will not give him the satisfaction of knowing this, so I tear my eyes away and keep on walking, all the while conscious of his mismatched eyes crawling over my body.

'Don't talk much, do you?'

Who is he to mock me? I think indignantly, throwing him a look that is meant to put him in his place. But when I see him standing there—hands on hips, cockily miming a silent whistle of appreciation—I feel my face flush with embarrassment. At that moment, a beautiful girl with waist-long hair comes out of the caravan. She carries a sleeping baby in her arms and appears hot and bothered; but when her flashing eyes alight on me there is a welcoming smile on her sultry mouth, as if she half recognises me. *Or do I imagine this?* But when her glance takes in my red cheeks and the gypsy's amused expression, she scowls.

Chapter 8

The House By The Sea

My father's house is as dark and as quiet as it ever was. Just as he likes it. I've lost count of the number of times I've been punished for laughing, crying and running within these walls—another of Frank's laws. Even the old-fashioned wall clock dares not make a ticking sound; yet memories lurk in every shadowy corner. *Try stopping them, Father.*

I thought about this kitchen, the so-called heart of any home, a lot when I was in Thornhaugh and it is exactly as I remember, yet a feeling of loss overwhelms me. This is my home. I was born here. Obviously, it feels smaller now, but the house knows me. I sense this. *Whose side is it on?* Does it remember my *mother's soft touch or does it answer only to my father's bullish hands?*

A mahogany trestle table runs the length of one wall and its chipped surface reminds me of the times I used to sit, legs swinging, waiting for my mother to take me to school. She was late for everything and my impatience with her sometimes got the better of me, leading me to gouge out bits of wood with my fingernails. My yellow anorak used to hang above the table, right next to my mother's fur-edged coat, but neither is to be seen now. This hurts in a way I didn't expect it to, so I move across the room to lay my hands on the back of one of the wooden rocking chairs that are parked either side of the fireplace. They are too uncomfortable to sit in but I recall the sound of their squeak on the floor from many years ago, and suspect my mother may have cradled me in one of them. As usual, whenever I think about her, the scent of her perfume surrounds me. The delicate floral fragrance is far more agreeable than the stale cooking smells that linger here now.

The Belfast sink overflows with dishes. Greasy roasting tins are stacked on the wooden drainer next to it. A grubby curtain beneath the sink houses white porcelain crockery. From here, I used to pass imaginary cups of tea to my mother who would pretend to sip from the heavy earthenware, even though she hated the feel of it against her mouth. My mother's preference for fine china lives on in the willow-patterned plates and serving dishes that take pride of place on the shelves of our farmhouse dresser. I am pleased for her sake that they have survived but doubt they have been taken down and dusted in years. Already, my eyes are smarting from the dust motes leaking in through the partially open back door.

Through this gap I can see part of the garden that was once my mother's pride and joy. Here, she would grow things that were "Good for nothing, except looking at", according to my father—sweet peas, lavender, daffodils, poppies and grape hyacinth. "Something for every season," she used to say. Whenever she entered the house, she would bring the smell of the garden in with her, and it remained long after she passed, fooling us into thinking she was still among us. Eventually, my father dug up the flowerbed and planted vegetables in it but his enthusiasm did not last long and the garden soon reverted to the wilderness it is now. I may decide to take it over myself one day, but first things first.

Reminding myself that houses do not clean themselves, I try not to be overly critical of the home that was considered good enough for my mother but I cannot deny how depressing the small airless windows are, never mind the years of accumulative neglect, evident in the filthy range, grease-streaked walls and hanging cobwebs. The grandeur of Thornhaugh and years of being waited on are behind me and if I am to make a success of my homecoming, I must do something about the general grubbiness of the place.

Somewhat begrudgingly, I start with the dishes and realise that I am having to bend to avoid the low wooden beams. It occurs to me that at five feet nine inches tall, I have outgrown my mother, who never once had to stoop in this kitchen to take care of her brood. At six feet three, my father still towers over me though. On that depressing thought, I roll up the sleeves of my shirt, exposing white skin that rarely sees the sunlight, and tie my hair into a loose ponytail. As I do so, I cannot help thinking about the gypsy's thick black ponytail and the way it swung against his muscular shoulders.

***

I have my back to my father when he comes in, noisily banging the door behind him and shutting out what little light there was. My unruly hair has escaped from the ponytail and my skin is glistening with sweat but that doesn't stop me feeling empowered. Back at Thornhaugh, I was always being told to rest and take it easy. "You are not well, Natalie," became like a chant in my ear, and for many years I believed this.

Climbing down from the chair, where I have been perched, dusting my mother's dinner service on the top shelves of the dresser, I wipe my cobwebbed hands on my jeans and stare at my father, who is cradling a bloody package against his chest. The sight of blood immediately makes my stomach churn but although he is finally looking at me, *exactly what I wanted him to do earlier,* my eyes are the first to drop away. His fierce expression is too much for me to handle. We are so close I can see the open pores on his skin glow red with sweat but at the same time we have never been more distant.

Eventually, he lowers his own eyes and drops the parcel of meat on the table I have spent a good hour scrubbing and bleaching. Only then does it occur to me that my father might be sick rather than angry. There is a yellow hue to his skin that is less healthy than the white flesh belonging to the shoulder of pork on the table. While he washes his hands at the sink, I warily eye the meat but find I cannot throw off the past as easily as I would like, because the butcher's daughter in me is already assessing how expertly it has been prepared.

'I see you still insist on bringing your work home.' The words are out of my mouth before I can stop them.

He turns to gawp at me, water carelessly dripping off his fingers onto the flagstone floor.

Drip. Splat. Drip.

I close my eyes and dig my fingernails into the palm of my hand, numbing the memory of that day in the slaughterhouse. Blood. So much blood. When I open my eyes again, my father is looking at me as if he is seeing me for the first time.

'Are you trying to be smart?'

Like him, I am baffled as to where my outburst of sarcasm came from. Clearly, he does not approve of my acid tongue, so I stay on safer ground.

'I tidied up.'

His eyes do not falter, nor swing to the side to investigate the room. So I try again.

'What do you think?'

'I think things were all right as they were.'

I feel myself giving up. Everything is so much harder than it has to be. That is my father for you. *One last attempt to make friends and then I am done.*

'I thought I'd cook something special tonight to mark my homecoming.'

I watch my father's eyes grow smaller than ever as he scrutinises me.

'You thinking of staying then?'

'If it's all right with you, Father.'

'People around here have long memories,' he snarls.

I do not know what to say to this, so I stay silent. As I watch him drying his hands on a grubby towel I get the feeling he would rather do anything than look at me. Sideways on, I can see his cheek pulsing angrily.

'There's sausages in the fridge if you want to cook something,' he concedes at last.

'I don't eat meat, Father. I haven't for a long time.' I break this news gently, knowing that it will matter to him. It certainly gets his attention, because his eyes are rolling around in his head, like marbles tossed any old how into the air.

'Whoever heard of a butcher's daughter not eating meat?'

His eyes search my face, but avoid clashing with my dark eyes, which I know must remind him of my mother. Perhaps for a moment his face softens. 'You'd better not let on to folk around here.'

***

My bedroom has not changed in thirteen years. The single bed with the patchwork quilt is still there. The books and glass-eyed dolls—still there. Unlike the clutter downstairs, the bedrooms, including this one, are sparsely furnished, frugal almost, and the walls in here are painted an icy blue, making the room seem cold even on a hot day. *Blue for the boy my father always wanted,* I remind myself. Even after mother disappointed him by giving birth to a dark eyed baby girl, he refused to change the colour.

Without knowing how I got into this position, I find myself sitting cross legged on the bare floorboards, imitating the girl I used to be—as I go through a cardboard box of old photographs. Having found the box under the bed where it has been gathering dust all these years, I am longing to reunite the one picture of my mother I *was* allowed to keep with me at Thornhaugh with the others.

I sense his presence long before I see him. As a child, I used to think that the room grew dark at any mention of him. I find nothing has changed. Sure enough, when I look over my shoulder, his awkwardness is before me.

Father has changed into grubby overalls and wrings his hands nervously, as if unsure of himself. Yet this is *his* house. I am *his* daughter. And it is *his* rules we abide by. Taking pity on him, I throw him an encouraging smile, as if to invite him over the threshold, but he won't come in proper, just stands there hovering in the doorway.

'I'll be out and about till late. Don't wait up.'

This is a command. Not a request. Clearly, neither of us wants to spend any more time together than is necessary after the silent meal downstairs; when the chink of cutlery frayed both our nerves. I do not blame him for making his escape but when I notice his eyes resting on the box of photographs, I *do* blame him for my mother's disappearance.

'Some things don't change, huh?' His chin juts out defiantly, indicating the photographs.

'Why won't you talk about her?' My own voice is barely a whisper.

'Leave the dead where they belong, Natalie. And you and me will get along fine.'

'Where *do* the dead belong, Father? If it's in the cemetery, I'd like to know.'

Chapter 9

Little Downey Cemetery

Little Downey's graveyard might be the smallest of cemeteries, but it is the only one I have ever known. One day I shall be buried here, in the shadow of the church that keeps its distance from the dead. But with the cemetery facing the sea, I can think of worse places to end up. A solitary ash tree provides shade for the lucky few, and rooks, brave as you like, hop from gravestone to gravestone. Their calls are heard more often than church bells. It is a solitary place, a mile and a half's walk from the village, and I have never come across another person here. Nobody comes to lay flowers for the dead in Little Downey.

The grass is overgrown and ivy clings to the crumbling gravestones, making the epitaphs difficult to read. Some of the writing has faded away completely and I feel sad for the people who have been forgotten about. The cloying smell of decay is ever-present, but it is not altogether unpleasant; better than bleached corridors and old urine, smells I have grown accustomed to. On that depressing thought, I realise I have been wandering around the graveyard for a good half hour, moving from one gravestone to the next, tracing my fingers against the engraved lettering and still haven't found what I am looking for. The truth is, I never expected to.

Giving up, I walk over to the wooden bench that has its back rudely turned on the dead; preferring instead the view of the bay. Because it is still early and the sun is not properly out yet, the bench is damp, but I sit down anyway, so I can face the sea. Up here, the wind is fierce even on the warmest of days. I feel its cold seep into me and liken its numbing effect to an injection of sedative travelling around my body; a familiar sensation for someone like me. With the cliff edge a few meters away, it is dangerous for me to imagine my mother is calling out my name, but I hear its whisper all the same; carried along on the breeze. I feel her with me. She is close. Yet not in the graveyard where she is meant to be.

'Where are you, Mother? What did they do to you?'

Chapter 10

Little Downey Beach

I could have avoided coming this way. *Why didn't I?* It is not as if pushing a bicycle along a pebbled beach is easy. After skulking around the house for what felt like the longest week of my life, I had at last ventured into Little Downey, on my mother's old shopper bike, to buy some essentials. The sort of thing I cannot ask my father for, although admittedly I did have to ask him for the money. Thankfully, he did not question why. Explaining that I needed tampons would have been embarrassing enough but any mention of razors would have raised alarm bells.

In the space of a week, we have hardly said a dozen words to each other. He goes to work early every day and comes home late; drinking in The Black Bull or working late in his workshop. If we do eat together, we do so in silence. Occasionally, we pass each other on the stairs and every time this happens, it is as awkward as the first. Making eye contact is avoided, accidental touching even more so. Since that first day I arrived home, when I openly challenged him about my mother's whereabouts, I have been good; repeatedly biting my tongue so as not to antagonise him. So far, this seems to be working. How long I can keep it up is another matter, as by nature I am not a submissive person.

I see the gypsy long before he sees me. As before, he is shirtless and has on the same pair of tight jeans but today he is barefoot and wears his hair loose around his shoulders. He is browner than I remember and busy flexing his muscles, testing out an axe on a wooden chopping block, which I do not recall seeing before. I am horrified to discover there are three hens and a cockerel in a cage close by; clearly awaiting the most brutal of fates. Their clucking excites the two dogs who paw at the cage and whine softly.

My stomach is in knots as my eyes dart from the chickens to the gypsy. Now that he has noticed me, I find I cannot look away. I do not know which eye bothers me most, the blue or the brown one. The answer is both. There is something lustful about the way he is looking at me, which I have never experienced before, and it terrifies and excites me at the same time. The most worrying thing is he seems to know it.

He has already spotted my unease and I can tell, by the mischievous sparkle in his mismatched eyes, that he is amused by it. Holding my gaze, he walks over to the cage and pulls out the cockerel. He does this in a surprisingly gentle way, the bird hardly making any fuss at all, but as soon as he heads for the block, I break my self-imposed silence.

'Don't, please.'

The dogs, closely following on his heels, stop to gaze at me, as if worried I might jeopardise the chance of a kill, but when their master pays me no heed, they lick their lips and jostle for position. The gypsy places the bird on the block. It struggles and he stops its wings from flapping by placing a hand over its feathered body. Feeling myself shudder, my gaze is drawn to the cutting edge of the axe in his other hand. I tell myself that it is just a chicken, but I believe that *all life* is precious and I even consider pleading with him again. But when I see the smirk on his sun-bronzed face, I realise there is no point. This man will do exactly as he likes and to hell with anyone else.

I might be powerless to save the chicken but I will not watch him kill it. Doing what I did not think was possible, I mount the bike and set off ungainly over the pebbles. It is hard going but I manage to stay in the saddle, legs pedalling furiously to put as much distance between us as possible. When I hear the axe hitting the block, the bike swerves beneath me but I keep on cycling. *Don't look back, Natalie, whatever you do.* The sound of the gypsy's laughter stalks me all the way home and I try, but fail, to shut it out.

Chapter 11

The House By The Sea

I sweep this porch at least once every day but the dust and sand return like an unwanted dog as soon as my back is turned. It creeps into the house too, leaving ghostly footprints over the floor. The dust is in my hair and up my nostrils and when I catch a glimpse of my reflection in the windowpane, I look pale and exhausted. I feel much older than when I first arrived home. *Has it only been a week since I returned to Little Downey?* Sometimes, it feels as if I have never been away at all and at other times, I am sharply reminded of the fact I am considered an outsider, at least by the villagers.

My jaunt into Little Downey was not a huge success. One or two people nodded and said a polite but formal "Good morning" but most, especially the likes of Mrs Abbot in the post office-cum-grocery store, glared at me as if they wanted me dead. At one stage, I thought she was going to ask me to leave, that she was going to refuse to serve me. If that had happened, I would have died of embarrassment. My heart was in my mouth when I paid for my purchases and when our fingers collided over the money, my hands shook uncontrollably. She did not even acknowledge my timid "Goodbye and thank you" when I left, just tutted. I half expected her husband to come through from the back of the shop, where he could be seen counting his takings, with a rope meant for my neck.

In hindsight, which everyone says is a wonderful thing but truly isn't, I wonder if I am making too much of their hostility towards me. Isn't Dr Moses always telling me I have too vivid an imagination, inventing slights that were never intended or hearing unspoken insults? I miss him dreadfully, of course. The thought of my old protector is enough to make me feel tearful and I am not one for tears as a rule, never have been. *Frank's Law, remember.* Funny how for years I yearned to escape the claustrophobic atmosphere of Thornhaugh and now find myself longing for human company. Back then, being alone, properly alone that is, was a luxury I could only dream of.

I sigh and run a hand through my dirty hair. There is no escaping the fact I am lonely here, that I need a friend. I have my housework of course, which is the only thing keeping me sane at the moment. *I must stop using that word to describe myself.* Keeping house seems to agree with me. I find it both therapeutic and satisfying, and if it ends up becoming another addiction, it will be less harmful than some of my other disorders. Going back to the villagers, I suppose I will have to be more patient. Isn't time meant to be the greatest of healers? It is only natural that they should be wary of me.

Hearing a vehicle approach, a sound so rare I barely recognise it for what it is to begin with, I shield my eyes with my hand to avoid the harsh sunlight, and peer out. An unfamiliar pickup truck is making its way along the winding sand trail up to the house, a cloud of dust gathering behind it. We have a visitor and without knowing who it is, my heart is already pounding. *What will I say to them? What do they want?* Just a few minutes ago, I was complaining of loneliness and longing to meet new people but now there is a real chance of that happening, I find myself panicking.

When the pickup truck comes to an unhurried halt in front of me, I can tell that beneath its dusty surface it is shiny black and new. My eyes are drawn to the fierce use of the word ANIMAL printed on the side of the truck but when the door is pushed open and the driver steps out from the glare of the sun, I am relieved to find he is not at all animal-like.

My father's good-looking assistant strides over confidently but does not step foot onto the porch. I get the impression he refrains from doing so out of politeness and will wait for an invite before presuming anything. I like him even more for it.

'Hi.'

After such a build-up, his greeting is a bit of a disappointment. However, with a face like that, I could forgive him a lot worse; maybe even the cold blue eyes that state his allegiance to Little Downey.

'Hi,' I mumble begrudgingly, hating to be caught out looking so unkempt. Looking as I do, dirty and dishevelled, means I cannot be my true self with him and I wish him miles away.

'You work for my dad, right?' Just like my father, I am sparse with words.

'Daniel. Dan. Frank and I are partners.'

Daniel, Dan holds out a hand, but it is a few seconds before I take it. I am not used to this sort of contact; not used to men full stop, unless they are doctors or orderlies. My hand is hot and moist, his dry and cool, having stepped out of an air-conditioned vehicle. The comparison makes me feel even more at a disadvantage. We look at each other for a second too long and our eyes dart away at the same time. There is an awkward pause between us that does not have any right to be there, seeing as we do not know each other. Then I remember that we are all socially awkward in Little Downey. It is what we are known for.

'You don't remember me, do you?' he asks candidly.

'No, sorry. Should I?' I hate it when people talk in riddles. This is another failing of Little Downey's. Again, like my father, I prefer plain speaking.

'Dan Harper. I was only three years above you at school.'

'Harper? Didn't you have a younger sister? Debbie.'

'That's the one.'

He seems inordinately pleased that I remember this. I cannot imagine why, but all is revealed when he speaks again.

'Remembering my sister is the next best thing to remembering me,' he states.

'Is she still around?' I change the subject because I do not remember him but do not want to hurt his feelings.

'Uh uh. She married a dentist, lives in Devon.'

'That's unusual.'

'What? Marrying a dentist or living in Devon?'

'No, I didn't mean...' I shake my head, annoyed with him for deliberately misunderstanding me.

'You mean it's unusual for anyone in Little Downey to move away.' He finishes my sentence for me, then winks. 'You don't need me to tell you that we do things differently around here.'

There's that smile again. It changes everything. The way I feel about him. The way I feel about Little Downey even. There is goodness in him, I know it. A joker with a heart. Nothing like the gypsy. *I don't even know why I am thinking about him.*

Realising I still have the sweeping brush in my hand, I casually put it to one side, hoping he won't forever associate me with the mundane task of cleaning. It startles me that I should find myself wishing I'd put on a dress, something I rarely do, and a touch of make-up, nothing too heavy. Out here, I could sit around for days without seeing a soul, so there is hardly any need to look glamorous, yet this is exactly what my mother had done. Ironically, I don't think my father paid any attention to what she wore or once complimented her on her looks. She was a beautiful woman with an inattentive husband. This alone must have been enough to drive somebody as flirtatious and playful as her, quite mad.

'I hardly remember you. Yet you must know everything about me,' I admit, feeling suddenly flat and distrustful.

'Don't let that worry you.' He appears unphased.

'It worries most people,' I exclaim, trying not to stare at his wonky smile and icy blue eyes.

'Not me.' He shakes his head and buries his hands in his pockets.

'Why?' I am relentless, but I know exactly where I get this trait.

'Stick around long enough, Natalie, and you'll find out I'm not like most people.'

He throws me his best grin and I smile back. There is something irresistible about Daniel Harper and because it feels as if we have known each other for years, I believe him.

Chapter 12

Hours later, I am still sitting there, staring into the distance with a stupid grin on my face, when my father arrives home. Because today feels different. *Correction, I feel different,* I do not get to my feet when he steps on to the porch, nor do I immediately apologise for my existence when his eyes narrow at the two empty beer bottles on the table.

'Somebody been?'

'I thought he might have mentioned it.'

'Who?'

There is something about my expression that my father objects to. I can tell this by the way he is frowning but I have done nothing wrong, so I stretch lazily and yawn.

'Daniel.'

Father looks at me as if I am stupid and I am keen to avoid pointing out that he is the one acting dumb. He must know who I am talking about.

'Daniel Harper.' I am more abrupt than I intended.

'What did *he* want?'

I do not hear the veiled threat in my father's voice, so I get to my feet, surprised by how tipsy I feel. I may only have had one beer but it has me beaten.

'Just to say hello.'

I resume my sweeping, *anything is better than having my father scowling at me,* but when I do sneak a glance in his direction, I see that his focus is back on the beer bottles. They appear to unsettle him more than my dreamy expression.

'Don't go getting friendly with the likes of him,' he growls.

'Why not?' I straighten up and give my father my full attention. 'I thought you'd be pleased. He *is* your business partner.'

'Business partner be damned. You'll do as you're told and keep away from him. You hear?'

He spits angrily, the phlegm landing inches away from my foot. I put down the broom and cross my arms, every bit as angry as he is.

'You can't stop me seeing him. You can't stop me doing anything. If Mother was here...'

'Well, she ain't.'

As far as he is concerned that is the end of the conversation and to prove this, he stomps off towards the outdoor workshop. But I am not done yet.

'That's it. Walk away!' I shout after him. 'Like you always do when I try to talk about her.'

Chapter 13

The Whitewashed Building

A silence has descended on this hot and humid afternoon that feels unnatural. The house by the sea might be remote, situated one mile from the nearest other property and three from the village, but it is never usually as quiet as this. The stillness is eerie. Shielding my eyes from the sun, I search the sky for signs of life but there is not a single bird in sight. I listen out for the reassuring sound of waves crashing against the shore in the distance but the sea is likewise silent. The only thing I *can* hear is the crackle of the sun-scorched grass beneath my flip-flops as I tiptoe towards my father's workshop.

Because I have always been afraid of the whitewashed building, I would never normally venture out here alone. Since coming home, I have not been anywhere near it. I won't even glance its way when I walk past it, which I am forced to do every time I go down to the beach or cycle into Little Downey. It may have started out life as a seventeenth-century Welsh longhouse; a long low single-story building that would once have accommodated people at one end and cattle at the other, with a passageway between the two parts— but to me it represents the stuff nightmares are made of.

The building has been neglected to the point of appearing dilapidated. The once-white walls have yellowed over time and the roof sags lazily in the middle. At either end of the building there is a solid wooden door with heavy iron hinges. My father only ever uses the door on the right, but each entrance retains its own set of crumbling concrete steps. The frames on the small black windows have rotted away, exposing the rusted bars on the inside. Nobody has ever explained what the bars are for. To this day, I do not know if their purpose is to keep people in or out. The thought of being locked inside, of not being able to get out, fills me with the same dread I felt as a child, whenever I went near it.

Judging by the way my heart is hammering, I do not think I will ever outgrow my fear of this place. My father is nowhere to be seen. No sound comes from within, so I push open the door, jumping at the sound of its unfamiliar squeak. Peering inside, I see nothing but blackness. The smell of decay takes my breath away.

'Father.'

My hair is sticking to the back of my neck and I want, more than anything, to run back to the house, but if I do not apologise to my father there is a very real chance he will report my behaviour to Dr Moses. I *cannot* and *will not* promise never to see Daniel again but I can't risk news of our quarrel reaching Thornhaugh either. Dr Moses would make too much of a drama out of our father-daughter row and I am ever mindful of his parting words: "If you screw up, Natalie. You could end up being sectioned indefinitely."

Hovering in the open doorway, I look around, conscious that I have been holding my breath for too long. My nerves are frayed beyond endurance. It is an unnatural trait of mine, I know, but I would choose pain over emotional torment any day of the week. *Where are you, Father?* His van is parked under the shade of the Dutch barn, so I know he hasn't gone anywhere. He is not in the house either, so he must be inside the building. Making up my mind that he is ignoring me on purpose, I decide I cannot blame him. I might not have been the one in the wrong before but I should never have spoken so disrespectfully or raised my voice. If my mother *was* still alive today, she would be ashamed of me.

Bracing myself for I know not what, I give a determined shake of my head before stepping inside. *Get a grip, Natalie. It is just a smelly old building. It cannot hurt you.* The first thing I feel is a cobweb breaking against my face, making me flinch. The first thing I see is a row of jangling rusty metal meat hooks suspended from the ceiling. They are stained black from old blood. At once, I am a child again; afraid and in need of adult protection.

'Father.'

It is dark inside and there are flies everywhere. I swat them away, promising myself that if my father were to show himself right now, I would forgive him anything. I would even welcome a soft cuff of the head, the nearest thing to affection I ever received from him.

My eyes are drawn to the tools on the butcher's block. I know exactly what each saw, knife or cleaver is used for. Mesmerised by the jagged edges and shiny curves of the knives that gleam in the shadows, I run a finger along one of the blades and stare at it for a long time. It means something to me, I realise, but I do not remember what. Then I hear the sinister sound of a butcher's saw at work; flesh and bone being cut—and blood dripping.

Drip. Splat. Drip.

Taking a giant breath, I close my eyes and try to think back to my first memory of this building. I know the sounds echoing around me cannot be real, yet in this moment, they are more tangible than anything else. They take precedence over everything—my mother, my father, Daniel, Little Downey, the gypsy. They are also disturbingly familiar. I would give anything to be my younger self again, to see what she saw, and hear what she heard. So much is missing from my memory. If only I could remember—

***

I can smell the rain. Taste it on my tongue. My hair is wet and bedraggled, and I shiver from the cold. Above me, the sky is grey and patchy with black clouds that are heading towards the village, having already paid us a visit. I wipe the snot from my nose and peer inside the whitewashed building. I have been sent on a fool's errand by my mother as I am meant to tell my father that he is needed back at the house, because we have a spider. He is going to be furious, of course, and is bound to take his temper out on me.

It is hard to pass on a message to my father when I am not allowed to enter his workshop. He might be anywhere inside and would not hear me even if I yelled at the top of my lungs. He never does when he is working. Neither me nor my mother understand why he must bring his work home with him. You would think working all those hours in the butcher's shop would be enough for anybody. Luckily, the door to the workshop is wide open, a rarity, and I spot him straight away. He has his back to me but I can tell by the way his elbows are moving like pistons that he is chopping up meat on the butcher's block.

He is not yet aware of me, so I have a good look around, something I never usually get the chance to do. If caught, my father will once again accuse me of spying, but I am only six, seven in a few weeks' time, and I do not know what he means by this.

There are metal hooks hanging from the ceiling. They are so shiny I am sure I could see my face in them, if I wanted to. But I don't because I know they are used to hang dead animals, and this is something I do not like to think about. When I grow up, I am meant to take over from my father and become a butcher too. But I console myself that this will not take place for hundreds of years.

A single ray of sunshine pokes through the clouds and sneaks its way into the building through the metal bars at the window. The light reflects on my father's bent head, making him appear like an angel.

'Daddy!'

I watch him spin around, eyes blazing with fear and alarm, looking more like the devil than an angel. At the same time, the knife in his hand clatters to the floor. I didn't mean to frighten him, and I am about to tell him so when—

'How many times have I told you never to come in here?'

I should be frightened, and of course I am, but I am even more terrified by what I can see on the butcher's block—a severed finger. A bloody torn human finger! Unable to breathe or move or react to my father's angry expression—all I can do is break another of Frank's laws, by opening my mouth and screaming.

Capable of moving athletically when he wants to, but only when he wants to, he reaches me quickly. His warm bloodstained hand clasps a silencing hand over my mouth but I fight back, kicking and squealing.

'Stop that screaming. Stop it,' he commands.

I bite down on his fleshy finger and scream even louder, pointing hysterically at the dismembered finger. Why doesn't he see it? Why doesn't he do anything about it? I feel myself being shaken like a rat and my mind goes cloudy for a while. I do not realise I have been dragged outside until I feel the cold rain running down my neck.

Before I know it, I am back in the house, sat at the kitchen table with snot running out of my nose. I am told not to cry but I cannot help it. My mother is nowhere to be seen. She never is in such moments. My father stands by the sink, running water over his hands, which is an odd thing for him to do when I am sat here sobbing my heart out. I watch him take a pocketknife out of his apron and jab at something. A sharp intake of breath cuts through the silence and then my father slips the knife back in his apron. His movements are sly, like a cat stalking a bird. When he looks over his shoulder at me, I quickly turn my head away, so he cannot accuse me of spying.

'It's all right. My finger is fine. See. I didn't lose it.'

My father thrusts his hand in my face, a hostile action that does not match his conciliatory tone. Seeing the deep bloody gash on his finger makes me whimper even more, and unable to help himself, he resorts to shaking me again.

'I saw. I saw.' I am beside myself with fear and confusion. I do not trust my father. After what I saw, I cannot believe anything he says. All I know is somebody is missing a finger and it is not him.

'Forget what you thought you saw, Natalie. Do you hear me? Damn it.'

He slaps my face. Hard. I do not know who is more surprised—him or me. In the stunned silence that follows, we both stare open mouthed at each other.

***

I am surrounded by my mother's whisper. It has a way of bringing me back to the present like no drug can. I feel as if I have been floating on a calm ocean and now find myself in dangerous waters, because when I open my eyes, I realise am still touching the knife. Quickly, I withdraw my finger but I am a second too late and it nicks me anyway. The trickle of crimson blood makes me tremble, yet I remain hypnotised by it.

My body feels hot and cold at the same time and there is a dull ache in my head, a sign that I am late taking my medication. I cannot even be sure I took my first lot of pills this morning, so it is hardly any wonder I feel as I do. What would Dr Moses say if he could see me now, staring into space and drifting in and out of different timelines?

Wanting to escape the building, the jumble of confusing memories, all thoughts of Thornhaugh and Dr Moses' subtle threats, I bolt out of the building. The need to flee is overwhelming and I run as fast as I can towards the house but I do not get far— because the desire to retch is stronger. Coming to a breathless stop, I vomit up saliva and beer. That is when I see my father coming out of the other door of the whitewashed building, the one he swears never to use. When he sees the state I am in, he barks a sarcastic laugh.

'Perhaps now you'll keep your nose out of what doesn't concern you.' He wags a warning finger at me.

Chapter 14

Little Downey Beach

I plod despondently along the deserted beach, swinging my flip-flops in one hand and shielding my eyes from the sun with the other, watching the rocky curve of the coastline getting further away from me. Putting distance between myself and the house by the sea has never felt so important.

Further out, the sea is choppy and black but the water I am paddling through is cloudy and calm. On the hottest of days, the water remains cold and I am glad of this, because my feet are scorching from walking too long on hot pebbles. After what happened in the whitewashed building, I came down to the beach, as I always do when I am troubled or *in trouble*, to escape my father. The sea is a much better parent.

When I come across an upside-down crab, I crouch to take a closer look. It is about the same size as my hand and is a familiar visitor to the Welsh coastline, this being a spider crab. The crab's shell is a mottled brown, which cleverly mimics the colour of the seaweed that has been left behind by the tide. Today though, the crab is out in the open and has nowhere to hide. I am surprised it has not already been picked up by a hungry gull. Deciding that this discovery is the nicest thing to happen to me today, I watch the crab wriggling to be free, happy in the knowledge that I can help it. When I attempt to flip it over, its salmon pink claw comes out to swipe me but having shared this beach with crabs much bigger than this one, I easily outwit it.

As soon as it is upright again, it scurries away in a jerky sideways motion towards the water's edge and I hear the gentlest of plops as it disappears into the ocean. The smile on my face vanishes when I see the gypsy and his dog coming towards me. When the dog spots me, it freezes, then barks in alarm before running towards me with its hackles raised. The gypsy does not call it back, even though it looks as if it might bite me. Instead, he carries on whistling through his fingers and searching the coastline with troubled eyes.

Having deliberately avoided going anywhere near the gypsy camp, I am angry with him for being on this part of the beach. *My beach.* I am angry at his dog too, which continues to circle me, growling uneasily whenever I move. I am not afraid of the dog, but I will not risk antagonising it, so I keep still and lower my eyes to show that I am no threat.

When it suits him, the gypsy eventually comes over, barely registering the fact that I am being held captive by his dog.

'Have you seen my other dog? He's a lot like this one, only smaller.'

Deciding that words are too precious to waste on him, I shake my head. This is all the answer he is going to get out of me. I should feel sorry for him because he has lost his dog but I do not. The image of the chicken on the block is still fresh in my mind; besides, I am sure the dog will turn up. They usually do.

He runs a hand through his hair and it occurs to me that he appears genuinely concerned. There is a kind of appeal in his clashing eyes that is new. Because I have only ever known him to be sarcastic or cruel, this surprises me. *Could I have got him wrong?* What comes out of his mouth next convinces me otherwise.

'I guess there must be a bitch in heat somewhere.'

The teasing grin is back. His hands are in his pockets and his head is cocked to one side, both eyes on me at once. He is much too close. I can see sweat trickling down his chest. I am about to say something when—

'Jed!'

We both turn to see the beautiful young gypsy woman climbing down from a sand dune. As before, she looks hot and bothered—and no wonder, she is wearing a long off-the-shoulder dress that hinders her every move. She has bunches of it in her hands to stop her from tripping and keeps looking back over her shoulder as if she has left something important behind. *Surely not the baby.* As she heads towards us, I notice that the scowl on her face does not diminish her dark beauty.

I turn back to the gypsy and watch him shrug comically, his eyebrows shooting upwards, as if the sudden appearance of the gypsy woman tickles him. I cannot think why, when she is clearly angry with him. I certainly would not want to be in his shoes. I watch him walk over to her, his dog following on his heels.

Keen to avoid any conflict with the fiery gypsy woman, whom I suspect would beat me hands down in a fight, I carry on walking, but cannot resist one quick look back. They are still in the same spot, arguing. Tossing her hair about angrily, the gypsy woman gestures wildly with her hands, while he stares at the sand. *He has his comeuppance,* I cannot resist thinking. And I am glad he is in trouble. I cannot think of anyone who deserves it more.

***

I am back on my rock, looking out to sea, and struggling to make sense of everything. The sun, low in the sky, dips its blazing toe in the ocean and I feel eager for it to set. *The sooner this day is over the better.* I cannot stop thinking about the gypsy, trying to work him out. One minute he is everything I detest in a person—cruel, sarcastic, taunting, nothing at all like Daniel, and the next, let's say he's the opposite. *His name is Jed.* I repeat the name over in my mind until I feel used to it. It suits him. I do not think I could have come up with a better one. I do not ask myself why I am wasting my time thinking about him. Deep down, I suspect the answer might shock me.

I hear it for some time before it registers—the sound of a dog barking and whining. At first, I try to ignore it but in the end I give up and go to investigate. Before I get very far, I find myself hoping that it is not the gypsy's dog I can hear, because I do not want to be the one that has to return it, not after the way his woman looked at me on the beach. As soon as I see the scruffy wire-haired lurcher digging in the sand dune my heart sinks, because of course it is the gypsy's dog. Just like he said, this one is a lot like the one from before, only smaller. Friendlier too, because when it sees me its tail moves from side to side but it does not pause in its digging. Sand flies everywhere, including on me.

'Hello, boy. What are you doing there? Trying to dig your way to Australia?'

Hearing my voice, the dog's head shoots up and sand pours off its biscuit-coloured snout, making it sneeze. Tail wagging frantically, it backs away, play bows and yelps in excitement. I know enough about dogs to guess that it wants to show me something.

'What is it? What have you got there?'

Chapter 15

I do not know what happened to the dog. My screams must have frightened it off because it is nowhere to be seen. There is no one chasing after me or nipping at my heels. Only the sun is behind me as I run towards the gap in the cliffs and the well-worn sand trail that leads up to the house by the sea, where safety of sorts awaits. My heart is hammering against my ribcage and there is a lump in my throat that I cannot swallow. God, I wish I could unsee what I have seen. The thought of it makes me want to vomit. But I dare not pause, even for a moment. Not even to catch my breath. I must get home, to my father.

When I see a tall familiar figure striding confidently towards me, I do not give up on my screaming. Fear keeps me at it. When the sound reaches him, it brings him to a halt but only for a second or two and then, like me, he is running.

'Daniel!' I yell, picking up pace so that I can reach him quicker. I am so relieved to see him, I could burst.

He catches me in his arms and I sob almost immediately into his shoulder. Physically, my rescuer is in far better shape than I am; his body muscular and unyielding. But as upset as I am, it disturbs me that I can smell meat on him. The romantic girl in me is disillusioned and I for one could strangle her. *Honestly, Natalie. Talk about ungrateful.*

'What's wrong? Are you all right?'

While I try to get my breath, sucking in great gulps of salty sea air, I can tell Daniel is already trying to work out what has happened. I watch his intelligent blue eyes flitting across the empty beach and scanning the rocks before coming to rest, almost with dread, on the protruding cliff edge that looks down on us. I guess what he is thinking. Another suicide. Another jumper. I shake my head at him, but the words will not come—

'The... The...'

'What, Natalie?'

He pushes me away and I stumble a little, surprised by his tone, because he sounds annoyed with me. But in the next second, he pulls me close again. I realise after all that he is simply concerned and possibly frightened for me.

'What is it? Tell me.'

'The gypsy'—is all I can manage.

A long pause, and then—

'Scum gypsies. I'll make sure they're run out of here for good.'

As I watch his eyes narrow with hatred, I realise his response is exactly as I predicted. There has never been any love lost between Little Downey and the travelling community. Already, Daniel's scowling eyes are on the lookout, wanting to do harm to another human being and I feel suddenly protective of the gypsy and his way of life.

'No,' I say, but I can tell Daniel is no longer listening to me. 'It was the gypsy's dog I saw... It was... It had... It was eating something. It looked human.'

There. I finally get my words out. I say them aloud all right—I can tell this by the quizzical way Daniel is looking at me, as if he's not sure he should be taking me seriously or not. Now he *is* going to think I am insane. Soon, he will be like everyone else in Little Downey, even though he swore he was different.

'Wait for me here,' he instructs and I nod. There is no way he or anybody else will catch me in those sand dunes again. Not after what I saw.

***

He is gone longer than I imagined. *What can he be doing? Surely, he's found it by now.* When there is still no sign of him, I scratch at my arms. The skin there is pitted from old scarring. It feels ugly to touch and I roll my sleeves down again, ashamed of myself. Waiting makes me a bundle of nerves. I understand why I am like this. I have had it explained to me enough times.

My mother was late for everything and as a child I was traumatised by this; wrongly assuming I had been abandoned and that she was never coming back. My hysteria was therefore unfounded, they said. Except I don't believe what they told me at Thornhaugh, because isn't that exactly what my mother did in the end? If throwing yourself off a cliff edge and committing suicide is not abandonment, I do not know what is.

When Daniel finally returns, I am at first relieved, then horrified, to see him carrying something in his arms. I think of the blood and the battered human flesh with its torn endings. The clawing fingers. The putrid stench. *My God, why is he bringing it back? Surely, he should leave it where I found it, for the police to examine.* Then, I remember that involving outsiders, even the local constabulary, is not how things are done in Little Downey.

When I see his mouth curl into a smile, I know something is not right. He would not be grinning if he had seen what I saw.

'Is this what you saw?' he asks gently.

Bracing myself, I look down at what he is holding and I shake my head in disbelief at the dead branch covered in slimy seaweed that has bits of grasping twig sticking out of it. I suppose it does look a little like an arm but I am still not convinced this is what I saw in the sand dune. *I could not be that mistaken, could I?* When I glance up at Daniel, I can tell he never believed me in the first place but did not want to hurt my feelings. *He can save himself the bother*, I think resentfully, because I do not want or need his pity. That would change everything between us. We would no longer be equals. Suddenly, I realise how important it is that he does not look at me the way I am used to being looked at.

'I could have sworn...' My voice sounds lame and unpersuasive, even to my own ears. The evidence is right there in front of me but I was so sure of what I had seen.

'You'll laugh about this later, I promise,' he jokes.

Chapter 16

Little Downey Coast Road

I am wearing my mother's favourite red dress. I can never hope to look as beautiful in it as she did but I spent a lot of my childhood imagining myself in it and so today, I went into the room she once shared with my father and slid it off its hanger. As soon as the cool silky fabric was in my hands, her scent and laughter were everywhere. How many times have I watched her sitting in front of the dressing table mirror applying bright red lipstick, with a romantic story to tell?

I sometimes think my mother was more in love with the idea of being in love than anything else. She may have had a grown woman's responsibilities—a house, husband and a child to look after, but in her heart she remained a young girl. I take after her in looks, at least that is what people say, but otherwise we have nothing in common. Is this why she went away? Who could blame her for wanting to escape her oh-so-serious tomboy child and domineering husband?

At Thornhaugh, the colour red was prohibited, at least as far as I was concerned. "It's like a red rag to a bull," they used to say but it was years before I understood what this meant. I look down at my bony knees and bare white legs and realise the dress could not be more blood red if it tried. Immediately, I think about the severed arm and wonder if I was mistaken, as Daniel says I am, or if it is floating in the sea somewhere along the coastline.

I turn to look at Daniel, who has both hands on the steering wheel but only one eye on the road and I reward him with a trickle of nervous laughter.

'See. I told you I could make you laugh.' He grins.

I like the way he is looking at me. It makes me feel warm inside, as if I were submerged in a hot bath, not in the same way my heart races with fear whenever I come face to face with the gypsy but it is a pleasant feeling, nonetheless. So far, Daniel has noticed every bit of effort I have made for him – the strapless dress, lip-gloss and painted fingernails.

'I guess it was pretty stupid of me,' I finally admit, all thoughts of the severed arm and gypsy disappearing from my mind.

'No more talk of bodies being dug up though. Otherwise you'll give me nightmares,' he jests, choosing that moment to casually place a hand over mine.

We have the same white skin and softness of flesh but I remain uncertain about whether I should allow the touch to go unchecked. I am an old-fashioned girl at heart, at least that is how I imagine myself, never having been on a date before. When I catch Daniel glancing at me, I sense I am being tested. Deciding I am not ready for this, I am about to gently withdraw my hand, when something runs out in front of us—

I see the dog first, in the pickup truck's headlights, before he does.

'Look out!' I shout.

There is a sickening thud, the sound of flesh and bone hitting hot metal. I clasp a hand over my eyes, not wanting to witness a defenceless animal being crushed to death or worse still, dragged along under the truck.

'Did we kill it?' I ask fearfully, as Daniel pulls the truck over to the side of the road.

'Not sure,' he mumbles, killing the engine and swinging his long rugby-playing legs out of the vehicle. I do not attempt to get out of my own seat, choosing instead to keep an eye on Daniel's shadow in my wing mirror as he searches up and down the unlit roadside. I feel bad for the dog. Really, I do. We should have been paying attention to the road not staring dreamily into each other's eyes. It has already occurred to me that this must be the same dog that I saw on the beach. The gypsy's dog.

When the sound of whimpering reaches my ears, I scramble out of the truck. My legs are wobbly when I hit the ground and I feel sick with fear, imagining the poor thing dying alone in the roadside with no one to help it. By now, Daniel has disappeared into the blackness and I am surrounded by the incessant murmur of night-time insects. In the far distance I can hear waves crashing against the rocks but no matter how hard I listen, there is no more whimpering. Perhaps I only imagined it.

'Daniel?' I call, fearful of what might be lurking in the shadows but I receive no reply.

Suddenly, I feel hot and feverish, as if I am coming down with something. The dress, all creased and misshapen, clings uncomfortably to the hot areas of my body. The fear that is upon me has nothing to do with my being afraid of the dark—more to do with the gypsy and what he will do if he finds out we have killed his dog, however accidentally.

'Are you there, Daniel? Can you see anything?' I call again, feeling quite scared. *I mustn't cry. Daniel's not like my mother. He won't abandon me. I'm sure of it.*

Then, remembering that my father always used to keep a torch in the glovebox of his van and suspecting Daniel might do the same, I reach into the truck, flick open the glovebox and grab the torch inside. It is nice to be right for once.

As soon as the torchlight comes on, it picks out all manner of unexplainable shadows and silhouettes but I ignore these and concentrate on Daniel's bent-over figure. He is some way from the roadside, amongst the rocks, and when he turns his head in my direction all I can see is a pair of white teeth flashing in the darkness. There is something about the set of his shoulders that reminds me of the stance my father adopts when breaking the bones of beasts in the butcher shop. As soon as I think this, I imagine I hear a distinctive snap—like the accompanying sound that goes with this barbaric practice, but then Daniel is on his way back to me, grabbing at handfuls of grass and wiping his hands against them.

'I couldn't see anything,' he admits, slyly glancing over his shoulder. 'It must have run off.'

Chapter 17

During the drive home, I undergo a hundred and one different emotions, ranging from being fully accepting of Daniel's explanations for everything that has happened to me today to becoming increasingly suspicious. Although the accident with the dog and the fact we were unable to find it played on my mind, we did end up having a nice evening.

Over a candle and three courses at the secluded beachside restaurant, which was far enough away from Little Downey to make us both believe we were free of the place, I talked about my mother and Daniel appeared genuinely interested. It turns out he is a good listener, hardly telling me anything of himself, except to suggest he has been the apple of his mother's eye ever since his sister left home.

He only broached the subject of my father once.

'I have to apologise for not mentioning my visit to your father sooner,' he'd told me. 'Knowing Frank as I do, I should have known better. It's no wonder he went off on one.'

'What did he say?' I gasped, unable to swallow the food in my mouth.

'Warned me off, that's all.' Daniel may have laughed the incident off, but he wasn't able to disguise the sadness in his eyes. 'Told me to stay away from his only daughter.'

'He said that?'

'Frank or no Frank, there was no way I was going to stay away after that. I couldn't even if I wanted to...' Daniel had almost blushed at this point. 'I had to check you were okay. And you are, aren't you? I mean look at you, you're beautiful, Natalie.'

His words had made me giddy. Nobody had ever said anything like that to me before.

'It's only natural that Frank should be protective of you,' Daniel gone on to admit. 'If you were mine, I'd feel the same.'

At this point, it was all I could do to stop myself from laughing. If Daniel knew what my father's true feelings were for me, or him for that matter, he would not be so forgiving.

After that, the rest of the evening raced by and before I knew it, we were pulling up outside the house by the sea, neither of us wanting our date to end.

***

The house is in darkness. For once, I hope my father is still at the pub. Not that it matters, as there is no avoiding what is to come. Tonight, or tomorrow, I will have to face his fury, knowing I have once again disobeyed him. I expect him to be angry but I also anticipate that he will not stay that way for long. Daniel is a good catch. Who better to take over the butcher's shop than a son-in-law of his own? On that thought, I feel myself blushing but Daniel seems to like the red in my cheeks. As I step out of the truck, our bodies accidentally collide and there is that familiar smell of meat again. It makes me wonder how we are to go on, because as things stand, I cannot imagine myself sharing the same bed with him.

We walk in single file onto the porch, the sound of his creaky tread on the decking much heavier than my own. He takes my hand again but this time I do not resist. This is the moment I have been looking forward to almost as much as I have been dreading. I have seen enough black and white romance movies at Thornhaugh to know what happens next.

He kisses me gently, taking great pains to make sure our bodies do not meet. The butterflies I had hoped for are there in abundance in my stomach but the lingering smell of meat fights for supremacy and wins. It is no good. I cannot help it. I move my head away but smile to take the sting out of my action, hoping he will put my aversion down to shyness.

'Thank you for putting up with me.' I am polite, a little distant in fact and I know he does not deserve this.

'No more conspiracy theories though.' He jokes his way out of any rejection he might be feeling. 'I know your old man is a bit on the scary side, but I don't think *even he* would invent a dead wife.'

'What if she *is* still alive though?' I persevere with the conspiracy he has warned me against. 'What if she just ran away?' I should not be putting this on him. It is not fair.

Naturally, he is a little shocked by my outburst but takes it in his stride. 'Who could blame her? I'd run away too if I were married to Frank.'

His laughter is short lived and I can tell he immediately regrets his words. I also get the impression he is moved by my sadness and feels protective towards me. I might not deserve it, but I grab at it all the same. He is everything I want in so many ways except—

'She didn't run, Natalie. My mother was there at the funeral. She told me all about it.'

This is news to me. *Why didn't he say anything before?* I feel hot tears running down my face. I am grateful to him, but I must ask again—

'Are you sure?'

Nodding, he reclaims my hand and I am shocked by how sweaty his skin is. His face is red and oily too and there are wet patches under his arms that were not there before. Everything about him suggests he is trying to hide something, that he might even be lying. Something in his cold blue eyes bothers me but I do not give it enough thought because I am too wrapped up in my own selfishness. This is because my heart is breaking all over again. It feels as if I am hearing about my mother's death for the first time.

'I wish it were a lie. For your sake. You must miss her.'

Daniel is back to his confident self again and I am quick to dismiss what I thought I saw in him earlier, putting it down to my overactive imagination. Swallowing deeply, I nod through my tears, wanting nothing more than to be alone, so I can sob out my anger and pain. Realising how ungrateful I am being, I work hard to disguise my selfishness because it is important that I retain Daniel's good opinion of me.

'I had a nice time tonight. Thank you, Daniel.'

'Just nice?' He is smiling again.

'Very nice.' I do not know what else to say. I obviously do not feel the same way he does.

'As nice as this?'

He kisses me again and I allow it, because he is a good guy, one of the best, but I do not reciprocate. Truthfully, it is all I can do not to push him away.

'I never had a boyfriend before,' I say to prevent him kissing me again.

'Is that what I am?' he teases.

'I don't know. Are you?' Unlike him, I am deadly serious.

'If you want me to be. Do you?'

I am not sure, and I almost say so, but I hold back. 'Goodnight, Daniel,' I say instead, coyly pecking him on the cheek.

Chapter 18

The House By The Sea

Having closed the porch door behind me, I watch the lights of Daniel's pickup truck bounce their way along the track that will take him out on the coast road into Little Downey, and long to feel more than I do. My first kiss was not the experience I had hoped for but that is not to say it will not get better. Perhaps I am being too harsh on myself and on Daniel. These are early days and I am not at all experienced in such matters.

It was foolish of me to suppose one kiss could change everything but I am determined to celebrate the event anyway, so I force myself to smile at the memory, shocked at how easily I am able to deceive myself. I wish Dr Moses were here so I could point out that an overactive imagination can sometimes come in handy. As I cannot, I put a finger to my lip and trace where Daniel has been. Tonight I have been touched by a man, kissed by a man, perhaps even loved by a man. Three firsts, all in one night. *So why don't I feel more?* It puzzles me that I do not, because Daniel is perfect for me in every way. *Almost.* But in a place as old-fashioned as Little Downey, where women are expected to settle down at a young age in order to fit in or run the risk of becoming an outcast—it is important that I have a boyfriend. As my mother found out, it is dangerous to be different here. Those who don't conform are more prone to throwing themselves off the cliff edge. For that reason alone, I plan on marrying as soon as possible. But if not Daniel, who else?

Deciding that I will not think about this now, that love is overrated anyway, and that I am more like my mother than I ever suspected, judging by the love-obsessed way I am behaving, I sigh and switch on the kitchen light.

My eyes go to the knife first, before I even register his presence. It is a razor-sharp Wusthof classic—spanning six inches in length; quite possibly the best boning knife on the market. Sitting at the table with a terrible face on him, my father's hand is wrapped around the yellow handle which matches the colour of his sleep-deprived eyes. He taps the knife menacingly against the table in time with his own angry heartbeat.

'You scared me! I didn't know you were there.' My voice is accusing, but this is for his benefit, so he cannot guess how scared I am.

'I told you I didn't want him sniffing around. Honour thy father. That's what the bible says.' He gestures to the dusty pages of an old bible lying conveniently open on the table.

'Honour thy father *and* mother,' I retaliate.

Angrily, he slams the knife into the table and gets to his feet, the chair scraping on the flagstone floor behind him. My eyes swing away from him and back to the knife. Its blade is embedded in the wood, where it continues to shake and vibrate, as if it has not done terrorising me yet. I am too frightened to move but I cannot take my eyes off the knife either. I would rather look at this than at my father, who is towering over me.

'You'd better start listening to Frank's Law around here.'

He is in my face, glaring at me, and I am so small beside him I feel sick with fear. I look for the knife again. It is still there. Without it, he can do nothing. I have been beaten before, but I will not allow him to beat me in the true sense of the word. *I am Natalie Powers,* I remind myself. *I am my mother's daughter.*

'I am not a child anymore,' I tell him. 'I can do as I like. See who I like.' I might sound fearless but I am shaking from head to toe.

'Over my dead body,' he snarls.

'I won't be bullied, Father. This is my home. I belong here as much as you do.'

'You *do not* belong here. Never did. Your home is back there—in the institution.'

He means every word of it. I can tell. As a result, something inside me dies.

'I'm not sick. Why won't you believe that?'

My pleading must have hit a nerve, because although he is still scowling at me, he is also searching for traces of sanity in my face. I sense that he almost believes me—

'I want to.'

There is a break to his voice that makes me want to reach out to him but I do not. He would see this as weakness. Nevertheless, I feel myself softening.

'What are you afraid of, Father? Losing me like you did Mother?'

At this, my father's head shoots up. The wary look is back. 'I ain't afraid of nuthin' or nobody 'cept you and your madness.'

Chapter 19

This is the third night in a row I have watched my father let himself out of the wrong door of the whitewashed building, *the one he claims never to use,* slyly glancing this way and that, before scurrying like a frightened mouse into the house. He seems to feel the weight of the full moon above him because he keeps his head low, while his heavy feet scrape a trail of sand into the house. As on the previous two nights, he closes the porch door quietly behind him, so as not to disturb me, but I could not *be more* disturbed. This is how I know he is up to something, because during the day, he usually slams the door shut.

It has been four days since the row and he still hasn't spoken to me. Daniel hasn't been anywhere near either, so I suspect he has been told to keep away. I wouldn't put it past my father to have warned him off with a loaded shotgun, but I am surprised, and hurt, that Daniel has not made more of an effort to see me. I suppose, when all is said and done, he *does* have to work with my father and is probably just biding his time. I hope so, because the loneliness and isolation of living out here is wearing me down. I used to think that Thornhaugh was my punishment for the things I did but I know the torture of returning home is far worse; that I am as much a prisoner as ever.

The nightdress I am wearing is my mother's and it hangs off me as it did her. In a few days of sitting around feeling sorry for myself, I have become a bag of bones that a starving dog would not want to pick over. Immediately, I am reminded of the gypsy's dog and wonder if it made it home safely. There is something bothering me about that night that my secretive self is keeping from me, so I do not stay on this subject too long. Instead, I run my hands over the satin nightgown that almost touches the floor and wonder why I am not like other girls. Most girls my age would not be seen dead in anything so old fashioned but I cannot resist anything that was my mother's, nor any attempt to bring her to life again. When I wrap my arms around myself, as I am doing now, I imagine it is her arms that are bringing me comfort. When I peer into the only mirror I *am* allowed to keep in my room, *because it is made of Perspex and cannot hurt me*, I expect to see her face—so I am shocked to find my own self looking back at me. My eyes are ugly from crying, I notice, and have black shadows under them. *My God, I look like a corpse*, I decide miserably.

I am about to move away from the window when I catch sight of something else outside—a shadowy figure flitting across the overgrown garden.

Holding my breath, I watch it move fast, yet awkwardly; zigzagging from side to side, as if drunk. The shape is too slight to be that of a man and it is certainly not my father, who I can hear mooching around downstairs. *What then? A fox or a deer perhaps?* As soon as I see a dim light appear in one of the barred windows belonging to the whitewashed building, I know that what I saw was no animal. Glancing firstly at the clock on my bedside table, noting that it is 2am, and back again at my ghostly reflection, I instinctively know that whatever is out there is far more sinister than anything I could imagine.

***

Having spent another hour lying awake, my mind conjuring up illusions of shadowy creatures creeping into the house and stealing up the staircase, I get out of bed and get dressed. I dare not put a light on in case it leaks onto the landing and disturbs my father who finally retired to his room an hour ago. I am praying that he is asleep.

As my legs find their way into a stiff pair of just-washed jeans, I slip on an oversized hoody, very apt for the sneaking around I am about to play a part in. On the landing, my plimsolled feet know how to avoid the creaky floorboards beneath the carpet but my heart is in my mouth when I push open the door to my father's room.

Inside, it is dark and shadowy, and it takes a while for my eyes to adjust. *Please be asleep,* is all I can think, because if not I will have some explaining to do and I haven't come prepared with any excuses. The sash window on my mother's side of the bed has been left open and the net curtain being sucked in and out by the sea breeze makes a sound like a kiss, something this house has not heard in a long time.

At last, I see him—asleep on top of the bedclothes, one arm above his head and the other tucked firmly in the waistband of his underpants. The moon through the window shines onto his sweating forehead and his eyelids flutter relentlessly, as if he doesn't rest peacefully. *Nor does he deserve to,* I can't resist thinking. As always, the blame for what happened to my mother is between us.

He wears a grubby vest, exposing tufts of black and grey streaked armpit hair and I am overwhelmed by the smell of sweat and dead flesh coming off his body. It oozes out of him like a disease, reminding me of Daniel, only this is far worse. Thinking back to the memory of my first kiss, I am almost sick in my mouth, so I force myself not to think about it.

Occasionally, the great fearless man that is Frank Powers whimpers in his sleep and I wonder which one of us is tormenting him in his dreams. *Me or her?* Not for the first time, I marvel at what my mother saw in him—she was beautiful and lively, and he quite the opposite. What can have been the attraction and why did their love die? This is what I want to know above all else; that and what happened to make her feel she couldn't turn to anyone in her hour of need, least of all her husband? *Damn that bloody cliff,* that's what I say, *and damn all the heartless reporters for renaming Little Downey "Suicide Bay". By romanticising what happened, they are as much to blame for my mother's death as anyone else. We all let her down. Every single one of us. But most of all—my father.*

'Father?' My voice seems to come from nowhere, appearing eerily ghostlike, even to my own ears.

'Father?' I say again, louder this time, not just to test he really *is* asleep, but to shake off the malevolent feeling that has crept into the room like an unwelcome shadow. Thankfully he goes on sleeping, so I slip away—gently closing the door behind me.

Chapter 20

The Whitewashed Building

Although I have brought a torch with me, I am nervous about using it, in case whoever is hiding out here sees it, so I am grateful to the moon for showing me the way. Without it, I would be alone in the dark, about to enter my father's workshop. *That's two of my worst fears about to happen in the space of one night.*

The hood pulled over my head stops my eyes from straying too far and I am glad of this, because I know if I stare at the shadows too long, I will start to see things that are not there. The stench of death reminds me that I am closer to the building than I first thought and when I see the same dim light that I saw from my room shining through the barred window, my heart sinks. I can't make up my mind if the flickering is caused by a candle or an oil lamp. All I know is I had hoped to find it gone and even imagined turning around and heading for home again but there is no chance of that happening now. When I hear a dog barking in the distance, I freeze, and a cold shiver runs through my body. I wonder if it is the gypsy's dog trying to find its way home. Out here, by the sea and the cliff edge, sounds get distorted, so I cannot tell how close the dog really is. It could be miles away.

I wait for the comfort of silence before moving on again and when I do, my body instinctively hunches over in an attempt to appear smaller and less visible. The thought of the intruder watching me as I approach fills me with terror. *Who can it be? What do they want?* Climbing on top of an old tin barbecue,

I try not to make a sound but the torch in my pocket scrapes against the flimsy metal and the light inside the building is immediately extinguished, reminding me once again that I am not alone out here.

All I can hear is my own breathing and I want more than anything to abandon this mission and go home but something bigger than my fear drives me on, so I brace myself for I know not what, switch on the torch, and shine it through the rusting bars of the window.

Once my eyes adjust to the gloomy interior, I find myself staring at crumbling brick walls. When one of the metal hooks on the ceiling moves slightly, creating a sickening clunk, my breathing becomes so loud it hurts my ears. As the blood drains from my body, I sense an invisible presence surround me. The same one I haven't been able to shake off since leaving the house, or even before that, when I first saw the shadow flitting across the garden. I am so afraid I don't think I could scream if I wanted to. I close my eyes, wishing I was anywhere but here but they flash open again when I hear a shuffling sound coming from inside the building. I cannot bear not knowing what made that noise, so I push my arm all the way through the bars and circle the room with my torch.

Expecting to see some dark otherworldly creature scurrying across the floor, I scour every inch of the concrete walls, floor and ceiling—but no such monster shows itself. I know that whatever made that noise can't have vanished; that it is lurking somewhere in the shadows. Perhaps it is creeping up on me. It could be standing beside me for all I know.

I want to cry. I want my mother. Every girl wants her mother when she is afraid.

The sound of the dog barking again startles me so much that I lose my balance and end up dropping the torch. It bounces noisily on the metal barbecue and the beam instantly goes off. *What now?* I think, as the barking turns to an anguished howling, causing the hairs on the back of my neck to stand up. There is something haunting about the dog's call. It is much closer than it was, I realise, and it crosses my mind that it would be impossible for it to have travelled so far so quickly, unless of course, it is a ghost dog.

Blindly, I scramble for the torch, and thank God when my hand closes around it. My gratitude is short lived when I switch it on and nothing happens. *Goddamn it. Don't you die on me.* Wiping my sweaty hands against my jeans, I shake the torch and pray for it to come back on. When it does, I am so relieved I could laugh out loud. The beam is weaker than before but I can live with that. Straightening up, I decide to shine the torch back through the gap in the bars one last time...just to be sure.

For a second, I think it is my own reflection staring back at me but I couldn't be more wrong. There, in front of me—showing absolutely no fear—is the face of a woman with balding hair, rotting teeth and haunted yellow eyes.

When my mouth opens to scream, she mimics me. In my eagerness to escape, I tumble off the barbecue and hit the ground hard. When I get up again, I think I am about to black out with fear and this feeling intensifies when I realise I have lost the torch. I give up looking for it sooner than I would like because the thought of that monstrosity coming after me is more terrifying than running blindly through the dark.

I run, petrified, away from the whitewashed building, but the house by the sea plays hide and seek with me. One second I can see it and the next it is gone. Realising that the moon has abandoned me, I aim for where I think my father's house should be and pray that I am right. This is one time I wish I had broken one of Frank's laws and left a light on to find my way back. Beneath me, my legs, already wobbly with fear, stumble often.

When I run into someone, I scream louder than I ever thought possible and immediately fight back at the arms that are trying to pin mine down. When a hand presses against my mouth, effectively silencing me, I claw madly at whatever I can get hold of.

Hearing a sharp intake of breath, I take pleasure in knowing I have left a mark on my attacker. But when the hand wraps itself more firmly around my face and I find myself struggling to breathe, I try to bargain with God. *Please don't let me be suffocated. Anything but that.* But, as usual He isn't listening, so I remind myself that this person's skin and blood is under my fingernails. They will not be allowed to get away with this. My father will see to that. I am surprised that I am so sure of this when he makes no attempt to disguise his hatred of me.

A woozy feeling comes over me and it dawns on me that today might be my turn to die. I ask myself if this matters. *Will anyone miss me? Not my father, that's for sure.* With all the fight gone out of me, I focus my attention on a distant star. *Am I to live?* I ask of it, *or die?*

"Everybody has to die sometime, Natalie." I hear her voice. Of course, I do. My mother—

I want nothing more than to go to her, but when the pressure is released from my mouth and my lungs fill with air, I realise I am not about to be murdered after all; that it is my stillness and silence that is required, so I give in to the body that has captured mine and make myself familiar with its scent. It has a clean earthy smell, reminding me of woodland, campfires and the sea. I sense that this person is not the same witchlike creature I saw in my father's workshop. That thing, *that thing*, whatever it is, could not possibly smell so good.

'It's okay. I'm not going to hurt you.'

His voice comes out of nowhere, like a stray bullet that might take someone's ear off. I recognise it immediately. Who could not, after the impression he has left on me. Clearly, he doesn't trust me to remain quiet because he keeps one finger pressed to my mouth. In the dark, I notice that one of his mismatched eyes shows up more vividly than the other.

'I think it's gone,' Jed whispers.

'You saw it too? I'm not going mad?' I ask.

Both our heads are cricked in the direction of the whitewashed building as I say this but he cannot know that everything depends on his answer.

'It's not safe out here,' he says after a long pause. 'Not with that thing about.'

'I think that thing is my mother,' I acknowledge, hardly daring to look at him.

Chapter 21

The House By The Sea

I can hardly see for the steam but I could find my way around this bathroom blindfolded if I had to. I know, for instance, that my father's shaving brush will be on the windowsill where he always leaves it and his worn grey flannel will have been put back beneath the bar of soap that has his black and grey hairs stuck to it. The double-edged razor blades he uses to shave his face will of course be nowhere to be seen.

These are things only a family member can know about a house and its inhabitants. *My God. What kind of family do I belong to, if what I saw last night was real?* I do not want to think about last night, yet it is *all* I can think about. *Can it be true? Or am I losing my mind? I must not think about my mother. Focus on something else, Natalie.*

The window has a crack in it that runs from corner to corner. There is a bullet-sized chunk of glass missing from the bottom of the pane. I know if I put one eye to it, I will see the whitewashed building outside and be reminded once again of what happened. *That thing cannot be my mother. I know this to be impossible yet last night I didn't think so. Last night was last night,* I remind myself, and I wasn't myself. *Nothing new there then!*

The sound of the shower spilling a continuous stream of water into the cast iron bath beneath it is meant to be soothing, but it isn't helping.

Drip. Splat. Drip.

I put my hands over my ears and close my eyes, wanting to shut out the slaughterhouse scene in my head. Death and blood. All my life, death and blood.

Above the window there is a wooden beam, which dates to when the house was first built. I have imagined myself hanging from it many times. I wonder if my mother also considered it an option before finally settling on the cliff edge. *She is not dead, Natalie. You know she is alive. You saw her. She did not take her own life. It was a big lie.*

It has been a long time since I imagined coming across my father's oxygen-starved face writhing at the end of a noose on this beam. Many thought he would take his life after Mother died, *went away*, but he carried on going to spite everyone, he said. The thought of my father dying a slow and agonising death used to keep me awake at night. He might not have loved me but he was all I had. Now I know that he has been lying to me all these years, I am not so sure he doesn't deserve such a terrible end. I know I will eventually take this horrid thought back. I love my father and always have. I just wish he felt the same.

***

Because I have been hunched up in a naked ball on the floor for too long, my feet are numb with cold and my knees feel as if they will never unwind by themselves. I do not care about the growth of black hair on my legs or the way my greasy hair sticks to my shoulders. I know that what I am about to do is unacceptable, unforgivable even, after all the psychiatric help I have received. If Dr Moses were here, he would try to talk me out of it. But he is not and I am glad because his disappointment is something I do not want to witness again. Letting people down is something I have grown good at.

I look down at my clenched fist, noticing how pink the tips of my fingers have become. When I try to unravel them, they resist. Clearly, they think they know what is best for me and do not want to relinquish the chunk of lacklustre glass hidden inside my palm. The size and shape of it is a perfect match for the hole in the window. I will put it back when I am done, so as not to arouse my father's suspicions. *He isn't the only one capable of keeping a secret.*

Before it even touches my skin, I feel the promise of a morphine-inducing high.

The glass is blunt, but I persevere, knowing that if I scrape it against the soft flesh of my thigh long enough, it will eventually tear and bleed. I feel little or no pain, even when my skin oozes with sticky blood. I have never experienced sex or had an orgasm but I cannot imagine a better feeling than this. I have been cutting myself since I was nine years old, on and off, and I know that makes me a social outcast, somebody quite disgusting, but I cannot stop. I do not do it to get attention, as many people mistakenly think, which is why I have learnt to do it slyly, to parts of my body that do not get exposed often. There's no hiding the scars from some people though. At school I used to get asked how I got my scars and I would say I had been in a fight. When asked "Who with?" I would reply "Myself."

If I am asked what it feels like to self-harm, I say: "It feels as if I am screaming but no one can hear me."

Chapter 22

Little Downey Beach

The bigger more aggressive dog does not bother getting to its feet when it sees me. It remains curled up in a foetal position with its head between its paws. There is something about its flattened ears that makes me think it is depressed. Jed has his back to me and is digging a large hole in the sand. Sweat runs down his bare shoulders onto the tattooed ladies on his arms, who, likewise, appear to weep rather than dance.

Today, I am not here by accident. This time, I am here to see him. And I will not let anybody stop me. On that thought, my eyes swing warily to the caravan. The door is pinned open as usual and I can hear music coming from inside, but so far, thank goodness, there is no sign of the feisty gypsy woman.

Only Jed can help me solve the mystery of what happened. He knows what I saw. It is our secret. All along, I was right. My mother never abandoned me. She loved me too much for that. Everyone else has been lying. Daniel. The villagers. My own father. But what made them fake my mother's death and why did my father allow it? This is something I have to find out, but I must tread carefully. My mother's existence proves I was never mad in the first place but who is going to believe me? Not the police, that's for sure. I dare not accuse my father of anything either. I would find myself back at Thornhaugh in no time at all.

'Hi,' I say, louder than I need to, because I do not want to startle Jed. Hasn't my father always warned me not to creep up on people and frighten them.

Jed turns slowly and I realise I am wrong. He *is* aware of my presence but is choosing to ignore me. He and the dog share the same sorrowful expression, I notice, but Jed's eyes hug the ground, intentionally blanking me. I want to ask him what is wrong but then I remember that we are still strangers. Last night, I thought there was a shared something between us, but I realise it meant nothing to him, whereas—

'Did you find your dog?' I am determined to remain friendly but I stumble on my words because I find his behaviour confusing. Although he is not looking directly at me, I can tell that his face is dark and grim, not at all welcoming. *What can I have done to upset him?*

'I think I heard it barking last night, before you turned up at the house...' I run out of steam because anger is making his blue eye twitch.

Clearing his throat, Jed spits into the hole in the ground. *What is it with the men of Little Downey and spitting?* Finally, he forces himself to look me straight in the eye.

'I think I liked you better when you didn't say much,' he grumbles.

Chapter 23

The House By The Sea

I have been sitting at the kitchen table staring into space for what seems like ages and I still cannot shake off the feeling of depression that has descended on me. I feel too numb to cry. It doesn't matter what I tell myself—*Take no notice, Natalie. He's not worth it. Forget about him. He's not important. Why should you care what he thinks?* —but I *do* think he's worth it, I *can't* forget about him, he *is* important, to me, and I *do* care what he thinks.

When I hear a knock on the porch door, I almost trip over myself in my haste to answer it. *It's him. I know it is. He's come to apologise.* But when I reach the door, I am alarmed to see the gypsy woman staring back at me through the glass. It never enters my head not to answer. If she wants a fight, bring it on; I am in the mood for it. Besides, I have done nothing wrong. I have not encouraged her man in any way.

I push open the door and we size each other up. There is no scowl on her face, just a look of intense interest. This is not at all what I was expecting. I can't seem to work either of them out. When I see she is holding a dead cockerel, I take a step backwards.

'I'm Merry,' she explains, as if I ought to know this.

Not waiting for an invite, she marches straight past me into the kitchen, where she stands, looking about her with unveiled curiosity. When I eventually catch up with her, she thrusts the dead bird at me.

'The chicken is for you.'

When I do not make any attempt to take the chicken from her, she frowns. 'It died of natural causes. His name is, *was* Fury.'

'I saw your husband kill it myself.' I draw myself up to my full height and jut out my chin. *I will not be lied to in my own house,* I think stubbornly, even though that is exactly what has been happening for the last sixteen years.

'Do you always believe everything you see? Sometimes, Natalie, the truth is different.'

'You know my name?'

'Of course. Take the chicken. It is a welcome home gift.'

I have no idea how she knows my name or that I have only recently returned to Little Downey but she doesn't know enough about me to work out that the gift of a dead animal is the last thing anyone could give me to win me over. However, I do get the impression she is the sort of woman who could twist anyone, Jed included, around her little finger. For some reason, this makes me feel sadder than ever. I am jealous of her I realise suddenly; because she is everything I am not—beautiful and womanly with the kind of hourglass figure I have always dreamt of. She also has Jed.

'Thank you,' I say to be polite, reluctantly taking the dead chicken from her. Placing it on the kitchen table, *which I will scrub with bleach when she is gone,* I realise that the poor thing's head is still intact. Perhaps she is telling the truth after all, because this bird certainly never died on a chopping block.

While I wash my hands at the sink, I watch the way she touches things; marvelling at this and that—the electric kettle and the modern washing machine which is a new addition to the household. Suddenly, she stops what she is doing, shrugs apologetically and laughs.

'Sorry. I don't know what it's like living in a real home.'

'I wouldn't call it that,' I say with an edge to my voice.

'I'm Jed's sister.'

'His sister! I thought...'

'I know what you thought, Natalie. You like him. And he likes you.'

'I'm not sure I believe you.' I do not know who I am angrier with—Jed for his earlier behaviour or Merry for her audacity.

There is no getting away from the fact that I am still smarting over Jed's putdown, but Merry, she doesn't even know me—

'You caught him at a bad moment. He was burying his dog.'

'It died! But last night, I thought I heard it…'

I pull out a chair and sit down, feeling suddenly tearful. Poor Jed. No wonder he spoke to me the way he did. *How could I have been so stupid? Whatever must he think of me?* And why didn't I cotton on to the fact he was burying his dog when I came across him, or guess at his relationship to Merry for that matter? They both have the same soft lilting Irish accent, both are dark skinned with hair as black as my own.

'We must have killed it after all, in the car.' I hesitate, scared to go on in case she or Jed should hold this admission against me but then I remind myself that I am meant to be an advocate of plain speaking. 'It ran out in front of us, you see. It was an accident.' I confess, hardly daring to meet her eye.

'It had had its neck broken. On purpose, if you ask me,' Merry snorts.

I immediately want to ask her if she is sure but I can tell by the outrage in her green eyes that she has never been surer of anything. Guiltily, I look away, realising I have known this all along. The truth has been hiding in the back of my mind, making me an accomplice of sorts. *What a coward I am.* Daniel killed the dog. I saw him do it, in the dark and from a long way away, but I still saw him. Yet I managed to convince myself I was mistaken; not wanting to spoil our night out or what I thought we had, which, in the end, turned out to be nothing. *How could I? How could he? Why would he?* I think up excuses for him. They come too easily. *He killed it to put it out of its misery,* I try telling myself. But if that was the case, why lie? *To protect you, Natalie.* But I am a woman, not a child.

'That kind of thing happens all the time around here. They don't like us in the village. But we're not the only ones.'

Taking this to mean I am equally disliked, I watch Merry take a crude necklace out of her pocket. It looks as if it has been made from a shoelace and has a row of chicken's claws and canine teeth attached to it. I have never seen anything so macabre or ugly.

'This is for you,' she tells me.

'What is it?' I ask, getting to my feet. I am not sure I want to know but I realise that I quite like her and do not want to offend her. There is something sultry and dangerous about her but at the same time she is childlike. I don't have to look far to realise who she reminds me of—my mother. *The real one. Not that other thing*.

'A lucky charm to ward off evil. Jed told me about your ghost.'

She is obviously referring to my mother and I feel surprised and a little hurt that Jed has shared this information with her. I try not to let this show, but she is incredibly intuitive—

'We tell each other everything. That's how I know he likes you,' Merry says with a knowing smile.

Hearing this makes up for everything, and I feel a smile creep on to my own face, as I hesitantly take the necklace from her.

'Now you have to give me a present,' she says, pointedly looking around the room.

I watch her eyes darting here and there, like a child's greedy hand in a sweet jar, before settling on a plastic bumblebee fridge magnet. I must confess that I am somewhat baffled and beguiled by this strange creature but I go along with the request anyway.

'Consider it yours,' I tell her, watching her quickly pocket the fridge magnet as if appropriating things that are not her own comes naturally.

'Shall I make some tea?' Merry asks, taking me by surprise all over again.

Feeling like a stranger in my own kitchen, I sit back down but do not take my eyes off her as she busies herself with the kettle, quickly finding cups, sugar and teabags. It occurs to me that she finds everything *too* quickly; as if she automatically knows where everything is. How she could possibly have known where to find the cups, which are hidden behind the curtain under the sink? I get the feeling I am deliberately being kept in the dark about something. I may have spent most of my life in an institution, where normal doesn't exist, but even I know this is not standard behaviour for the outside world. Feeling annoyed, I push the charm away from me, instinctively nervous of it, because I suspect it has more to do with witchcraft than good luck.

'You haven't forgotten how to find your way around a kitchen then?' I point out at last.

'Not this one,' Merry replies mysteriously.

She is not fazed by my question but her eyes remain clouded with secrecy. I do not appreciate her playing cat and mouse with me in my own home. My mother would not have tolerated this, nor must I, so I get to my feet and fold my arms to show I mean business.

What is that supposed to mean? I am about to reply, when out of the window, I catch sight of my father's van pulling into the yard. I am immediately fearful for Merry. Like most of Little Downey, my father hates gypsies.

'You must go,' I say panicking. 'There's no telling what my father will do if he finds you here.'

'Never mind Frank, Natalie,' she chuckles. 'His bark is worse than his bite.'

The suggestion that these two have crossed paths before doesn't go unnoticed. But, as much as I know this to be impossible, now is not the time to ask questions. I must insist she leave. Walking over to the door, I pointedly hold it open until she gets the message.

And with that, she is gone, leaving behind a trail of wonder and mystery, which I assume is perfectly normal for someone like her.

Chapter 24

Little Downey

Having braved the village shop again, receiving just as chilly a reception from Mrs Abbot as on my previous visit, but escaping her husband's ever-watchful scrutiny from out back, as he is nowhere to be seen, I collect my bicycle from the narrow alleyway where I left it and cycle through the village towards home. I'll never know what makes me turn right instead of left on the coast road. Perhaps my head is too full of Jed and Merry and my father, but mostly Jed, to notice that I have taken a wrong turn; but as soon as I see the ugly outline of the grey windowless building up ahead, I experience a numbing kind of terror.

I am back where I started—at the slaughterhouse. I say this is where I started, because I can hardly remember a time when it didn't feature in my life or give me nightmares. The place is as I remember. The doors might not appear as giant as they once did but they still clang ominously, as if announcing that death is on its way. The stench is overpowering; a mixture of faeces, urine and congealing blood. The building's familiar shadow falls onto a rough tarmac drive, broken down over time by the wheels of lorries bringing animals to slaughter. In an adjoining pen, tired-looking horses are squeezed tightly together. I dare not look at them, for fear of seeing a grey pony with kind eyes.

I stand in the lane, straddling my bike, wondering how I got here, knowing I would never have come here on purpose. *So, what made you, Natalie?* I resist the urge to stick a thumb in my mouth; reminding myself that I am a grown woman, not a frightened child. That's when I see Daniel's pickup truck hurtling along the pot-holed lane towards me. I consider standing my ground and challenging him over Jed's dog but when I see he has someone next to him in the passenger seat, I drop the bike and run.

It isn't until I reach the safety of one of the nearby outbuildings that I realise I haven't been spotted, because he drives straight though the double doors into the building, never once glancing my way.

I hear the engine being switched off, car doors opening, the clang of metal, shuffling of boots and the echo of male voices, but when I hear a distraught calf calling for its mother, I cover my ears. I have cried like that poor creature is doing. I know exactly how it feels.

I jump back when I see a tall thin ginger-haired youth come out of the building. Swinging a halter in one hand, he walks over to the pen of horses and goes inside. Patting one of the horses in a friendly enough way, he slips the halter over its head. There is something about his expression that is familiar. I cannot put a name to his face at present, but I am sure I will in time. The horse follows him docilely, ears pricked and tail swinging, as if anticipating a net of hay and a bowl of oats. *I cannot stand this.* I know what happens to horses once they are inside. The law says you can't kill a horse in sight of another horse—because they instantly *know* and freak out. Instead, they are shot separately.

I am about to run back to my bike and get the hell out of there before the single bullet rings out, when I hear my father's voice.

Chapter 25

Little Downey Slaughterhouse – Frank

Frank and Daniel are loading animal carcasses into the back of the pickup truck. It's a young man's job and Frank lets Daniel do most of the work. As the boss, he's earned that right. Already, his muscles ache. Stopping for a breather, he glances up at the freshly killed beasts that swing from metal chains above his head. After years of practice, he no longer sees dead animals, just meat. Good cuts and bad ones.

To the right of the double doors there is a small office with blinds at the windows. Through a gap in the blinds, Frank can see a woman he sometimes chats to sitting at a desk typing. Every now and again she picks up a green apple and takes a bite from it. She has a stomach stronger than most, he has to give her that. To the left of him, there are pens of restless frightened sheep, who bleat constantly and stomp their forefeet on the concrete floor. In a stall on its own, a brown calf circles agitatedly, its deep-throated moos noisily echoing around the draughty building.

A ginger-haired lad, one of Daniel's cronies, walks a skinny horse into the building. Frank doesn't know if it's just him but the blokes they're hiring these days keep on getting younger, barely out of school that one. He swings his eyes back to Daniel, who is wrestling with the last carcass. The lad is a grafter, he'll give him that. One day, if Daniel behaves himself and learns how to mind his own business, he will make a fine butcher. Frank is about to carry on minding *his* own business when the slaughterer, a man he knows well, shouts at the worker with the horse.

'Tie it up, Jono and bring me the calf instead. I can't hear myself think with that racket.'

Jono does as he is bid and ties up the horse, then slouches over to the stall with the calf inside. Frank grits his teeth at how slow he is. It's a wonder he hasn't had the slaughterer's boot up his arse before now. Daniel straightens up beside him, as if his interest is piqued by Jono's inexperienced handling of the calf, which is clearly giving him the runaround. Without so much as a "by your leave", Daniel jogs over to help him. That wouldn't have happened in Frank's day.

While they attempt to herd the bellowing calf between them, using arms, knees and the tips of their steel-toe-cap boots, Frank ambles over to Bob Black. They might go way back but they have never been friends. Frank has fought this man several times, pub brawls mostly, but once at his own wedding, much to his wife's displeasure, Frank ended up breaking Bob's nose.

Bob likes crossword puzzles and prefers Guinness over ale. He is also partial to a game of darts. More mysteriously, his wife Norma never leaves the house, having some form of agoraphobia that Bob doesn't like to talk about. The only other thing Frank knows for sure about Bob is that he is one sick fucker.

They both watch the calf stop to sniff its dead mother's body, which is lying on its side on the ground, steam and blood coming off it. This is a bit too much for Frank, but Bob laughs as if he might piss himself.

'Did you like seeing Mummy snuff it?' Bob taunts.

As if it understands, the calf glances in Bob's direction, raises its tail and lets a stream of loose green faeces shoot out of its rear end.

'You'll pay for that, you little fucker,' Bob gestures for the lads to hurry up but the calf only moves when a forklift truck comes forward to remove its mother's carcass.

Although armed with a large bolt gun, Bob Black is harmless enough looking but his enthusiasm for the job makes up for the lack of menace in his build. He smiles slyly at Frank's approach.

'The young and injured are meant to be slaughtered first,' Frank reminds him sternly. Now they're up close, Frank is surprised by how much he wants to pummel his fists into the man's face. Some battles are never forgotten.

'There's nothing wrong with having a bit of fun,' Bob points out sulkily. Clearly, he hasn't forgotten about the broken nose either. 'Then again, you always were a spoilsport.'

Deliberately clenching his fists in full sight of the man, but refusing to rise to the gibe, Frank wants to tell Bob that killing is one thing but to take enjoyment from it quite another but doesn't waste his breath. The man is a bully who no doubt terrorises animals and the young lads who work for him, but he is also a coward. He won't even look Frank in the eye.

Glancing nervously at Frank's fists, Bob shouts for Daniel and Jono to hurry up. Finally, the calf is manoeuvred into position. It has given up struggling and has fallen silent but its sides continue to heave with exhaustion. Daniel has it in a headlock so it cannot move, and his sleeves are soaked with its saliva. Aiming the bolt gun at the calf's head, Bob makes a friendly clucking noise to get its attention and is about to pull the trigger, when he pauses deliberately, almost for effect. This time he does look Frank in the eye—

'How's that daughter of yours, Frank? Tenderest bit of meat I've seen in a long time.'

'Mind your own, Bob. If you know what's good for you.'

Frank would give his right arm to take Bob outside and give him a good kicking but he can't do that in front of these youngsters, who look up to their elders. He changes his mind, when quite by accident, he catches Daniel passing a lecherous smile to Jono.

'That goes for you an' all. I want you to stay away from her,' Frank warns.

'You know I can't do that, Frank.' Daniel is all wide-eyed innocence, but a smile escapes him; the sniggering of the other two clearly egging him on.

'She don't know nothing.' Frank jabs a finger into Daniel's chest.

'Then you've got nothing to worry about.' Unsmiling, Daniel bats the finger away.

Chapter 26

Little Downey Beach – Natalie

My legs are tired from walking but my mind won't settle. So much for a long walk being good for you. I couldn't have picked a worst time to come down to the beach. It is swelteringly hot. Even the sea is subdued. There are no signs of birds or wildlife either. The saying "only mad dogs and Englishmen go out in the midday sun", a favourite of my father's, has never felt more appropriate.

They didn't see me watching them. Daniel or my father. Having caught me out in the past listening in to his grown-up conversations, Father should have known better. But he didn't glance my way. Not once. And I heard enough of their conversation to be on my guard. Having watched them through a small gap in the door, they might have had their backs to me, but I could see their blurred elongated faces reflected in the blood-splattered walls.

I cannot comprehend the meaning behind their words but I do know that they frighten me, these two men. Who would have thought that Daniel would square up to my father like that. Answering back and pushing his hand away. Even more of a mystery is the fact that my father allowed it. And what did my father mean when he told Daniel that I didn't know anything? *What don't I know?* Could they have been referring to my mother?

As for that man, Bob Black, I remember him from the first time I was taken to the slaughterhouse, when they found me hiding in the pigpen, covered in blood and straw, screaming "The animals don't want to die!" Like most men, my father included,

Bob Black is cruel. But more than that—I remember him looking at me in a way that wasn't natural. I might only have been seven at the time but I sensed there was something wrong with him, even then. Deep down, I'm sure my father felt the same. I once overheard him tell my mother that the only thing stopping Bob's wife from leaving the house was Bob himself.

But if Bob Black is the bogeyman, where does that leave the likes of my father and Daniel who are equally dangerous? I no longer feel safe in Little Downey. There is a mystery here that I have never been able to solve. It has everything to do with the cliff-top suicides. I sense this with all my heart, but I cannot run away, because there is my mother to consider. Jed and Merry too. What will happen to them if I disappear? Who will look out for them?

On that thought, I realise that the gypsy camp is where I have been heading all along. Subconsciously or not, I am drawn to this place and *them*.

***

I hear Merry before I see her. The sound of her splashing about in the water is what makes me glance towards the ocean, rather than the caravan. The sight of her hopping about in the freezing water brings a smile to my face, but it drops away again when I realise she is not wearing any clothes. Holidaymakers don't come here anymore, preferring the welcoming family-friendly resorts dotted further along the coastal path, which means she is in no danger of being spotted by anyone else. But I can't help feeling shocked and embarrassed. Berating myself for being such a prude, I am about to make a quick exit and pretend I haven't seen her when she calls out to me.

'Don't mind me!' she shouts. 'My body doesn't know what it is to be ashamed.'

As she wades through the water, more of her body is exposed. By the time she is on dry land and striding unashamedly towards me, I hardly know where to look. Noticing a frayed towel on the sand, I pick it up and hand it to her, but she shakes her head.

'I'm going straight back in. I just wanted to say hello. It's hot, isn't it.'

I try my hardest not to peer at her body, but she is so perfect it is impossible not to. She is the first young naked person I have seen. Those crazy enough to wander around starkers at Thornhaugh were old and infirm and I did not wilt in their presence as I am doing hers. I see that she is troubled by dark body hair as I am but does not appear bothered by it. The tuft of black hair between her legs is like my own, but unlike me, she has proper women's breasts. Being as flat chested as a boy, I long to touch hers; to find out what they feel like. When she smiles at me from underneath a tumble of long wet hair, I get the feeling she knows what I am thinking, and I feel my face flush.

I am sure my face turns even redder when Jed comes out of the caravan carrying the baby in one arm and rubbing the sleep out of his eyes with his free hand. He pauses when he sees me, and I think he is about to go back inside, but instead makes his way over; his dog trotting obediently behind him. This time, I thrust the towel at Merry.

'It's Jed,' I hiss.

She glances over at her brother and shrugs. 'Jed's seen me naked plenty of times.' Nevertheless, she wraps the towel around her, more to please me than anything else, I suspect. 'We are not a family for secrets,' she tells me, raising an eyebrow and I know that she is once again referring to the ghost that is my mother.

I watch her walk over to Jed and take the baby from him. She immediately clicks her tongue at it, much like a bird. There is something possessive about the way she holds her baby. I suspect she doesn't let it out of her sight often.

'There, there, little one. Mummy's here,' she coos.

Looking dishevelled and unwashed, as if he had just this minute woken up, Jed is more gorgeous than ever, but I purposefully ignore him, in case he still isn't speaking to me. If we are to be friends again then the first move must come from him. In the meantime, I pretend to show an interest in the baby, who has the same dark skin and hair as its mother and uncle. I think it is a girl, but I do not know for sure. I don't know much about babies, but I can tell this is a particularly beautiful one. When Merry flicks her wet hair to the side, I notice a prominent strawberry-shaped mark on her back.

'You're looking at my birthmark. The baby has one too. See.' Merry flips the baby over and sure enough there on its back is the same mark in miniature. I have never seen anything like this before and wonder if Jed has one too.

Sensing that he is looking at me, I feel my skin burn. Only when I am sure he is no longer looking do I risk glancing his way; in time to see the remains of a smirk vanish from his face.

'Are you coming in for a dip?'

He isn't looking at me when he says this, so I can be forgiven for thinking he is addressing his sister. It is only when Merry gives me a push that I dare to think otherwise.

'Me? Oh no, I couldn't.'

'Fair enough,' he mutters, making it sound as if the loss is all mine.

My eyes don't know what to do with themselves when he undresses in front of me. Taunting me with the same knowing smile I have seen on his sister's face, I watch him kick off his jeans, then remove his cotton boxers. I will not, must not, look at what is between his legs. It wouldn't be seemly. I ignore the pointed way he is looking at my clothes; daring me to join him. Behind me, Merry laughs, and I fire her a look of contempt. Her face tells me she is enjoying my discomfort but, in the end, she decides to take pity on me.

'Don't be shy, Natalie.'

Because I feel as if my shameful secret is there on my face for all to see, I do not answer straight away. I rub my scarred arms, visible to no one, not even myself, because as usual they are hidden beneath the sleeves of my shirt. For the first time, I hate the cutting and the fact that the scars are preventing me from doing something I desperately want to do. Merry is wrong about me being shy. With Jed, I don't think I would be. With Daniel, yes, most definitely, but the thought of him touching me fills me with disgust. I am ashamed, humiliated even, to have ever considered him as a potential suitor. Jed is a different matter. I would give anything to join him in the water. *But what would he say if he saw my scars? Or Merry, for that matter? Would they view me differently?*

'I can't. I have scars,' I finally admit.

'Nobody will mind about that. Go on.'

Again, she gives me a push. There is nothing but kindness and sincerity on her face, and not a jot of pity either. My whispered confession has not made her recoil in horror. Can I assume then that her brother will feel the same? When I turn around to look for Jed, I see that he is already at the water's edge and that the dog isn't far behind.

'Last chance!' Jed shouts, throwing me a wave.

I know all about last chances. Dr Moses issued me with the most important one of all when I left Thornhaugh—the threat of being permanently sectioned.

Chapter 27

The House By The Sea

It is dusk and the gentlest of breezes fans my face as I climb the sandy path up to the house by the sea. My step is lighter than it was when I first set out for my walk and the smell of the sea in my hair is a reminder of the good time I had on the beach this afternoon. Carrying my wet clothes in one hand, I go barefoot in the sand, naked beneath the over-sized shirt that Jed has leant me. The damp material clings to my skin and my body has never felt so alive; nor have I ever walked so tall or felt so majestic. The sense of liberation I am feeling is both new and exhilarating. I wouldn't swap it for anything.

When I catch sight of my father messing about with a metal dustbin by the side of the house, *lurking in the shadows as always,* I immediately feel self-conscious. Reassuring myself that there is no way he can know what I have been thinking, where I have been or who I have been doing it with, I pull down my shirt and claw a hand through my tangled hair. Being in my father's presence has the power to bring me back down to earth until I am an anxious-to-please child again.

Making my way over to him, I remember that I was supposed to ask Merry what she meant the other day when she told me not to mind my father, that his bark was worse than his bite. There is no point in demanding answers from my father. He would ignore me as he always does. Nonetheless, the mystery has been eating me up and I had every intention of raising this with her as when I saw her again, but as soon as I was among them, I forgot all about it. Easy enough to do when Jed is around. When I am with him, there is no heartache, no killing and, best of all, no ghosts. I may only have known them a short while but Merry and Jed are my people in a way that the villagers in Little Downey have never been.

'What are you doing, Father?' I ask nervously, in case he can see right through me.

'Rats.' A grunt, nothing more. He doesn't even turn to look at me.

Silently, I watch him. An angry vein protrudes prominently on the side of his right eye as if he is thinking too hard. You and me, both, I want to say to him, but I do not, because deep down, I suspect I do not ask my father about Merry because I fear the truth as much as he does. We Powers, we like to think we speak the truth and shame the devil, but the truth of the matter is, we run from it like the cowards we are.

'Rats?' I ask in confusion. *What sort of answer is that?*

Knowing better than to expect a rational reply, I join him at the dustbin, going down on my knees so we are side by side. I get the impression that we may have kneeled together like this before, only in prayer, but as soon as the memory stirs, it is cruelly whipped away again. *Was my father ever kind to me?* Sometimes I think so. Other times I'm not so sure. *Just because you want to believe he is capable of loving you, doesn't make it true, Natalie.*

When I finally investigate the dustbin, I am shocked to discover there are two large rats inside, each squaring up to the other and viciously baring its teeth. I may have made a Sunday School promise to love all of God's creatures but rats are another matter.

'Ugh.' I immediately recoil from them. Nasty, horrid creatures they might be, but I don't want them to come to any harm.

'What are you going to do to them?' I demand.

'Me? Nothing.' My father shrugs innocently, as if surprised by my question. He scratches his stubbly chin and frowns at me, as if I should already know this—

'Put two alpha males like this together and they end up eating each other. The surviving one gets a taste for its own kind and ends up killing all the other rats.'

My father spits into the dustbin and his phlegm hits one of the rats square on the nose, making it squeal noisily in protest.

'End of rat problem,' he states, dusting his hands together.

'Is that another one of Frank's laws?' I ask suspiciously.

'It's nature's law,' he replies, appearing puzzled by my ignorance.

Chapter 28

Time stands still in Little Downey. Nowhere more so than the house by the sea, which has seen too many deaths to care about the living. I am sitting at the kitchen table, pondering how many have been lost to the cliff edge in the last twenty years. Twenty? Thirty? More than that? Is anyone keeping count? For the first time, I ask myself if the suicides are real. They could be a cover up for other missing people—a conspiracy of sorts. And why not? If they issued a fake death certificate for my mother, and I assume that they did, then how many others has this happened to?

In a place as isolated as this, where nobody is in a rush to involve doctors, policemen or any other authority, it is entirely possible that they, the villagers, could get away with something like this. But why? And if the suicides never took place, then where are these missing people? What has the village done to them? Are they dead or very much alive, like my mother? Perhaps they are kept at Thornhaugh as I was. At this stage, I am not ruling anything out. Sighing with frustration, I realise I don't have any answers. All I know is living where we do, and how we do, can turn the shortest day into the longest, but the nights are worse.

Another long lonely night stretches in front of me. Already it is 9pm and soon it will be dark. I look at the congealing plates of food on the table and ignore the hunger pains in my belly. I must face facts. He isn't coming. So I get to my feet and scrape the greasy plate of fried eggs, sausages and beans into the bin. My father is in the pub again. He's never away from the place; claiming the food I serve up isn't worth hurrying home for. I do not disagree, as despite being famished, I have no appetite for my own meal of scrambled egg either. Unlike my mother, who was known for her culinary skills, I am not much of a cook.

As I put the crockery away, I am reminded of Merry and the fact that she seemed to know her way around this kitchen remarkably well. It was as if she had been in it many times before, knew it intimately even. Just because I didn't question her or my father about this doesn't mean I am not deeply curious. Absently, I wonder what my mother would think of another woman being in her kitchen. I shudder at the answer, because I know she would not like it any more than I would. Pausing at the window, my hands gripping the sink, I imagine her out there, alone in the dark. She could be watching me right now through the bars of the whitewashed building.

That's when I see the rat. Even from here, I can tell it has been in a fight because its fur is stained with blood. I wonder if it is one of the two in the dustbin. The rat washes itself clean and doesn't appear in any hurry, which suggests it is master of its own surroundings. An alpha male. Fascinated, I watch it stop to sniff the air, as if it senses danger, before leaping onto one of the barred windows of the whitewashed building.

I jump back in alarm when a hand unexpectedly shoots out of the bars to grab it. Squealing in protest, the rat sinks its teeth into its attacker's flesh, but it gets squeezed so hard, black blood erupts from its mouth. Tearing my eyes away from this gruesome spectacle, I tell myself that what I am seeing is not real. It can't be. It would be impossible for me to hear the sickening sound of the rat's bones being crushed from all the way in here. This is nothing but a psychotic imagining, the kind Dr Moses likes to warn me about. If he was here, he would no doubt go on to explain that the defenceless rat somehow represents my poor mother and that the eating of any kind of flesh awakens a primal fear in me, instilled at an early age.

I was just thinking about her, so I suppose he could be right. The fact is, I am always thinking about her, but at the same time I am intent on pushing her away. I want to go to my mother, of course I do, but I am afraid. Of so many things. Will she know me? Would my approaching her put her in even more danger? If the villagers and my father find out I know their secret, they could hide her elsewhere, where I may never find her again. I don't want to be responsible for them doing something even more terrible to her.

A noise behind me, the scurrying of a real rat perhaps, not an illusory one, breaks my concentration. *God forbid, it is not one of my father's cannibal rats.* Add to that, the sudden dipping of the yellow lights above my head and I am immediately on edge. A power cut is the last thing I need. I don't think my nerves could stand it. Reaching automatically for the drawer where the candles and matches are kept, I wish again that my father was home.

I picture him propped up at the bar in The Black Bull, getting drunker by the pint, no doubt angry with me as usual, *when is he not?* I dare not think about what he would do if he found out I had spent the afternoon with the gypsy. He would be furious. Much more so than when he found out I had been out with Daniel. It occurs to me that I am not a good daughter to my father any more than he is a good parent to me. I have wilfully disobeyed him, and I should be trying to please him, not antagonise him. No wonder he is driven to such bad temper. Sadly, there is no suggestion of him softening with age. I imagine that the other pub goers will be avoiding him as he glowers at them over his black ale, bristling for a fight to take his mind off the fact that his only daughter is a disappointment to him.

Chapter 29

The Black Bull – Frank

'Why don't you go home, Frank?'

Frank drags his bloodshot eyes out of his pint and glances at the plump woman behind the bar who dares address him when no one else will. As usual, she has too much flesh on display. Rather than peer down her crinkled cleavage, he stares into a pair of bright blue eyes that, on a sober day, perfectly match his own. Like most of the regulars here, he has known Barbara, or little Babs Owen as she was once known, since childhood. Except she is not so little now. The thought makes him chuckle, but this trickles away to nothing when he recognises the harsh blue irises of her eyes have paled with pity.

'I came here for drink. Not advice,' Frank grumbles, wiping away a dribble of beer from his chin and frowning at the lack of it in his glass.

'Have it your own way.' Barbara sighs, putting a fresh pint in front of him.

Somewhere in the back of his drink-addled mind, Frank owns up to the fact that he is in more of a foul mood than usual. Who can blame him? He's got a lot on his mind. That's why he drinks— to forget. Sometimes it works. Other times, not. Tonight is one of those nights when he can't shake off the past. The only thing he has managed to forget so far is the number of pints he's downed; not enough obviously, as he's still sober enough to make out one or two of the regulars breaking from their game of darts to turn their shifty eyes on him. Knocking back his beer, Frank stares them down. *Everybody would be better off if they minded their own goddamned business.*

Barely able to stand, Frank relies on the bar to keep himself upright, but his beer sloshes everywhere, making the counter wet and slippery. Every time he takes a swig from his pint, his elbows are in danger of disappearing from under him. He already has a split lip from the last time his face encountered it. Wiping blood from his mouth and smearing it drunkenly across his face, Frank slams his empty glass down with such force it shatters, causing more faces to turn and glance in his direction. When Frank spots Bob Black's grinning face among the crowd, his temper increases.

'Had enough of this damn place. I'm getting out,' Frank mumbles incoherently.

'Shush, Frank. They'll hear you,' Barbara hisses from across the counter.

Staring over at the stony-faced regulars, Frank thumps his fists on the bar. 'So what if they do. I don't care. I don't care anymore. Do you hear me? Do your worst, I tell you.'

Frank's tirade causes him to lose his balance and unable to stop himself, he tumbles heavily to the floor, where he lies in a prostrate heap, still mumbling.

'Sixteen years!' Frank chokes back an angry sob and covers his sweaty face with his hands. 'It's too much to ask of any man.'

Sensing that an unnatural silence has settled on the pub, and that all eyes are on him, Frank peers through his fingers at the regulars who have come to crowd around him. They won't want to miss seeing the big man cry. He can guess what they are thinking; that they never thought they would live to see this day. Bob has pushed his way to the front, his boot inches away from Frank's head. Dazed as he is, Frank watches the bloodstained boot tapping restlessly on the floor and guesses Bob would love to aim it at his skull. The mood in the pub has changed and sensing he is in real trouble, Frank tries to pull himself up, but his body has never felt so old or weary, and he sinks back down again with a sickening thud. That's when something falls out of his pocket onto the floor.

They see it before Frank does. He hears their gasps and sees them take a few uncertain steps backwards but it is not until Bob has it in his hand that Frank realises what it is. His head might be spinning, his vision blurred, but he would be a fool not to recognise his own necklace or the fact that the landlady's face above him is bleached with fear at the sight of it. Bob's cronies have formed a menacing circle around him, their faces twisted with anger and suspicion. If Frank wasn't in trouble before, he is now.

'You been hanging out with them dirty gypsies again, Frank?' Bob demands, shaking the charm necklace in Frank's sweating face.

'He wouldn't. Not after last time. You wouldn't. Would you, Frank?' Barbara sticks up for him yet again. Frank wonders why she bothers. Truth be told, she's always been sweet on him, even before he married Viv, but she couldn't hold a candle to his wife. Not then, not—

Putting in a super human effort to sober up, Frank fakes an unconvincing laugh. 'I'm drunk. I don't know what I'm saying.'

When Frank sees that this isn't working, he experiences a sickening but familiar fear, the kind he'd forgotten existed. Trying a different approach, he appeals to his lifelong rival, hoping for clemency.

'You know me, Bob,' Frank wheedles.

'That's right, Frank. I do,' Bob hisses cruelly, without a glimmer of pity.

Chapter 30

The House By The Sea – Natalie

The lights went out over an hour ago and the only half-decent candle I managed to light is threatening to go out too. Soon, I will be alone in the dark. The house, silent before, seems to have come alive, groaning and whispering, filling my head with ghostly voices that are impossible to shut out. That's why I am cradling the flickering flame with my hands, as if it were more precious than life itself.

Knowing that if I don't find a torch, I am going to have to spend a night in this house without any light, it occurs to me that I needn't be alone; I could go to the gypsy camp instead. There, I would be safe. *From what, or from whom, Natalie?* Jumping to my feet, I wonder why I did not think of it before, but my sudden movement causes the candle to go out, *exactly what I did not want, damn it,* and I am thrown into a world of moving shadows. A shiver of fear runs down my spine as I imagine I hear the familiar slaughterhouse sounds—Drip. Splat. Drip. Even so, I manage to fumble my way across the darkened kitchen, feeling for the cardigan I left hanging on the back of a chair. The night has taken a chilly turn and it is always cooler down on the beach.

When I reach the door, I see a face, twisted and blurred in the glass, looking back at me. Instinctively, I scream and jump backwards, my hand clutching at my racing heart. At first, I think it is my mother come to find me, because the face looks as if it has been there some time. My chest continues to pound with fear even when I realise it is Daniel.

'Sorry. I didn't mean to scare you,' he says, letting himself in.

Although he is smiling, I can tell this is not the same polite Daniel, who on his previous visit, would not step foot on the porch without first being invited. I also get the impression that he had every intention of scaring me. That this is exactly what he is here for. Because of this, I make up my mind not to let him see my alarm. His being here at night, without my father's permission or my consent, makes me nervous.

'It's a bit late to be running around in the dark, don't you think?' he states disapprovingly.

Every word sounds like a threat coming from him and I take a few paces back; put some distance between us. Playing for time, I slip on the cardigan and fiddle with the buttons, while I try to figure things out. *Why is he here? What does he want?*

'The power went out,' I offer, hoping to appear as casual as he does, although in the end my trembling fingers give me away. 'So I thought I'd go and find my father,' I lie unconvincingly, but rather than let me by, Daniel blocks my way. I am tall for a girl but he still manages to tower over me.

'He's in the pub,' he states with authority. 'And he won't thank you if you go looking for him.'

Daniel is right of course, and I nod in the dark to show that I have understood. 'I would invite you to stay, Daniel, but—'

'I've been thinking about you all day,' he interrupts, cracking his knuckles at the same time. A horrible intimidating sound, as if he might use them on me.

He is right beside me. Much closer than I can bear. I am surprised I did not smell him sooner. He reeks of blood, sweat and death. The smell is on his clothes, his breath, his hands— which are in my hair. Freezing at his touch, it's all I can do not to slap him.

'I'm booked in for a life-saving liver transplant tomorrow,' he sniggers unpleasantly in my ear, 'but I could always get out of it if you'd agree to come out with me instead.'

'I am not sure that's a good idea, Daniel.' I am forced to speak my mind. I am my father's daughter when all is said and done.

Daniel is not stupid. Even he can read a direct put down and he is quick to lose his temper. I feel him, rather than see him, step away from me.

'You seemed pretty sure the other night. You were up for it as much as—'

'I was not up for it.' My raised voice matches his. I must put an end to this. I should have done it sooner. Then I remind myself that Daniel is not the ordinary guy I first took him for. He is dangerous. It would not be wise to upset him any more than is needed.

'We had a nice time, Daniel,' I say more gently. 'But I don't think I want to do it again. Now I must go and find…'

Deliberately side stepping him, I walk determinedly towards the door, but he grabs my arm and pulls me towards him, his stinking breath hot on my face. I try to pull away, but he is much stronger than me. Pushing his face into mine, *I can't believe I once found him attractive,* our noses almost touch. This close, I can see that his eyes are full of hatred.

'You're a mental case,' he hisses cruelly. 'You don't know what you want.'

I am angry, rather than afraid, and as a result I find the strength to thrust him off. I don't know who this surprises more, him or me, but he backs off all the same, wary of me now. In the dark, we circle each other like sparring partners.

'You killed the gypsy's dog. I know you did. Don't bother denying it.'

'I put it out of its misery,' he sneers. 'What? You don't believe me?'

I shake my head furiously at him. *What kind of fool does he take me for?* Deciding that I am through being lied to, I go to the door and pointedly hold it open.

'And now I'm putting you out of yours. My father doesn't like you. I don't like you. And if that makes me a mental case, then I'm relieved to hear it.'

Chapter 31

Little Downey Beach

Up ahead, I can see the campfire burning. I am drawn to it like a lone wolf lured by the moon. Beside me, the waves break gently on the shore and the smell of sea salt in the air reminds me of Jed and our time spent together in the water. When I am almost upon the campsite, I pause in the shadows to watch the brother and sister from a distance.

Merry hugs the fire, while the baby claws at handfuls of her long hair. Jed, deep in thought, has his head bent low. I get the feeling that, like me, he likes to mull things over, but disguises this aspect of his personality behind a sarcastic smile. *Just like Daniel,* I can't help thinking. But Jed would never hurt me the way Daniel did. Nor would he harm any animal, let alone an injured frightened one.

I was wrong before, about the chicken on the chopping block. Jed didn't kill it. I know that now. Either I secretly wanted to think ill of him or I made the whole scene up in my head. This is what can happen when I forget to take my mediation. I should know better. Isn't Dr Moses always warning me about stuff like that. Shuddering at the memory of Daniel's hands on me, I rub my arm where he grabbed it and imagine I can still feel his fingers digging into my skin. Tomorrow there will be bruises. I hate that he has left a mark on me, as if I somehow belong to him.

Before walking into the warm glowing world the gypsies inhabit, I wipe my tear-stained face in the hope that Merry and Jed will not notice that I have been crying. They glance up when they see me approach but neither seems alarmed or surprised.

Rather, it is as if they have been expecting me. Merry hitches along the large piece of shipwreck debris they are sitting on and gestures for me to join them. Straight away, I figure out what Jed has been doing—whittling at a wooden carving of a dog, while his real dog rests its head in his lap. It opens its sleepy eyes fleetingly when it sees me, then closes them again. I do not blame it. I would not move from my place if I were it. Jed smiles at me with twinkling eyes, but goes on with his carving, leaving Merry to do the talking.

'I'll make some tea,' she says, as if this is her answer to everything, and I realise then that my red eyes have not gone unnoticed, at least by her. I am grateful for her silence but my gratitude does not last long, because before I can argue with her, she has placed the baby in my arms and disappeared into the caravan. I have never held a baby before and it shows. Afraid of squeezing it too tightly or dropping it altogether, I imagine I must look awkward holding it. Jed seems determined not to help me out. He goes on with his whittling.

'Can't keep away, huh?' He throws me an amused smile.

'I like being out here. It's peaceful.'

'That's Merry for you. She has that effect on people.'

He is inordinately proud of his sister, I can tell, and I feel a pang of jealousy that I know is unwarranted. Merry has shown me nothing but kindness and hospitality and doesn't deserve to come under my spiteful radar.

'Not just Merry,' I reply hesitantly, almost wishing my words unsaid. 'I am sorry about your dog.' I try again. 'What was its name?'

'It was just a dog. Didn't have no name.' Jed grimaces, not once looking up.

I do not believe him. I am not sure I am meant to, but one glance at his hardened jaw convinces me to change the subject. Even here, with Jed, I am at the mercy of men's moods.

'Does the baby have a name?' I try out a smile on him, but he doesn't look up to catch it.

'Merry calls it Darkly.'

'Unusual.' I pull a face, thinking what a strange pair they are. We are both silent for a while, each of us gazing into the fire, no doubt seeing something completely different there.

'They suit you.'

He is smiling at me again, all traces of his brooding mood gone, but I have no idea what he is talking about.

'What?'

'Babies. You look as if you should have a lot of them.'

My face reddening has nothing whatsoever to do with the heat from the fire but I cannot listen to Jed talking about babies without… Then, I realise I am being stupid. There is no hidden meaning to his words. He is simply speaking his mind.

'I would like that,' I reply, smiling back at him to show that I mean it. For some reason, it is important he believes me, although it does look as if I cannot tell one end of a baby from another. 'I always wished I'd had lots of little brothers and sisters to take care of.'

'Be careful what you wish for,' Jed warns, no longer smiling. I watch his eyes involuntarily dart to Merry's baby, before dropping away again.

His words hang in the air between us. *Whatever can he mean?* I glance at his bowed head, but he refuses to meet my eye, just goes on with his whittling, the knife slicing through wood and sending splinters of it into the flames. Then I look down at the baby whose bright blue eyes are looking back up at me with an easy kind of acceptance; as if it already knows me. *If I didn't know better, I'd think Jed was suggesting*—but even I know that babies are born with blue eyes and that this one will develop the same green eyes of its mother in time. When I see Merry coming out of the caravan, juggling three steaming mugs in her hands and looking as young and beautiful as ever, I know I am being ridiculous.

As soon as the herbal tea is handed around, Merry relieves me of the baby, pausing in her juggling of it, to glare at a spot on my neck.

'You're not wearing your lucky charm necklace.' She tuts.

'No. Sorry.' Guiltily, my hand goes to my throat. 'I must have forgotten.' I cannot bring myself to tell her that I would never wear anything so macabre.

'You must wear it, Natalie. Look. See.' Merry pushes her hair to one side so I can see the charm necklace around her own neck. It is like the one she gave me, only more elaborate.

'The villagers can spit at me or throw things but nothing can hurt me while I wear this,' she emphasises, as if she truly believes it.

Chapter 32

The House By The Sea

The silence between us, as we climb the steep sand trail up to the house, is anything but awkward. Few people can stay silent for so long, but I like that we allow our expressions to do most of the talking. I am looking at him now, sideways on, wondering if he is thinking the same as me—that I don't want this walk to end; but when the lights in my father's house came back on again after only an hour, I no longer had an excuse to stay at the campsite. Yet when I stood up to leave, I sensed Jed shared my disappointment. Things got better when Merry, with a knowing gleam in her eye, insisted he walk me home.

Merry might be on my side, but the dog isn't. It throws me jealous looks as if it considers me a serious contender for its master's affections. This action alone tells me more than Jed ever would. To reassure it, I reach down to stroke it, only to find Jed's fingers are already there, in the soft folds of the dog's fur. I leave my hand there, and so does he, which is equally telling. His skin feels leathery and warm, not cold and sweaty like Daniel's.

When I imagine Jed's hands on my body, I feel myself blushing, which makes me glad of the dark, but I am not the slightest bit ashamed. Unable to bear it any longer, I am about to tell him how I feel, when I realise we have reached the whitewashed building. Shame hits me then, like a bolt gun between the eyes, and I can hardly breathe for thinking of my mother. Instead of helping her, of trying to solve the mystery of what happened to her, I have been thinking only of myself. How could I have let my desire for a man get in the way of that.

Guiltily snapping my hand away from Jed's, I rake my hand agitatedly through my hair, ripping through knots. The pain is not enough but it is better than nothing. Meanwhile, Jed has come to a stop beside me, surprised by my sudden rejection of him. I don't have to glance at him to know that he is looking at me in a questioning way. The dog too.

'Why did you come back here?' he wants to know.

I get the feeling he already knows the answer to this but wants me to say the words out loud anyway. Perhaps he is right. That is exactly what I need to do. I look over at the whitewashed building again and feel myself shudder.

'There are things I have to know,' I tell him.

'Your mother,' Jed guesses intuitively.

Finding it hard to tear my glance away from the barred window where I first saw her, I wonder if she is in there now, watching us. She could be cold and hungry. *Should I go to her?* I ask myself for the hundredth time, but the same numbing fear prevents me. As Jed guides me away from the building, I question whether she is there at all or if she exists only in my imagination. But Jed saw her too, I remind myself, and he is as real as I am.

***

'They told me she was dead and for a long time I believed them,' I admit to Jed, who is sitting next to me on one of the dusty steps leading up to the porch.

'Them?' Jed doesn't follow.

We are hugging our knees, watching the flashes of silent lightning, which intermittently light up the night sky over Little Downey. If I didn't know better, I'd think the village was holding a firework display, to which everyone but us had been invited. While it is a pretty sight, I can't always see Jed's face due to the lights-on lights-off effect, but his arm, laid casually around my shoulder, is a constant presence.

'Father. The villagers.' I shake my head, not wanting to go on, all the while knowing I must. 'But there was no funeral. No grave. Nothing. One day she was there, the next…' I pause when another bolt of lightning illuminates his different-coloured eyes, which flash from blue to brown like multi-coloured fairy lights.

'I think they did something to her,' I finally admit.

'And you think Frank was involved?' Jed is incredulous.

We both get to our feet when we see car headlights approaching. My heart sinks when I recognise the familiar shape of the pickup truck hurtling along the lane.

Before it reaches the house, *for a minute I think it is going to drive straight at us,* the truck comes to a screeching halt. The revving of its engine is meant to intimidate. The next thing we see is a body being unceremoniously thrown out of the back seat.

'Father.'

I try to run to the lifeless figure on the ground, *he could be dead for all I know,* but Jed holds me back. Hating to be restrained, I am about to stamp on his foot when I see the truck crawling towards us again and I realise that Daniel has not come alone. Bob Black and the ginger-haired lad is with him. While they laugh like hyenas, Daniel's hate-filled stare zooms in on me, but I know his throat slashing gesture is intended for Jed, because I feel him tense beside me. I place a restraining hand on Jed's arm, in case he should decide to challenge Daniel, but before he can shrug me off, the truck's engine gives one last powerful rev, spins around, and reverses at speed towards the porch. Again, I think it is about to head straight towards us but at the last minute it changes course and tramples over my bicycle instead. When the truck has finished chewing it up, it takes off at speed down the lane.

***

I cannot remember the last time I touched my father's face. Tonight it is swollen from where somebody landed a cowardly punch on it, yet I long for more injuries to nurse. Ordinarily, he would not allow me to fuss around him the way I am doing now, as if this is how things have always been between us, but his drunkenness leaves him temporarily helpless. He might wince in pain when I dab at his split lip with cotton wool and antiseptic, but he does not struggle or lash out.

"Never known the village turn on one of its own before." Jed's voice, loaded with scorn, comes back to haunt me as I tend my father's wounds. Although I made him leave before my father regained consciousness, he is here with me in spirit and it is his voice I hear in my head. The fact that Jed was willing to protect me from a man like Frank speaks volumes, but I couldn't risk the two men getting into a fight. Jed's contempt for my father and the villagers took me by surprise until I remembered that this cruel sarcastic veneer of his was what I first glimpsed before I came to know the real person inside. This other side of Jed comes and goes as it pleases, like one of my father's rats, I realise with sudden perception. *You may not know him as well as you think you do, Natalie,* my head warns, but as usual, because I do not *like* what I am hearing, I ignore it.

But what if Jed is right. What if my father is one of them?

'I'm not one of them!' Frank hollers suddenly, as if able to read my thoughts.

'I'm not one of them, Natalie,' he repeats miserably.

'That's enough,' I urge, placing a restraining arm on his shoulder. But we both know it isn't. Not after the way he has treated my mother and me.

As soon as I see my father sag with exhaustion, my hatred crumbles. His wretched sobs do away with the past and I feel my heart melting. Whatever happened out there tonight, between him, Daniel and Bob Black—the old Frank Powers has vanished for good. I feel it in my bones. All I am left with is a glimmer of the giant he once was.

Grabbing my hand, he presses it against his chest, lowering his voice as if someone might overhear. 'You've got to believe me,' he pleads.

He is so convincing that I *do* believe him, but rather than tell him so, I heed the unspoken warning in my head. Jed is the only person I trust. My father doesn't come close.

'Why should I,' I insist, 'when you won't tell me what happened to my mother.'

I watch my father's eyes become more secretive. 'Whatever I did, it was to protect you.' He grinds his teeth.

'You're the one who had me locked away in a mental institution.' I have never forgiven him for this, and never will.

'It was the only safe place,' my father wheedles. 'Nobody could get at you there. They promised.'

'Who did? Safe from what, Father? Why would anybody want to get at me?'

'You're safer not knowing the whole story,' he whispers. 'All I can tell you is that it's what your mother wanted.' I watch him wet his lips, then raise a finger to his mouth, shushing me as if I were a child. 'She begged me not to let you come back here,' he finally admits.

Earlier, I watched Jed leave, wanting to be sure he was safe, that Daniel wasn't lurking in the shadows, waiting to take him down. In a typical Jed gesture, he left me with a conspiratorial wink that implied he wouldn't be far away if I needed him. Noticing that my father's eyes are returning to their familiar Little Downey blue, I drag myself over to the window again and become distracted by the menacing shadow of the whitewashed building, whose barred windows seem eerily to wink at me, in much the same way Jed did.

'I always knew she was alive, that she was out there somewhere. All along I have felt her with me.' I choke on my tears, finding it increasingly difficult to go on.

Then, anger takes hold, like a dead man's handshake that won't let go.

'All this time, I thought I was mad. You let me think that.' I spin around to confront my father, only to find that his head is bowed; he is sobbing once more. This time I feel no pity.

'Take me to see her,' I command. For the first time in my life, I am laying down the law. Natalie's Law.

Chapter 33

The Whitewashed Building

I cannot breathe. There is no room to move. No air. I seem to have lost my voice too because I cannot find any words for this moment. What we are about to do is terrifying, yet I wouldn't have my father stop for anything. While I wait for him to find the light switch, a claustrophobic fear grips me, and I am once again reminded of the time I was shut in the freezer with the dead animals. Shuddering at the memory, I stay as close to my father as possible. It is incredibly dark in here. But he is not hard to locate. The smell of sweat and blood on his clothing is all the compass I need. My father's breathing is like my own, heavy and out of control and when he eventually locates the cord above his head and a single bulb comes on, it casts eerie shadows on the whitewashed building's concrete walls.

When he pushes the dusty old butcher's block out of the way to reveal a secret trap door beneath, I am not as surprised as I should be. *So this is where he has been hiding her.* There are four heavy bolts holding down the door. Somebody has gone to a lot of trouble to make sure my mother cannot escape from whatever kind of hellhole is hidden below. I narrow my eyes at my father but he avoids my gaze; concentrates instead on undoing the bolts, the metal shrieking under his fingers as if warning us not to venture any further. When he finally lifts the door, it does not squeal off its hinges as it ought to, it creaks sleepily, and I guess this is because it has been used often over the years.

'Don't expect too much, Natalie. The years haven't been kind to her,' he advises.

114

Then, without warning, he disappears into the gaping black hole and I think I am about to pass out through sheer fright; that I won't be able to go through with this. I have never felt more like running than I do now. But I do not. I have been without my mother for sixteen years, and, while we might be strangers to each other, I will not abandon her, as she never really abandoned me. Whatever happened to make her stay away was nothing to do with her, *I know that now*, and everything to do with the villagers and my father.

After a few seconds, I make my way down the ladder, hating having to turn my back on my father, who is waiting for me somewhere at the bottom. I remain unconvinced by his claims that everyone but him is to blame for what happened. Time will tell I suppose.

Before I am halfway down, the smell reaches me. My God, the stench. I can only liken it to a revolting mixture of decaying flesh, vomit and human faeces. Taking my hand off the side rail to cover my nose and mouth, I feel the rungs of the ladder creak beneath me, from too much or too little wear and tear, I cannot tell. Stumbling awkwardly off the last rung, my feet hit a spongy surface and I guess, correctly, that this is natural ground where the soil has become compressed over time through constant use. I dread to think of how many times a day my mother must circle the confines of this cellar, prowling around it like a caged animal.

Even in the dark, I recognise my father's breathing, because like me, he is avoiding inhaling too much, due to the smell. It is so cold and damp down here, it crosses my mind that nobody could survive in such conditions. Surely it is impossible.

Then I hear somebody else's breathing and I know that it *is* possible. Their breathing is unlike mine or my father's, or anyone else's in fact, in that it sounds rattling and diseased. *What if I have found my mother only to lose her again to ill health?* The thought is intolerable and so is being down here. I do not think I can stomach it a second longer and I am tempted to flee back up the ladder when I hear the strike of a match. Even before the flame of an oil lamp appears, I catch a glimpse of a shadowy figure darting to the furthest corner of the cellar. While my father encourages the flame to soar higher, lighting up the open trap door, which points to our way out of here, I stare in disbelief at the woman with balding hair and rotting teeth who scrapes at the concrete walls with broken fingernails.

'Viv.'

My father puts down the oil lamp and approaches her, something I am incapable of doing. I can only stare in horror at the woman in front of me who is making an inhuman sound, something between a scream and a growl. Laughter lurks there also. I can feel its terrible tremble in the sound that she is making.

'Viv.' He speaks slowly, as if talking to a child, and she is in so many ways, but his voice is gentle too, a reminder that this creature is the woman he once loved. 'Look who's come to see you,' he encourages, pointing me out as if he were introducing us for the first time.

When he gestures for me to move forward, I progress slowly so as not to frighten her, but that doesn't prevent her turning her head away. It is obvious that she doesn't know who I am and wants to hide from me. She is painfully thin, and her face is smeared with excrement. *Good God, I will kill him for this*, I think vengefully. *As long as I live, I will never forgive him. I will put him down this hole myself and see how he likes it.*

But my father is looking at me in a trusting way, as if he cannot conceive that I could be angry with him. One would think, judging by his ridiculous expression, that he feels something special is about to happen. He is a fool. Deliberately ignoring him, I take a hesitant step towards my mother.

'Mother?' I find my voice at last even though it doesn't seem to belong to me. My words bounce off the walls, making them sound flat and cold.

'Mother,' I say again, after I've coughed and cleared my throat.

When I see the bloody scratches on the wall where she must have spent years trying to claw her way out, I glare at my father.

Shaking my head in disgust, I creep closer. Now that she is aware of my proximity, she tosses her head and moans like an animal in labour. In all my life I have never seen another human being so distressed, not even at Thornhaugh where everybody was considered crazy.

'Mother. It's me, Natalie.'

As soon as I say my name, she freezes. I take this as a good sign, even if she does still refuse to look at me. Relieved that the terrible moaning has stopped, I place one hand against the crumbling wall and bend down to her level, but I do not attempt to touch her. She is so fragile, I think her bones would snap under my fingers if I did.

'We've both been locked away, you and I, but I am here now,' I tell her, no longer able to prevent my tears from falling. I want to be strong, for my mother's sake, but I am destroyed by what has happened to her. *I will have my revenge if it is the last thing I do,* I promise myself. The desire to harm or kill another person is an entirely new emotion for me, but it feels like a missing friend, one who from now on will always be welcome at my door.

In the glow of the lamplight, I think I see a glimpse of recognition in my mother's haunted face and this gives me the confidence to move closer. When her head moves stiffly to the side, the bones in her neck snap like a chicken's carcass and her foul stinking breath wafts over me, but nothing will make me turn away from her. When I realise she is looking at me for the first time, I am so surprised I almost lose my balance. Her eyes are locked with mine, black on black, and I wonder if she recognises they are the same as her own. When her face creases with a frown, I can tell she is trying to figure things out. Clearly, she is not mad. Beneath the deeply etched lines on her face, there are signs of intelligence.

When her hands reach out to touch my hair, it is my turn to freeze. I feel her bony fingers wind a lock of my hair into a curl, and my heart breaks. *How could I have forgotten sleepy Sunday mornings cuddled up in bed with my mother who used to love playing with my hair.* I feel such overwhelming love for her and equal amounts of

117

hatred for my father and anyone else who might be responsible for my mother's lost life that I don't know how I am ever going to handle such strong emotions. Surely I am too damaged for that. I cannot bear to think of her being down here all these years. How could this happen to someone like her, who loved life and was once thought so beautiful? And how is a girl like me, who lost her mother, only to find her again, meant to react to such a discovery?

'Natalie. My Natalie?'

Her voice comes out as a pathetic croak, as if she has forgotten how to use it, but I recognise it all the same and a sob escapes me. Before it has finished echoing around the cellar walls, my head is resting where it has longed to be these last sixteen years—against my mother's bony chest. She pats me, awkwardly at first, like one would a dog. *I'm home at last.* The hand stroking me might smell of excrement and blood, but I do not, will not, recoil from her. The fast beating of her heart is soothing, and I feel my eyelids close. It is only when I hear my father shuffle from one foot to another, an irritating reminder of his unwelcome presence, that I open them.

Feeling like I never want to see or hear from him again, for as long as I live, I narrow my eyes at him, but when I realise that he has been moved to tears by our reunion, I am not sure what to think. His story will have to be good. But hear it out I will, when the time is right. For now, he can crumble all he likes. I will not comfort him.

When I turn back to my mother, I see that her expression has changed. She is looking at me blankly and her eyes have clouded over like grey marble. The face I am looking at is a mirror image of the woman I first glimpsed through the bars of this building.

'Mother? Are you all right?'

I cry out when I feel the first sharp tug on my hair but when she takes a fistful of it in her hands and viciously yanks it, I scream. The pain is indescribable. I try to pull away, but she has turned into a demon and is clawing at my face. I do not know what has happened to cause this sudden and alarming change in her, but I want her off me.

'Whore! Whore!'

As I try to protect myself from her insistent fingernails, *I dare not do more for fear of hurting her,* she continues to scream abuse into my face. Her eyes are ablaze with a kind of hatred I have never witnessed before, and I try to convince myself that she doesn't know what she is doing or saying, but when a drop of foul-smelling saliva drips from her toothless mouth onto my face, I find it hard to feel any compassion for the thing she has turned into.

'I've seen you. My bed. My sheets!' She screeches wildly, jabbing a proprietary finger at my father. 'My man.'

Snarling like a wild animal, she comes at me again, raining blows down on me this time. I put up my hands to defend myself but she catches the side of my mouth with her fist and I taste blood. She laughs at that, but just as she is about to lash out again, she is thrown up against the wall. Dizzy from the unprovoked attack, it is a few seconds before I realise that my father has intervened; that he has my mother pinned by the arms, where she continues to spit and snarl in his face. She can struggle all she likes, but she is no match for him.

'Natalie, are you all right? I'm so—'

I do not wait to hear my father's apology. I am out of there, already halfway up the ladder. Only when I reach the top rung, do I take one last fearful look back down; at my mother, whose wild eyes, a bloodshot yellow, burn into mine.

'Whore! Whore!' she screams again.

I climb out of the cellar, gasping for clean air, with my legs almost giving way beneath me. Trembling from head to toe, I do not think I will make it out of the building without collapsing but when I hear blows being delivered below, followed by my mother's pitiful sobs, I run from the place as fast as I can.

Chapter 34

The House By The Sea

I feel as if I have gone back in time, because here we are again—back at the kitchen table, where I was often made to sit as a child, so my father could berate me. He is standing straight backed in his usual place, with his back to the sink, looking down on me, and I am sat in mine, with my head bowed. But *unlike* then, I am not sobbing my eyes out and my nose isn't running with snot. Tonight, I am an adult with grown-up problems. To cure my trembling, I take a large slug of the whiskey my father has placed in front of me. I like how it burns my insides, where rage also lurks.

'You hit her!' I say at last.

'Sometimes.' My father becomes more interested in the floor than looking at me. 'It's often the only way to control her,' he mutters.

He is so matter of fact about this admission that I realise he too has lost his grip on reality. My mother's fake death, her subsequent imprisonment and his sickening behaviour have become the norm. I want to throw my glass at him, hurt him badly, but I do not. I shake my head because I can hardly believe what I am hearing. How can any of this be real?

'Is that another one of Frank's laws?' I finally mutter between gritted teeth. And then I turn on myself, because, *oh my God, that thing is my mother. I can't bear it. I can't.* I wanted so much to believe she was alive that I wished for it every day. Now that my dream has come true, I want only to undo it. As crazy as it sounds, I feel as if I have created a monster. *Am I going mad, like her?* A part of me, however ironic, can't help thinking that this outcome would please everybody. My father and Doctor Moses most of all.

'What did you do to her?' I demand, the deep distrust of my father spilling over into my scathing tone. 'Why is she locked away like an animal?' Anger is better than fear, I feel, but when my father storms towards me, his face screwed up with rage, I doubt myself, because deep down I am still afraid. Having lived in fear of him all my life, I have never once been able to breathe in this house without feeling scared.

Instead of pinning me to the wall like he did my mother, I am surprised when he reaches across the table and grabs hold of my hands, not gently but not forcibly either.

'Natalie, I want you to promise me something.'

It doesn't matter that I try to squirm away. He is insistent on being heard.

'Swear on your mother's life you'll do as I ask,' he implores, refusing to let go, but I am unable to look at his grazed hands without thinking of how he used them on my mother.

'What?' I ask incredulously. Before I've even heard him out, I know I am not going to like what he has to say.

His reply is slow in coming. 'Tomorrow you'll leave.'

'Leave?'

He is deadly serious, I can tell. Whatever I imagined my father might want from me— a promise to keep his terrible secret; to go on hiding the truth—it certainly wasn't this.

'You'll disappear. Never come back. It'll be as if you never came home.'

From the look on his face, I can see that he believes this is possible and for a moment I wonder if insanity truly does run in our family. My mother's disposition and mine have always been speculated on, with obvious reasons, but nobody has thought to question the paternal line before.

Wrestling my hands away from him, I scrape back my chair and get to my feet. 'How can I leave knowing Mother is down there? Locked up. All alone. I couldn't live with myself.'

I pace up and down the room like my mother must be doing, in her prison, while we discuss hers and mine futures. Agitatedly, I scratch at my arms, stopping only when I realise that my father is watching me, his cold blue eyes lingering too long on my scars. He doesn't like to see me like this. Makes him nervous, he says. So he should be.

'We'll take her to Dr Moses,' I say decisively, as if it is the most obvious thing in the world to do. 'He'll know what to do. He can make her better.'

Without warning, my father throws the bottle of whiskey at the wall where it shatters. 'Are you mad?' he bellows.

'Why not?' I ask, torn between fear and curiosity.

'Because she's as good as dead if you do. Is that what you want?'

Suddenly, I am a long way away. There is a ringing in my ears, like white noise, and I feel unsteady on my feet. I shake my head, to try to clear it, but there is a fogginess there that I cannot shift. *Am I mad like my father is suggesting? Is there no hope for me or my mother?* The tears start to fall as I think about my father's words.

'First Mother. Then me. Locked up. Driven insane.' Rage stirs within me again. I will not allow my father to blame me for this. He must not be allowed to run riot inside my head.

'You're the one that's mad.' I spin around to confront him and almost lose my balance. 'I'll go to the police. I'll tell them everything,' I say, feeling victorious, even though I am slurring my words.

'I can't let you do that, Natalie.'

My father's voice sounds distant but he is just across the kitchen from me. The look of regret on his face is enough for two men, I can't help thinking. Suddenly he has two heads. Everything has become distorted, little more than a blur. I cannot seem to focus on anything properly. Blaming the drink, I gaze stupidly into my glass as if the answer to my troubles can be found there. Feeling increasingly woozy, I vow never to touch a drop of alcohol again.

Swaying from side to side, I reach out to grab hold of a kitchen chair but miss and almost take a tumble. If my father wasn't there to catch me, I would have fallen flat on my face.

'Don't feel well,' I admit, as he helps me into the chair.

'You won't. But it won't last long.'

He has moved out of my line of vision. I suspect him of playing cat and mouse with me, but the only thing that matters are the two glasses of whiskey on the table. Having made such a fuss over how a tipple of Scotland's finest would settle both our nerves, his glass remains suspiciously full. Why didn't I notice this before? Never having known my father nurture a glass so long, the penny drops too late.

'Something in my drink.'

Chapter 35

Thornhaugh

'So, you see, Natalie. Your father didn't drug you. He's concerned for you. We all are. As you know, he gave a very different account of what happened that night, but we'll soon have you remembering things correctly.'

I am sitting up in bed, ignoring the pile of pills in my hand and the silvery eyes of my protector, Dr Moses, who is trying to reassure me that all is as it should be. But for once, I see through and beyond him, my glance settling hypnotically on the familiar green lawns of Thornhaugh in the distance, where long-term patients like me parade up and down; some alone, some escorted by nurses. *What am I doing back here? Have I been away at all?*

Eventually, I take the pills, *like a good girl*, and swallow them obediently enough, but not in one go as Dr Moses would like. To delay the inevitable dulling of my senses, I take my time; sipping dainty gulps of water in-between, even though I know this will put Dr Moses' nerves on edge. As expected, he drums his fingers on the bedside table. He has never said so, but I suspect that I am a growing burden to him. I can only hope he never tires of me completely. I do not know where I would be without him.

As if he knows what is on my mind, he reaches across to pat me in a fatherly way. Although his hands are as smooth and white as ever, I am immediately reminded of another pair of hands with bloody fingernails, but I cannot think who they belong to. My own are pink and healthy and my nails, though clipped short, are not broken or bloody.

Suddenly, a woman's voice, familiar but unrecognisable, appears out of nowhere.

Whore! Whore!

There is something deeply distressing about the crying that follows. It brings me close to tears, leaving me feeling restless and uneasy. At first, I question if it is one of the patients in a nearby room but I can tell from the unflinching way Dr Moses is looking at me that he does not hear the cries as I do, so I do not give myself away. If I confide in him, he will say that the voice is in my head, and I suppose he would be right. Dr Moses is always right.

'And my mother?' I ask without any enthusiasm. I have been asking the same question for so long, we are both tired of the repetition, yet it is a game we continue to play.

'Died sixteen years ago. I have a copy of the death certificate here if you want to see it.'

He flaps a piece of paper at me but I do not ask to see it. Feeling incredibly tired, I slip further down in the bed for extra warmth. No matter the weather, Thornhaugh, with its tall ceilings and draughty hallways, is always cold. *Am I doomed to spend my whole life in this sterile institution? Am I back here for good? If so, what am I meant to have done this time? More importantly, is my mother dead as they would have me believe, when earlier this morning, or was it yesterday or the day before, I felt certain she was alive?*

'You told me about the funeral yourself. Don't you remember?' Dr Moses' silver-tongued voice is as smooth as ever. It wraps me in cotton wool. The way it always has.

***

The rain lashes down on us, stinging our upturned faces, as if we have not yet suffered enough. I want it to stop. If the sun comes out, then everything will be a lie. Funerals don't take place when the sun is shining. Everybody knows that. Yet here I am, staring at my mother's coffin which is being carried by six men I do not know and I am clinging to my father's leg, terrified of being shrugged off so he can shake someone else's hand, while they whisper hateful condolences in his ear. They should be punished for the terrible lies they are saying about my mother, who isn't dead, and who hasn't abandoned me.

But the cliff edge, situated a few measly feet away from Little Downey's overcrowded cemetery, does not lie. It is a terrible reminder of the tragedy that has befallen us.

I have been warned not to slouch, so I stand up straight, but nobody can stop me counting the long line of black cars parked on the rocky incline. To my mind, they look as if they're the ones that have been abandoned and the cemetery gates, which hang off their hinges, have downturned mouths like my own. In the trees, crows try to hurry us along with their bossy caws and a boy with blond hair and blue eyes, like my father's, throws stones at them. When the boy catches me frowning, he winks cheekily at me, as an older boy might.

The ground is riddled with rabbit holes, which means the men carrying the coffin stumble often, drawing gasps from the mourners gathered around the open grave; my mother's last resting place. As we watch her coffin, which doesn't look anywhere near fancy enough for her, being lowered into the earth, I stare at the expressionless faces in the crowd. Some, like Andrew Muxlow, who is the closest thing to a friend my father has—I recognise. Swamped in a long black coat, he appears considerably sadder than anyone else and for that reason alone I smile at him, but he turns away from the black eyes that remind everyone of her.

Others, like the obese woman and her blond-haired son, the one who hates crows, I have never met before. Forcing my fingers into my father's rigid hand, we do not throw flowers as others do. Nor do we cry. Not once. Not then. Not afterwards. Frank's Law.

***

'There were sandwiches at the house afterwards. Everybody came,' I murmur in something of a childlike trance, the tears spilling off my cheeks, as I recall the wake.

'That's right.' Dr Moses nods his encouragement, as if this alone will prompt further memories to return.

But then I remember that the villagers came only to snoop, to sip sherry and to whisper behind their hands, which angered my father; made him mad enough to sweep an entire table of sandwiches onto the floor. I do not mention this part to Dr Moses, as I do not think he will believe me. Suddenly, I experience a more painful flashback and I clutch at Dr Moses' sleeve, not giving him a chance to pull away or call out for assistance.

'And there is no mad woman in the cellar. The village isn't out to get me,' I plead.

I can tell by the way Dr Moses is looking at me, *kindly and patiently*, that my eyes must be rolling around in my head again. *The madness is never far away*, he will be thinking. But then he proves me wrong, by laughing out loud. Actually laughing.

'As I have never been to Little Downey,' he jokes, 'I cannot vouch for the majority. But look at all these gifts and cards. It seems to me that you have a good many friends there.'

I glance over at the bunches of flowers, still in their cellophane, and the dozen or so Get Well cards on the windowsill, as if I have never seen them before. How long they have been there, or who brought them in, I have no idea, but I do not let on.

'I do?' I ask, feeling emotional.

Dr Moses pats me a second time and I notice that his eyes are as watery as my own, which makes me sadder still. He has always been kind to me, yet I continue to hide so much from him. I can never hope to deserve him.

'You've suffered a relapse, Natalie. But we'll soon have you back on your feet again.'

***

Back on my feet again. Soon have me back on my feet again, I think drowsily, not sure if it is night or day. There is a heaviness on my chest that is pressing down on me, which prevents me from getting out of bed. I am unsure of what drugs they gave me, but as I am so tired, I suspect I have been given a sleeping pill.

Thornhaugh is a few miles from the coast, but I imagine I can hear the waves crashing against the rocks. I can even taste sea salt in the air. As I fall into a restless sleep, I dream about a line of black cars disappearing off the cliff edge into the water below and wonder which one of the crumbling gravestones in Little Downey's cemetery belongs to my mother.

Chapter 36

Little Downey Cemetery – Daniel

In the darkened cemetery, Daniel and Jono work quickly, throwing up a wall of sea mist around them; stopping only to wipe sweat from their brows or to pull up their sleeves. Trampling on an assortment of crushed wreaths and flowers that have been carelessly tossed aside, they take it in turns to attack the ground with a shovel. Working silently and without any light, the sea glinting in the distance behind them is as glossy as spilt oil.

Somewhere close by an owl hoots, making Jono flinch, but when the metal edge of Daniel's blade scrapes on something hard, they stop what they are doing and stare at each other. This seems to act as a signal for Daniel to jump into the open grave, while Jono keeps watch, shiftily turning his head this way and that, on the lookout for God knows what. Meanwhile, Daniel flicks on a torch to illuminate the high walls of the grave. Crouching over an exposed wooden coffin, he looks up at Jono and winks.

'What you waiting for? Chuck it down!' Daniel calls out impatiently, shining the beam upwards, into Jono's face.

A crow bar is passed down and Daniel wastes no time prying open the coffin lid. It cries like a drowning kitten before finally splitting. Through a crack in the wood, a dead man's face peers out in a creepy game of hide and seek. Not put off by this, Daniel levers the rest of the wood off with his hands to reveal more of the corpse—an elderly man with a sparse comb over, who wears a jacket much too big for him.

'Good to see you again, Ted.' Daniel shakes the dead man's hand and laughs.

Like a buffoon who knows he is being too loud, Jono clasps a hand over his mouth and sniggers through his fingers.

'Shut up, idiot,' Daniel warns.

The sound of a rock crashing down to the sea below causes them to stop what they are doing and turn alarmed eyes on each other.

'What was that? Did you hear that?' Jono asks nervously, edging closer to the open grave. His face is as white as any dead man's.

'It's a graveyard. It's the middle of the night,' Daniel hisses. 'We wouldn't be normal if we didn't hear things.'

***

An hour later, they have got what they came for. The flowers are back on the grave and the earth has been patted down neatly again, as if it had never been disturbed. The same can't be said for Daniel, who can't shake off the fear that somebody had been watching them the whole time. Jono is already in the pickup truck, fingernails drumming on the paintwork, impatiently waiting to get the hell out of there, but Daniel cannot leave without knowing.

'Come on,' Jono hisses, leaning out of the window.

Ignoring the terror in his friend's eyes, Daniel picks his way over the rocks in the dark, sending shards of smaller stones off the cliff edge, where they can be heard bouncing down on the sand below, like ghostly raindrops. He doesn't have to look far. Sees it straight away. As if it had been left there deliberately for him to find—a chunky necklace made from chicken feet and canine teeth lays discarded in the rocky soil. He doesn't know what a find like this means. He only knows it doesn't belong here; that whoever left it behind had no right being here. He looks in the direction of the house by the sea, which stands tall and proud, like Frank Powers and his difficult daughter, and senses that trouble is afoot.

Chapter 37

Thornhaugh – Natalie

The residents' lounge where long-term patients like me are sent in our Sunday best, to reassure loved ones that all is well in our world, is lavishly furnished, unlike our own rooms. Each comfy armchair is covered in a shade of tartan that goes well with the forest-green carpet. The heavy curtains are draped with fancy swags and pelmets, and an original fireplace, dating back to the sixteenth century provides a focal point for people to stare vacantly at. The tall windows, eight in all, look out onto the woodland that lurks at the back of the house, casting a permanent shadow over certain parts of the room, even at night. For some reason, the trees were planted too close together, giving it a claustrophobic air.

As always, there are nurses on hand to dish out cups of tea. If you have ever had the unpleasant experience of visiting a mental institution or asylum, then you will know that there is an abundance of tea to be had. It solves everything, apparently. I know that we are not supposed to call them institutions nowadays, but that is exactly what Thornhaugh is. Don't let anyone tell you otherwise. Our privileges are thin on the ground, but in here at least, we can drink from real china and are even allowed to stir our tea with a metal spoon.

I sit away from the others and do just that—stir my milky tea. As I watch the liquid circling around in the cup, I think about slipping the spoon into my pocket, *it would feel good rasping against my skin*, but I do not. One thing I have learned during my time here is that you are never truly alone at Thornhaugh. There are eyes and ears everywhere.

Unlike the others, who sit next to visitors who vaguely resemble themselves, and who do not attempt to disguise how bored they are, I am not expecting anyone. Who would visit me? Dr Moses told me that I have a good many friends and loved ones in Little Downey but so far, I have not seen any evidence of that.

I cannot stop thinking about my dream, with the two men digging up a corpse in the graveyard. Could it have been real? A memory from before? Have I previously witnessed something like that, which traumatised me so much as a child that I have since blocked it out of my mind? With a start, I realise that there is a good reason why the tall ginger one in my dream felt familiar. He is the same lad I saw at the slaughterhouse. I am sure of it. Now that I come to think of it, he reminds me of an orderly who works here; who sometimes brings me my medication. They could be related for all I know. If so, that probably means he is from Little Downey too. Although I do not know what any of this means yet, I decide that it wouldn't be wise to ask the orderly about this, in case he is a spy, sent by Dr Moses to find out what strange tricks my mind is playing on me.

If only I could remember everything, not just bits, including the things they don't want me to. My mind might be hazy from prescribed medication but the one thing I *am* certain of is that something sinister is going on in Little Downey; something to do with the cliff-top suicides. Whatever I hear to the contrary, I keep coming back to the same conclusion, however insane that sounds.

Every time I close my eyes, I see flashbacks of gruesome scenes that back up my theory. Dismembered body parts, including a severed arm floating out to sea, a bloodied finger on a butcher's block and a dog with a broken neck. And the sounds. Oh God, the sounds. The metallic scratching of blades coming together, of bones being broken. Blood dripping.

Drip. Splat. Drip.

My mind is not a pleasant place to be.

Then I see him—

He carries a bunch of flowers that look as if they have been plucked out of somebody's front garden and wears trendy ripped jeans and a collarless shirt, breaking Thornhaugh's stuffy dress code. I find myself staring at him, not because of this, but due to the fact he has different-coloured eyes. They are mesmerising.

When he spots me tucked away in the corner and heads in my direction, I immediately panic. *What can he want of me?* His stride is too confident for my liking, and judging by the expression on his face, I rather think he expects something of me. He has the look of a man who feels he does not need any introduction, that he would be impossible to forget. I do not know what entitles him to this opinion, for he is a stranger here.

Before I know it, he is standing in front of me, holding out the flowers and grinning. I stare blankly at him, confused and angry, yet find myself surprised by the latter emotion. *He is nothing to me. Why should I feel angry?*

'Do I know you?' I enquire rather formally.

'Jed. Remember?'

Some of the sparkle from his eyes is lost when I shake my head. One eye is blue, the other brown, I notice. Not wanting to give away how awkward I feel in his presence, I glance at the others, who gawp at us as if we were not of this world.

'Are you from the village? Did my father send you?' I keep my voice low, not wanting to be overheard.

'Natalie! You don't know me?'

He sounds hurt but disguises it well by pretending to look around for a nurse to take the flowers from him, but as nobody approaches us, he places them down on the coffee table and pulls up one of the comfy armchairs. Once he is seated, I stare stupidly at the flesh oozing out of his ripped jeans. I don't know where else to look. Eventually, I glance up and our eyes meet. Close up, his are even more hypnotic.

'Are you my boyfriend?

There I go again, with the plain speaking. Somebody once told me, *I've forgotten who*, that it isn't an attractive habit for a woman to have, but that doesn't stop me. I suppose there is no harm in hoping; after all *he is* a strikingly handsome man.

Rather than laugh at my suggestion, he leans closer, *his face just inches from mine,* and smiles sadly. For one electrifying moment, I think he is about to take my hand in his, but he does not. I cannot help wondering what that would have felt like.

'I was kind of hoping to be,' he admits at last, making me feel hot and cold all at once.

When that news has sunk in, I stir my tea again. He watches me so intently it makes me uneasy, not in an unpleasant way, anything but...

'I fixed your bike. The one that got all chewed up. You remember?'

'Vaguely,' I lie, wondering where he is going with this.

'I took it, stole it, from the house, the night they brought you here.'

'You were there?'

'I was around. This place gives me the creeps, Natalie.' He shudders for impact. 'They can call it a psychiatric hospital all they like but it feels more like a house of horror to me. Even I would go mad in a place like this.'

'The bike was easy to fix but the same can't be said of me. Is that what you are thinking?'

He forces a smile, but his eyes remain cloudy with concern. 'First the dog goes missing, then Merry...' He pauses as if he has said too much.

I watch him stretch out his long legs and wonder if he is playing with me, because not only have I never heard that name before, I cannot believe someone like him, who looks like a movie star, could be interested in someone like me. Deciding not to give too much away, in case he *is* teasing, I take a sip of my now-cold tea and feign disinterest.

'Who?' I ask casually, as if the identity of this person is of no importance to me.

'My sister.' He frowns as if he cannot believe what he is hearing. 'The one with the baby,' he adds dramatically, as if that should nail it.

He's right. Something in my memory stirs—a small pair of blue persistent eyes staring up at me; imprinting on me, as if they know me.

'An unusual name,' I say without thinking.

'That's right.' Jed sits up straight in his chair. 'Darkly,' he says, filling in the gaps.

The name is familiar, but I do not know why. Once again, I am filled with fear of the unknown. Sensing that something from my past is about to leap out at me, my fingers go unconsciously to the ugly necklace around my neck. I remember someone telling me that it was put there to protect me, but I can't remember who. None of the staff has commented on it, which is strange, but that doesn't stop them looking at it as if they would like to rip it off me. Because of this, I know it is a thing of interest, of power even.

Suddenly, I see a flick of long black hair, wet and peppered with sand, green flashing eyes and perfect golden skin. A beautiful woman naked on the beach, laughing. A raised eyebrow and the words "We are not a family for secrets". The memory lasts only for a second, but it is enough. *Merry, who doesn't know what it is like to be ashamed of her own body. Merry and some kind of exchange over the kitchen table. The bumblebee magnet for something else. What was it? Think Natalie. Think.*

'She has a lucky charm necklace, like mine.' I gasp, finally making the connection.

Chapter 38

The House By The Sea – Daniel

Daniel struggles alone with the heavy trap door, while Jono hovers inside the doorway of the whitewashed building, as if too terrified to come inside. Daniel doesn't blame him. For years, this house, that family, this building, and the creepy cliff edge have put the fear of God in him too. Even from here, the stench rising out of the underground cellar makes Daniel want to gag. He doesn't know how Natalie's mother can stand it, not that she has much choice. Doesn't get the fascination with the dumb necklace either but even so he hasn't let it out of his sight since they came across it in the cemetery. He's convinced someone was spying on them, that they left it behind on purpose, to freak them out. Their plan certainly worked. If he's right, the only way to make sure it doesn't happen again is to go through with what he is about to do.

Waving the necklace over the trap door, Daniel makes a clucking sound in the back of his throat. Anybody would think he was calling a pet dog, not…

Jesus Christ. She is climbing out of the cellar. He can see glimpses of balding hair and a pair of black eyes that look as if they could turn you to dust. He feels himself shrivel up with fear as the "mad woman from the cellar" he's heard so much about climbs further up the ladder. Soon she will be at the top. Soon she will be in the building with them.

'Come and get it,' Daniel calls playfully, trying to man-up to his fear. But even he backs away when she reaches the top rung of the ladder. He's not sure if it's the creaking of the ladder he can hear, or the sound of her bones cracking.

'That's it. Good girl. Come and get it.' Daniel entices her with the necklace.

As soon as the woman's eyes land on it, he can tell straightaway that it means something to her. Her eyes never leave it.

As her sickly elongated shadow creeps into the room, seeming to dwarf both him and Jono, Daniel takes a couple more steps back to avoid it passing over him. He's superstitious about such things and with good reason. The death count in Little Downey is never discussed openly but every house in the village keeps a private tally. Some have died who didn't deserve to, like his own sister, while others, like this mad bitch…

He watches her take a few zombie-like steps towards him, but he has the sense to throw the necklace as far away from him as possible before she gets too close. Ignoring their presence, the mad woman moves at a speed he would never have guessed at. Falling to her knees, she pounces on the necklace and holds it close to her heart. Rocking on the spot, like the crazy people do in the movies, she hums some unknown tune to herself.

Finally, Dan darts Jono the look he has been waiting for. "Let's get out of here," it says. Relieved beyond belief, Jono doesn't argue.

Chapter 39

Thornhaugh – Natalie

'So, you *are* a family for secrets after all,' I state, still recovering from shock after what Jed has told me. Part of me, a huge part actually, is furious with myself for being blind to what has been going on under my nose, but I am also overcome with a new emotion—a sense of belonging that I have never experienced before.

'I have a sister,' I say again, unable to digest such unexpected news. Yet strangely, I am elated. 'A baby sister.'

Jed has his head tilted to one side like a playful puppy and is smiling at me in an encouraging way. If his watery eyes are anything to go by, he is almost as happy as I am. I might not know him, as he seems to know me, but I do not doubt what he has told me is true. As ridiculous as it sounds, it even makes sense. Kind of.

Then, as I realise the not-so-pleasant consequences of what this new addition to my family means, my smile fades away to be replaced with a deep frown.

'But Merry and my father!' I gasp, unable to keep the disgust from my voice.

'It's your father I wanted to talk to you about.' Jed picks his words carefully.

'What about him?' I snap, angry with my father without knowing why.

'I went up to the house looking for Merry. Knowing that you were…' he pauses, 'in here, I assumed she had gone to spend the night with Frank.' He coughs uncomfortably and I wince at the thought, knowing how much my mother would have hated another woman spending the night in her house, her bed. Touching her things.

My man. Mine.

'But Frank said he hadn't seen her.'

'And?' I prompt him.

'He's lying, Natalie. The baby was there. I heard her crying upstairs. Merry wouldn't have left her there unless…'

'Unless what?' His words frighten me more than he can know.

'She lost her necklace. I think she went back to look for it. She saw something in the cemetery that frightened her, but she refused to tell me what it was. Said she had to talk to Frank first. The only thing she was clear on was that without the necklace, we were all in grave danger.'

Chapter 40

The House By The Sea – Vivian

Vivian has been outside so long, watching and waiting, that the wildlife, silent at first, has resumed its night-time chorus. The flapping of wings, scuttling of vermin and rustling of rabbits in the overgrowth does not frighten her. Nothing can. Her eyes have acclimatised to the darkness and she can even pick out certain objects: the whitewashed building and the solid shape of Frank's van in the open barn. The house remains invisible though, as if it has decided to keep its distance from her. It is Frank's domain now.

Shivering with cold, Vivian finds the end of her bloodstained dressing gown and ties it around her, no longer liking the feel of fresh air on her skin. The air has changed. The sky has become blacker. The moon is like a pool of bad blood dripping down on her head. Warily, she glances around. Her eyes darting this way and that; ever conscious of the fact that her freedom could be taken away from her at any moment. Because of this, she remains convinced that the rustling noises around her are closing in, circling her.

But if they have come to find her, they will soon realise that they are too late. Gypsy scum are not to be tolerated round here. Everyone knows that. This time she will not be punished. As a wife and mother, not to mention a homeowner protecting her own patch of soil, she did what was expected of her. She had every right.

Hands shaking, through rage rather than fear, she fingers the charm necklace around her ravaged neck as if it were an old friend.

She does not believe in its power. The serrated edge of the bloodied knife in her other hand is another matter though. Ignoring the blood oozing from cuts on her own body that have been made with the same knife, Vivian sways on the swing that creaks when nobody is looking, her legs dangling in mid-air, like a schoolgirl's.

A rotting stench follows her everywhere. She has grown accustomed to it but not the darkness of her mind. *Who am I? Where am I? Is this home?* Her eyes blink. Not once but several times. She chuckles softly, a threatening sound that doesn't travel far. Her movements are jerky and disjointed but always ready to pounce.

Vivian has no idea that she is no longer beautiful. She hasn't caught sight of her own reflection in years. But she doesn't need a mirror to know that anyone seeing her eyes for the first time would instantly recognise that there is something familiar about them. Frank once told her that they looked as if they have been borrowed from a loved one and dropped thoughtlessly into the face of a monster. But what does he know? All men are fools. Thinking only with what is between their legs.

'I've seen you touching my things. Wearing my things. Whore.' The creature, who *is* Natalie and who *isn't* Natalie, jabs the knife in the air and works herself into more of a state with every hate spewed word.

'My things. My man.'

Chapter 41

The House By The Sea – Frank

Frank has no idea what woke him, but whatever it was, it also disturbed the baby. The cooing sound coming from the Moses basket prompts him to swing his tired legs out of bed. *They ache more than they used to, blasted rheumatoid arthritis,* but first he has to unravel them from the sheet wrapped tightly around his lower half. The blankets are all over the place, as if he had been having a fight with himself before falling asleep. His whole life is one big battle, he can't help thinking. Can't remember the last time he slept through the night. The baby makes up for this. She has got under his skin in a way he never expected. Not at his age. Yawning lazily, he stretches his arms above his head, and experiences a rare feeling of contentment when he sees the baby gurgling happily away to herself.

She doesn't look anything like him, thank God, but there is something about the eyes that are familiar. She has more of a look of Natalie about her than anyone else. Like Natalie, the baby is happiest on her own and often cries when he picks her up, so he doesn't attempt it now. Nor does he wrap her in the blanket, knowing it won't last two minutes before being thrown off again. He never says her name out loud if he can help it. He can't imagine why anyone would choose such a name for a baby. Sounds too mystical and mysterious for his liking. But his curiosity is piqued when her eyes swing back and forth from his face to the window, as if trying to tell him something.

Rolling a shoulder to relieve his aches and pains, Frank moves towards the window. As a rule, he's not one for superstitions or old wives' tales, but the hairs on his arms are pricked. The room closes in around him, making him feel claustrophobic. He notices things he has never seen before, like the tall shadows marching like soldiers going to war over the walls and the flashes of silver seen through the sash window, as bats fly past. Their delicate wings flapping against their small bodies sound like the pages of a book being turned.

"A feeling" is how some people would describe what he is experiencing. A feeling he doesn't like because a chilling fear is creeping into his bones and making him sweat. The closer he gets to the window, the more convinced he is that something is wrong.

Chapter 42
Thornhaugh – Natalie

The murmur of muted voices dies away when Dr Moses walks into the residents' lounge. His authority is felt immediately, resulting in bowed heads from patients who do not want to be singled out. They needn't concern themselves, because Dr Moses only has eyes for me, but I notice that his eyes instantly darken when he spots Jed sitting next to me. In fact, his whole posture changes.

If I didn't know better, I'd think Dr Moses recognised him from somewhere, but I know this to be impossible as Jed is a stranger here. When Dr Moses parades the room, stopping to talk to visitors, I think I must have been mistaken because nothing flusters Dr Moses. Even so, his eyes continue to dart back and forth to my mouth as if trying to lip-read what I am saying. I might as well be talking to myself at this point, because Jed is only interested in returning Dr Moses' look with an equal amount of animosity.

'Who's that?' Jed's narrowed eyes follow Dr Moses' progress around the room.

'Dr Moses,' I reply smiling, mostly out of gratitude, but partly because I think everybody should know this.

'I've seen him before,' Jed tosses his head irritably, 'going into the butcher's shop in Little Downey.'

'Dr Moses has never been to Little Downey,' I state dismissively. 'He told me so himself.' I quote this matter-of-factly, as if it is the gospel truth, because in my eyes it is, but Jed remains suspicious.

'In that case he's got a dead ringer in the village,' Jed replies ominously.

Chapter 43

White on white. A sterile barren environment without any windows or natural light. Just a set of flickering fluorescent strip lights making eerie patterns on the walls. In places, the paint peels to reveal blood-red brickwork beneath. Somebody has scratched the words "Help me" over this wall. I do not know if I am the author of these words or if somebody else, *one of them*, is responsible. In here, there are no mirrors to catch me out.

The communal shower block has floor-to-ceiling tiles and multiple shower heads that each pump out a weak supply of water, ranging at best from cold to lukewarm, never hot. Having turned every one of the showerheads on, I am huddled under the most powerful stream of water. It trickles down my white and blue-veined body onto the tiled floor, before disappearing with a gurgle down a brown-stained plughole.

Drip. Splat. Drip.

I am back in the slaughterhouse, where the cows don't want to die. Some things you never get over, right? Next, I am in Dr Moses office, which at the age of thirteen, felt more like a head-teacher's domain, arguing about the ethics of so-called *humane* slaughter and the human capacity to forget that the meat on their plate was once a living animal.

'Just because you didn't hear their screams, doesn't mean you didn't participate in their killing,' I remember telling him. *How clever I felt.*

As so often happens, one memory triggers another, only this time it makes me start, causing me to almost drop the thing I am holding in my hand.

'We'll take her to Dr Moses. He'll know what to do.'

The voice from the past is my own. I distinctly remember screaming those very words at my father. Recall even the sound of glass breaking a split second afterwards.

Then, Jed's voice, loaded with doubt— 'I've seen him before, in Little Downey, going into the butcher's shop.'

Too well, I recall my own response. 'Dr Moses has never been to Little Downey. He told me so himself.'

'In that case he's got a dead ringer in the village.' Jed's words come back to haunt me.

I have no reason to doubt what Jed told me. He seemed sincere enough. *Is he right? Is Dr Moses lying about his connection to Little Downey? If so, what else has he been lying about? My mother, perhaps?* I long to find out what else Jed knows. I still can't get over the fact that I have a half-sister. Although knowing this brings me comfort, I can't stop worrying about Merry and what might have happened to her. As yet I remember very little about her, but I sense that she was important to me. *Has Jed found her by now? Is she safe? Can my father be trusted to look after a baby?* He didn't do a very good job raising me that's for sure. So much is going through my head, I feel like screaming.

When I look down and see a trail of blood in the bottom of the shower, the desire to scream dies away. I cannot risk anyone finding me like this. Although horrified, I do nothing to start with. Simply watch the blood disappear down the plughole. Then, with a sense of foreboding, I open my palm to reveal the broken end of a plastic lip balm inside it. Subconsciously, I have been rubbing it against my upper arm until the skin there is sticky with blood. From experience, I know it will sting like hell later. I do not want to acknowledge, even to myself, how much I am looking forward to that.

Dead ringer. Dead ringer. Dead ringer.

I look at the pathetic piece of bloodied plastic and drop it like it is poison. It immediately fills with water, diluting the blood around it. Soon, all traces of self-harming will be gone. Will I also disappear in the end? *Is this what they want? My father and Dr Moses?*

Something doesn't add up. I have always known this, but Jed's suspicions seem to confirm what I already know. There is something sinister going on in Little Downey and possibly here at Thornhaugh too. After Jed's visit yesterday, I stopped taking my medication. If I am to discover the truth, I need to keep my wits about me.

During my thirteen years at Thornhaugh, I have come to understand that homes may change, but people don't, and I have an overwhelming desire to return to the home and father I still fear, knowing that forgotten memories wait for me there. I feel certain that my father's house is the key to everything.

***

An hour later, I am gliding down the grand oak staircase. This is a first for me, since residents are not allowed in the listed parts of the house. Secretly, I always imagined being married from Thornhaugh; pictured myself coming down the steps in a swirl of ivory—my father in a blue suit and pink carnation waiting for me at the bottom. Today, I transverse it unhindered as there is nobody milling about in the reception hall below. No father to greet me. No photographer to take snapshots of my special day. No husband waiting in the wings. Better still, no Dr Moses to whisk me back to my room on the third floor, the one with the depressingly long grey window.

I know better than to try opening the huge Gothic entrance doors as they are always kept locked. I will have to find a different way out. When I hear the clunk of a sturdy pair of nurse's shoes approaching, I duck through a fire door into a narrow unlit corridor which brings me out on the north side of the building, by the old kitchen, which is used as a storeroom. When the sound of the footsteps grows louder, I duck into the storeroom. It is dusty enough to make me want to sneeze, so I move towards the metal door that opens into an industrial-sized walk-in blast freezer. I have no choice but to hide in here for now. Sliding open the dead bolt locking handle, I step inside.

The lights flicker on automatically to reveal an all-grey metallic interior. Obviously, it is freezing cold inside and my breath instantly fogs up. Some things I expected to see, like white-ice forming over metal racking where packages and boxes of frozen vegetables are stored. I do not know what else I expected to see until I walk straight into it—

Racks of meat suspended from meat hooks.

The pale flesh, visible through its transparent packaging, is stamped "Slaughtered in Little Downey" but these cuts of meat resemble no animal!

Stumbling backwards, until my spine smacks into one of the metal walls, I feel as if someone has plunged me into an ice-cold bath, sucking all the breath out of me. Never taking my eyes off the grotesque joints of flesh that dangle like hanging victims in front of me, I cling to the metal racking, accidentally knocking off frozen packets of peas, which split from their seams and sprinkle on the floor, creating a ghoulish carpet of green at my feet.

Knowledge comes slowly. Hundreds of different thoughts rush through my mind. No matter how I try, I cannot deny the horror in front me. *This cannot be real,* I tell myself. Yet, God help me, I find myself walking towards one of the monstrosities, inexplicably drawn to it. There is something familiar about the shape of its carcass, the angle of its jaw.

Black eyes. The same as my own.

Could this be my mother? Have they already got to her, while I have been wasting time at Thornhaugh, sipping tea and daydreaming of Jed?

I close my eyes and pray that I am mistaken. This is one time I do not want to be right. It wouldn't be the first.

When I open my eyes again, I thank God that I am indeed wrong. On closer inspection, I can see that the partially open eyes are not black like my mother's, but Little Downey blue. More terrifying though is the fact that I recognise the owner of those eyes. I may only have seen him once since my return to Little Downey, but I am sure it is Ted Abbot from the post-office-cum-grocery store, the one I saw counting his takings out back. *Why is his body here? What can he have done to warrant such a cruel ending?* Nobody deserves to be treated like a slab of meat. Did he betray the village in some way? Now that I come to think of it, I believe this is the same corpse from my dream. The one I saw being dug up. I have no idea what is going on, nor what the body is doing here. But I can guess.

I almost want to say the word aloud, but fear prevents me—

You must get away from here, Natalie. I cannot bear to look at the glazed over blue eyes a second longer. They bulge at me as if trying to tell me something. But I think I already know what that something is. I cannot hide from the truth any longer. I only have to look at what has been going on behind my back all these years to know this.

Having had my worst fears confirmed, I slip out of the blast freezer, panicking about which direction I should take next. To be caught now is unthinkable. I no longer know who I can trust. Not my father, not the villagers, and probably not Dr Moses either, who I can see through a slit in the blinds of his office, further along the corridor. Somebody must be issuing fake death certificates for all the people that go missing. Who better than Little Downey's own resident physician.

He is on the phone and like before, when he saw Jed for the first time, Dr Moses appears flustered and anxious. He even runs a hand through his well-groomed hair. Something I have never seen him do before.

Another first. He's left the key in his office door. Guessing that Dr Moses must have popped into his office for only a second or two, I quickly turn the key in the lock, thrilled by my own daring. He is too preoccupied with his phone call to hear its quiet clink.

'No. I don't know where she is,' I hear him say, all the while pacing up and down a well-worn track in the carpet.

'What do you propose I do then?' he snaps into the phone.

Dr Moses chooses exactly that moment to stare in my direction. I quickly bob down, making myself invisible behind the slats in the blind but I am too late, he has spotted me.

'Natalie.' He gasps, dropping the phone.

In half a dozen long-legged strides, he's at the door. On finding himself locked in, he angrily rattles the handle, then hammers on the glass with a clenched fist.

'Natalie! Natalie!' he shouts.

Knowing it won't be long before Dr Moses is released and has everyone chasing after me, I burst into the dining room. From here, I should be able to slip out of the French doors and escape. I know this room well, although I always preferred to eat my meals at the table in the corner, away from the others, but today it is as if I am viewing it, and *them*, for the first time.

A little girl with wild hair, aged about nine, raises a fork to her mouth. I watch in fascination as a stringy piece of meat dangles enticingly above her mouth. She has a fixed smile on her face and rocks her chair so hard, I think it will topple over.

My eyes switch to the man sitting at my table. He is chasing peas around his plate with fat sweaty fingers and wears a look of deep concentration on his jowly face. His cardigan buttons are done up wrong and parts of his hairy belly protrude through the gaps. As if he knows he is being watched, he stops what he is doing and turns slow slothful eyes on me.

I gasp when I see who it is. I haven't set eyes on Andrew Muxlow in years, not since my mother's funeral. But then I remind myself that there wasn't any funeral. What memories I have of that day are as fake as my mother's alleged suicide. *Is she dead as everyone would have me believe or should I listen to my own instinct that tells me she is very much alive?* Realising I do not have the answers to these questions yet, I focus on the living breathing person in front of me. Most of his hair is gone, I notice, and he is older of course, a great deal heavier too, but having always suspected him of having a soft spot for my mother, he is not somebody I would ever forget.

His eyes, once as blue as my father's, are milky white. There is no recognition in his eyes, as he continues to watch me, just a look of hunger. His mouth opens and closes, as if he is about to say something, and I see that his tongue is stained green from the peas.

'You don't know what they're feeding you,' I gesture to the plate of food in front of him, unwilling to say the damning words out loud. *As yet, I cannot admit the full horror of it myself.*

But my words do not stop him. Nothing will, I fear, judging by the gluttonous expression on his face as he scoops up a handful of meat and shovels it in his mouth.

'I know,' he says.

I watch spellbound as undigested bits of flesh spill out of his mouth onto the plastic tablecloth. I cannot take my eyes off him, or the other patients who have all turned to stare at me. Sidling hesitantly towards the French doors, a chilling fear enters my bones as I watch each pair of eyes flare with sudden darkness.

I am not safe, I realise. I cannot help him, nor others like him, who are long gone. I cannot help myself either. Not while I am locked up in this place.

Chapter 44

Little Downey Beach

Stumbling along the coastal path that stretches for 186 miles, I am grateful to be heading in the opposite direction to Little Downey; towards the headland where my father's house is. It is almost dark, and sheep in the adjoining fields appear from nowhere, like clouds of dust, to frighten me. Their startled bleating alerts me to the very real danger I face—I could easily fall from the cliff edge to the pebbled shore below. Nobody but a fool, *or a mad woman*, I think ironically, would come up here in the dark without hiking boots and a torch. It is such a sheer drop, I have to cling on to whatever bit of prickly yellow gorse or long grass I can, ignoring the dark patches of shadow that fall across my path.

Up here, the sea breeze whispers through the bramble and trees that cling to the side of the cliff and I imagine I hear Jed, somewhere in the distance, calling for his sister.

'Merry! Merry!' His voice sounds desperate, I realise. Not like Jed at all. I can see the beam of his torch shining up and down the beach and among the sand dunes. The sea, at his heels, sounds angry tonight, almost as frustrated as he is. The waves seem to want to hush him, but he won't be silenced.

'Merry!' He shouts again. But again, there is no response.

Standing dangerously close to the cliff edge, I realise I am too far away to make myself heard. The wind would whip my screams out of my throat should I attempt to get Jed's attention. On the beach below, I can make out the shape of his dog, but tonight it doesn't cling to its side as it usually does. Jed is intent on following the path up to the house by the sea, but the dog is behaving erratically. Despite Jed whistling for it, it runs off in another direction altogether, ignoring him.

The twinkling of the oil tankers out at sea remind me that there are other people in the world besides me, but somehow it doesn't feel that way. Longing to be among my own kind again, I climb down from the towering cliff edge that may or may not have been responsible for taking many lives and thank God when I am back on the beach.

As ever, the past is nipping at my heels, like a rabid dog, keeping me going, making me ask questions, but even though the walk back to my father's house is only a mile or two away, I am already exhausted. Weakness and fatigue are all I ever feel when I am at Thornhaugh. They keep me this way on purpose, I suspect. I feel safer on sand but cannot shake off the sensation that somebody is following me. At times, I was certain I was going to be pushed from the cliff edge to my death. The flashing image of my body being carried away by the sea caused me panic and stumble often. I feel lucky to have made it down at all.

Relieved to see the looming shadow of the house come into view, I realise that it has never felt more like home. It might look like a daunting place to live but it is where I was born. Where I belong. Not even my father can take that away from me. I laugh when I see that he has left a light on, in a downstairs room, as if to welcome me home.

Chapter 45

The House By The Sea – Frank

The room is cluttered, a relic of time gone by, with horsehair sofas and crochet cushions. The furniture is dark and shabby, the carpet threadbare. There are no family portraits on show but above the fireplace there is a large framed drawing of a cow, demonstrating where the various butchered cuts of meat come from. This rather sad homage to a living creature takes pride of place on the chimney wall and is the only modern thing in the room.

The voice of Nina Simone floats upwards from an old-fashioned record player. The twelve-inch vinyl wobbles on its turntable and the words to *I Put A Spell On You* are accompanied by a gentle hissing sound, lending authenticity to the jazz recording.

The door opens and a bright overhead light comes on. As if frightened of entering his own living room, Frank hovers on the threshold. His eyes are wide with alarm. Looking this way and that, as if expecting somebody to leap out of the shadows, he enters cautiously.

Appearing hypnotised by the music, Frank walks over to the player and stares at the record on the turntable; his face tight and unreadable. He has aged overnight. The blue in his eyes is all but gone and his face is grey with worry and something else— fear. Jumping at nothing, he gently removes the needle, making sure it doesn't scratch the vinyl, and places it back in its sleeve before closing the record player lid. Then, hearing a sound outside, he turns off the light and heads into the utility room, just off the kitchen.

Unlocking a metal cabinet, Frank takes out his Winchester bolt-action rifle. Handling it with care, Frank points the muzzle away from himself. Then, grabbing a box of ammunition, he goes into the kitchen and loads the gun before sitting down at the table.

Looking desperately ill, as if he might keel over any second, sweat pours off his face, landing like tears on the gun's glossy brown handle. On the table in front of him is a large glass of whiskey. He takes a double slug, wipes his mouth, rolls his eyes as it takes effect and tries to still his trembling hands. It is clear from the expression on his face that he believes something bad is about to happen.

Chapter 46

Little Downey Beach – Natalie

Something runs past me. Almost touches me. Jed's dog? I cannot see it, but I feel it. Holding my breath, I freeze, terrified it might come back to bite me. I wait. I listen. I imagine I hear a soft growling but tell myself it cannot be real. There. See. It has stopped, proving me right for once. *Is it safe to go on*? I am so near to home, yet still so far away. At least another quarter of a mile. And I still must cross the part of the beach that isn't under water as well as climb the steep trail up to the house.

Grappling over large wet rocks that feel familiar to my touch, I realise that this is the Old Sheep Wash part of the beach where I used to swim as a child. Suddenly, I am flooded with memories— the sound of laughter, the sensation of being thrown up in the air by arms stronger than my own, of being caught again. Not my father. It couldn't have been him. I scorn the very idea of that. Then I remember holding hands with someone in the water and I realise this is the sheltered cove where Jed and I swam. This is one memory I *can* trust because it feels like it happened a long time ago, even though it didn't. I have been told that this is the true test of a genuine memory. Even Dr Moses agrees with me on that score.

I am about to continue my journey when I am unexpectedly blinded by a savage white light that causes my eyes to screw up in pain.

'Going somewhere, Natalie?'

I recognise the voice immediately. Of course I do. *Daniel Harper.* As soon as the name is in my head, I quickly build up a damning memory of everything that has happened between us. Once my eyes grow used to the searchlights on the grill of the pickup truck, I can make out Daniel grinning at me from behind the wheel.

Realising I was right all along about being followed, I make a bolt for it, hoping to catch him off guard. But Daniel is after me in an instant. First, I hear his mad scramble to get out of the truck, then the muffled thump of his footsteps on the sand behind me. He is much faster than I am.

I never stood a chance, I realise, as Daniel tackles me effortlessly to the ground. Luckily, I fall on soft sand, not harsh rock. Though temporarily winded, I am unhurt.

As he presses his body into mine, the smell of butchered meat overwhelms me. But when he touches me through my clothes in ways that I do not want him to, I fight him. Of course I fight, I am a Powers, but he is stronger than me. My efforts to escape do exhaust him though and I take pleasure from this fact. Collapsing in a heap on top of me, our eyes shine with equal amounts of hatred as we catch our breaths. Behind him, I glimpse a skinny grey silhouette that is almost invisible to the naked eye. Nose to the ground, the dog's hackles rise when it sees us rolling around in the sand. I watch it sniff the air, as if searching for a familiar scent, before disappearing from view.

'We've got unfinished business, you and I,' Daniel threatens, getting his breath back.

'I want nothing to do with you.' I spit, literally I spit, and then I try to bring a knee up into his groin, so I can roll away from him, but my attempt fails, amuses him even.

'Yet something tells me the time is right for us to go into business together.' He chuckles.

***

I am hunched up in the passenger seat, as far away from Daniel as possible, but we do not take our eyes off each other. Because of this, his driving is erratic. We are travelling too fast along the coast road and the truck swerves, changing lanes as if it has a mind of its own. I am terrified but I will not let it show. Something tells me this would make him drive even more dangerously. I have no idea what is about to happen, or where he is taking me, but I do not want to die. Realising that I will do anything I can to survive, *and yes, I really do think of the worst things that I may have to do,* is an affirming moment in the life of someone who has thought often about suicide.

When I finger the charm around my neck, hoping there might be some truth in its protective powers, I notice Daniel frowning at it. When he turns his head and keeps his cruel eyes fixed on the road ahead for once, I realise that the necklace unnerves him. I think about unfastening it and throwing it at him, but then I see a shadow, something on the backseat, and recoil from it. I am too frightened to look over my shoulder in case I really have conjured up a dark force that is about to kill us all.

A vicious growling coming from the rear of the truck seems to confirm my suspicion, but then I realise rather stupidly that it is Jed's dog, not a demon. I know I haven't imagined this, because Daniel hears it too, and is as surprised as I am. I watch his eyes swing to the rear-view mirror and whatever he sees there alarms him.

'What the fuck.'

Ears flattened, and teeth bared, the dog's head appears between us, causing us both to scream at the same time. The truck swerves again. When the dog sinks its teeth into Daniel's forearm, he screams and loses control of the wheel.

***

I am lucky to be alive, is the first thought that creeps into my mind when I regain consciousness. At first, I have no idea where I am, nor what has happened, but I do not think I am back at Thornhaugh, nor yet in my bedroom at my father's house, because the overpowering smell of diesel fills the air, making me want to gag. I can taste blood and there is a sharp pain in my shoulder that I cannot reach. Looking down, I see the reason for that—I am restricted by a tightened safety belt, and I thank God for it, because when I spot Daniel next to me, his head resting on the wheel, I quickly piece together what happened. As I do, my fingers fly to my neck, and I am relieved to find the lucky charm is still there. I won't be so quick to dismiss its power in future. Then I remember the dog, and I look behind me, but if it is still there, it must be hurt too, because it remains silent.

I turn back to Daniel, wondering what I should do. Does he deserve to be rescued? Probably not. *You can't leave him here to die, Natalie.* My inner voice denies me the pleasure this would bring. I think about shoving him to see if I can wake him up, but I am scared he will attack me again. Realising the truck could catch on fire and that we could both burn to death prompts me to get out of the truck. As far as I can tell, Daniel is still breathing, even if his eyes are closed, so he is in no immediate danger.

It is a struggle to climb out and as soon as my feet hit the tarmac I realise why. The front end of the truck is buried deep in the side of the cliff and steam pours out of its crushed bonnet. I stagger around to the other side, limping badly on my right leg, to try the driver's door handle but it won't budge. Peering through the window, I notice that Daniel has a sizeable gash on his forehead. I do not pity him, but despite my previous evil thoughts, I am not the sort of person to leave someone to die. I am also worried about the dog.

'Daniel. You've got to wake up. The truck…'

I make the mistake of hammering on the window, which rouses both the dog and Daniel; something I hadn't considered. I hear, rather than see, the dog attacking Daniel again and when a fresh spray of blood appears on the glass, I stagger backwards, unsure what to do. Then from behind me, I hear a distant gunshot coming from the house, and I make up my mind to flee. Everything becomes a blur after that and I limp away as fast as I can, not just to save myself but to escape Daniel's terrible screams for help.

Chapter 47

The Whitewashed Building

I watch Jed backing dazedly out of my father's house with a look of astonishment on his face. Blood spurts from his chest and sprays the ground. When he sees me standing there, motionless, unable to believe what I am seeing, there is such disappointment in his eyes, I am reminded of the cow in the slaughterhouse, and I have to look away. When I glance back again, Jed is gazing in disbelief at the gaping wound beneath his ribs. Instinctively, he presses down on it with one hand, then raises the finger of his other hand to point at the door he has just staggered out of. My father is nowhere to be seen.

'He… He… 'Jed stumbles over his words, as if he still cannot take in what has happened to him, before collapsing.

I move quickly. Putting an arm around Jed, I help him to get to his feet.

'We have to get out of here.' I warn. 'Before…' My eyes dart toward the house and Jed nods in agreement. He appears more shocked to see me than I am him; as if I am a ghost or an illusion. But having limped all the way here battered and bruised, I feel more alive than I ever hoped to. Plus, I have every right to be here, whereas Jed does not. What can he have been thinking to come here? While it is obvious that the quarrel with my father, which resulted in Jed getting shot, must have had something to do with Merry or me, I have been through too much today for my mind to process things clearly. First, the discovery of what they are feeding the residents at Thornhaugh, then Daniel, then the dog, and finally the car crash. Now this!

Jed opens his mouth to say something. I think his lips stretch to form my name, but I cannot be sure. Next, his beautiful mismatched eyes fill with confusion and I get the impression he wants to warn me of something. But there is no time. If I don't get him to safety soon, he could die. My father's house is obviously out of the question.

'This way,' I tell him, allowing him to lean heavily against me as I drag him toward the nearest building.

Chapter 48

Little Downey Coast Road – Daniel

If Daniel doesn't get out soon, he's a dead man. Either the dog will rip out his throat or the truck will explode in flames and he will burn to death. Mad as hell that he is unable to do anything about the situation he finds himself in, he has given up trying to beat off the dog and is concentrating solely on protecting his head from being savaged. The dog continues to shake him though, ripping through layers of skin on his arms and chest. The pain is excruciating but Daniel realises he is lucky the dog hasn't so far damaged any vital organs.

Deciding he cannot allow a dog *or a girl* to get the better of him, that he'll live to spite them both, he braces himself for an even more ferocious attack before diving across the seat, to wrestle with the door handle. Try as he might, he cannot get it open. When he sees flames flickering over the bonnet, heading his way, he screams in fear and throws his weight at the door. This time, it swings open and Daniel falls out onto the road, gasping for clean air; wanting to laugh and cry at the same time. When he looks around for the dog, it is nowhere to be seen. Crawling away from the truck on his hands and knees, constantly checking over his shoulder in case the dog should show up, he thinks about how much he will enjoy making Natalie pay for leaving him at the mercy of a fucking dog, or worst still, being burnt alive. Just wait till he gets his hands on her. As for that dog—

Behind him, Daniel hears a savage snarling and instantly freezes in the hope that the dog won't see him. It is completely dark out on the road and if he keeps quiet and doesn't move he might stand a chance. But the growling keeps on getting meaner and louder. Bracing himself for the inevitable, Daniel's face twists with fear. He cannot bring himself to look. He doesn't have to. The dog appears from nowhere to pin him to the ground; sinking its vicious teeth into his flesh. This time he hears the crunch of bone.

'No fucking way!' Daniel screams.

Every time he moves or tries to defend himself, the dog attacks him with renewed fury. Its foul-smelling slobber saturates his clothing, until he's no longer sure how much of it is saliva and how much of it is his own blood. He's in a bad way, that much he can tell. Feeling as exhausted as he does, he guesses he's running out of time. If he doesn't do something soon—

Managing to roll over on his back in a bid to face up to the dog, Daniel is surprised as well as relieved when it unexpectedly backs off. It doesn't go far, and it continues to observe him with flattened ears, bared teeth and a bloody face, but it's a start.

'Good boy,' Daniel cajoles in the fake tone he reserves for customers' dogs; secretly he cannot stand them. 'You have no idea what I'm going to do to you…' he warns in the same deceitful tone.

And realises his mistake when the dog stops circling and makes a sudden lunge for his throat. Bastard dog knew what it was doing all along, Daniel realises. It was simply biding its time. Drawing upon his last ounce of strength, Daniel kicks out with all his might and feels the soles of his boots connect with teeth and bone.

Terrified of being set on again, he pulls himself to his feet, ignoring the pain coursing through his body. Spitting out an angry trail of blood on the roadside, he finds the dog over by the truck. It's not dead, but it's not far off. It lies whimpering with its long wiry legs going to ten to the dozen. Its snout is covered with blood and it looks as if it is missing some teeth.

'Picked on the wrong bloke this time, didn't you.' Daniel laughs smugly.

In response, the dog weakly lifts its head and growls in recognition. Realising it would still kill him, given the chance,

Daniel staggers to the back of the truck, ignoring the gathering flames and cloud of black smoke, to take out a shovel. Raising it above his head, he notices that the dog doesn't take its eyes off him. As if it knows what is about to happen, it whines pitifully and licks Daniel's boot in a gesture of surrender, but it is too late for that.

'I fucking hate dogs!' Daniel yells, bringing down the shovel.

Chapter 49

The Whitewashed Building – Natalie

'I can't believe Father shot you. Left you for dead,' I exclaim for the third time since dragging Jed inside the whitewashed building. I stop blathering only when the distant sound of a dog crying out in pain cuts through the suffocating silence. As Jed doesn't respond to this eerie echo, I cannot be certain it is real. I am finding it hard enough to believe what I *am* seeing.

As always, it is dark and damp in here and the stench automatically has me covering my nose and mouth with my hand. I use my other hand to reach for the cord that I know is dangling somewhere above my head and I am relieved when my fingers curl around it. A dim light appears when I pull on the cord, creating shadows in corners that do not exist. I almost faint when I see that the butcher's block has been moved aside and the heavy trap door is swinging open. This can only mean one thing—

'She's out.' I gasp.

Instantly, I revert back to when I was a child again; not wanting to see, not wanting to hear, not wanting to believe. But I have to see. Have to know. So, I take the smallest of steps towards the gaping black hole in the floor, but Jed, writhing in agony on the floor, almost trips me up, on purpose I suspect, to bring me to my senses.

Not so long ago, I longed to put my hands on his body. Now, I recoil from it. I can smell the blood congealing on him. If he opens his eyes while I lay his head down on the floor, I am sure I will faint. I do not faint. As always, I am stronger and more resilient than I give myself credit for. I hold Thornhaugh responsible for my self-doubt, and so much more. Having had it drilled into me from an early age how weak and fragile I am, I almost came to believe it myself.

Never taking my eyes off the trap door, I rip open Jed's shirt and put pressure on the wound in attempt to stop the bleeding. Meanwhile, Jed drifts in and out of consciousness. Every so often his mouth opens as if he is about to say something or his eyelids flicker.

Convinced he is going to die, I dig my nail into my thumb as hard as I can and concentrate on watching the skin pale to white. I do not know what else to do. I am unable to cope with this kind of situation. I hear Jed's voice, barely a murmur in my ear, but I do not know what he is saying. His words grow louder inside my head until I cannot stand it a second longer.

'Merry wouldn't take off like that. Not without the baby,' Jed states stubbornly, staring pointedly at the open trap door. 'Frank swears he doesn't know what happened to her, but I think he's protecting someone. Why the gun, if he's got nothing to hide.'

I try to hush Jed, but he won't have it.

'I warned Merry, but she wouldn't listen. Thought nothing could harm her as long as she wore that damn stupid charm necklace,' Jed chokes.

'What do you think has happened to her?' I ask tearfully.

He shakes his head. 'There's something going on this village, Natalie. Everybody seems to have a secret.'

'Not everyone.' I grip his hand, determined that he should believe me.

He pauses to frown up at me. 'Yours is the biggest of them all.'

At first, I do not understand what he means by this, then I realise he is referring to my mother. He is right of course. But before I can agree with him, he's off again, slurring his words.

'You've got to find out what they did to Merry. Before it's too late.'

I cannot bring myself to tell him what I know in my heart, that it is already too late for his sister. Instead, I check his forehead. He is burning up. This is not good. Not good at all.

'You're delirious,' I say, willing myself not to look at Jed. If he dies, my father will go to prison and I will end up back at Thornhaugh, for good this time. The possibility of this fills me with such dread, I rock my body from side to side. Usually, this action brings me comfort, but not today.

'Natalie!' Jed's voice jolts me out of my self-induced trance. If Jed is to survive, he needs all the help he can get. This is not the time to think about myself.

'What shall I do?' I shake him awake when I realise that his eyes have dimmed again. 'Tell me what to do Jed, please,' I beg.

'See if you can find a first aid box. Some bandages or something.' His voice fades away as he passes out again, leaving me alone with my demons in the whitewashed building.

***

Keeping one fearful eye on the open trap door, terrified in case my mother should make an appearance, I search my father's workshop for a first aid box, never really expecting to find one. At the same time, I experience a hazy memory of being out here on my own quite recently and a shiver runs down my spine. I cannot think of any reason why I would come out here in the dark unless I was searching for something, as I am doing now.

Not something, Natalie. Someone.

Where would my father store a first aid box? Where? Where? For some reason, my eyes keep returning to the butcher's block with the rusty cutting tools that have always unnerved me. Luckily, there are no animal carcasses hanging in here for me to bump into. I will not think about what I discovered back at Thornhaugh. Every time I close my eyes, I see the swinging joints of milky white flesh and the "Slaughtered in Little Downey" stamp.

Natalie. Natalie.

I imagine I hear my mother's haunting whisper, calling out to me from the cellar below, but I fight against it. I must keep my wits about me if I am to be of any help to Jed.

Ignoring the scratches on the floor where the butcher's block stands, I do not stop to stare at the knives as I pass by, but I do catch a glimpse of my own blurred reflection in their blades. I immediately think of my mother again. We are so alike.

Natalie. Natalie.

I find bandages in a cupboard on the wall that also houses poisons and jars of suspicious-looking liquid that look as if they should have been thrown away years ago.

Something in my drink.

Your father did not drug you, Natalie.

From behind me, I hear a creaking sound followed by a secretive shuffling. I know it is not Jed. He is well out of it.

After a few seconds of silence, I dare to glance over my shoulder. That's when I see it—not my mother God forbid—but a mound over by the window with a tea towel thrown over it. I am not naive enough to believe that someone has left a tray of cakes out here to cool by the window, although that is exactly what it looks like.

Besides, it is swarming with flies. I watch them buzz around then land on the gingham fabric before disappearing underneath. Breaking the seals on the cellophane packaging, I unwind the rolls of bandages but do not take my eye off the tea towel. It doesn't matter that somebody else's life is in my hands, I will not return to Jed until I have found out what it is hidden underneath it.

Chapter 50

The House By The Sea

My body shakes with rage as I tiptoe into the room. My father has collapsed into a chair at the kitchen table and has his back to me, holding his head in his hands. He doesn't see me. Doesn't hear me. Nothing changes. I have always been able to creep up on him in this way; fool that he is. Sweat is coming off him in buckets, forming dark patches on his clothing. His smell fills the room. I pause when I notice the gun resting on the table, inches from his hand. I want to pick it up and bash him over the head with it, for what he has done to Jed, but I do not. Haven't I been brought up to be a dutiful and obedient daughter?

As if sensing he is not alone, my father twists around in his chair to look at me. His eyes, smaller and shrunken than ever, are swine like. I see something in them that is not new, now I come to think of it. He is terrified of me. But I remind myself he is the monster. Not I.

'I take it you're not going to ask how Jed is?' I spit.

Father is immediately on his feet, jumpy and anxious, but does not speak, just stares blankly at me. I know him well enough to guess what he is thinking. He will be telling himself that if he says nothing, he will get away with it. I doubt he thinks anything of shooting a gypsy. Probably thinks Jed deserves a bullet in the chest for simply being on his property.

Eventually, my father breaks his silence. 'What are you doing here, Natalie?'

He sounds as if he cares. I am tempted to laugh out loud at that, but I do not. I watch him glance behind me, as if checking I am alone. He is probably wondering where Jed is.

'Where have you come from?' my father wants to know.

I want to tell him "Hell and back" but of course I do not do that either. Such dramatic words would result in a raised eyebrow from Dr Moses, I cannot resist thinking.

When my father notices the blood on my hands and the cold guarded expression on my face, he makes a great show of being puzzled. 'Natalie?' He cannot fail to notice my fury, yet he is stupid enough to take a step towards me.

'Don't come near me!' I yell, recoiling in horror. I would rather drown, face down in the sea, than have any contact with him.

'Natalie,' he says again, confused by my behaviour.

He is wondering why I won't look directly at him; why my knuckles are locked white with anger, with strips of bandaging stretched tightly around my wrists, like restraints, which we both know I am no stranger to. As if my hands were wrapped around his neck, I squeeze the taut piece of fabric until it cannot stretch any further. I am sure this is the only thing stopping me from lunging at him. *I will no longer refer to this man as Father.* When the material eventually rips, he nervously licks his bottom lip.

I watch his mind at work. His eyes flit from the shredded bandages, to my face, then to the darkened window. I can almost see his train of thought. He is in the whitewashed building, glancing around, trying to figure out what I might have seen there to make me react like this. When it eventually dawns on him, his eyes pop wide with disbelief.

'That's…' I stumble on my words, my voice choking with emotion. 'Merry out there.'

A shutter of deceit comes down on his face, making me hate him even more.

'Merry's birthmark!' I scream. 'I'd know it anywhere. You killed her. Cut her into pieces.' The bandages fall from my hands, scattering on the floor like petals on a coffin.

I think Frank is about to pass out. He struggles for breath and gulps at the air like a fish. 'I don't know what you're talking about,' he admits finally.

I can tell by the guilty look on his face that he's determined to make me think I have imagined all of this. As if that will get him off the hook! I wonder why he bothers. It's clear that he feels nothing for no one, me included. Isn't that what I always suspected?

Refusing to look me in the eye, he stares at his boots instead. I think the pulsating blue veins on his face are about to explode. But he, at least, is alive, I remind myself bitterly. Unlike poor Merry. As soon as I saw the slab of white meat hidden under the bloodstained cloth, I recognised the distinctive strawberry mark on it. At first, I couldn't make the connection. It was only when I traced the mark with my finger that the memory of that day on the beach came back to me—when a naked laughing Merry showed me her birthmark for the first time. *The baby has one too, see.*

Darling Merry, who was young and beautiful and so full of life. She was everything I wanted to be and more. My eyes well with tears thinking about her.

'You cut her up. Murdered her. You're going to do the same to me,' I sob.

'No, Natalie. It's not how it looks. I swear I never touched anybody. After… I'll tell you everything but right now we need to get the hell out of here.'

I dodge his outstretched arms. *Since when did my father want to hold me?*

'I'm not going anywhere with you!' I shout, backing towards the door, pausing only when my elbow scrapes against the handle. 'Don't come near me,' I warn, looking around for something to arm myself with. Then, I remember my father's gun. But he is closer to it than I am. I would not be able to reach it first.

My father's guilt-ridden eyes are everywhere, trying to second-guess me. I back out of the door but dare not turn my back on him until I am in the hallway, where I stand a fighting chance of getting away from him. Fearing he will soon be upon me, I make a bolt for the front door. This door is rarely opened and I fumble with the lock for a few wasted seconds. The silence is unbearable. Inside my head I am screaming but all I can hear is my own breathing. Convinced that my father is going to chop me into tiny pieces, I feel overwhelming relief when the door finally creaks open.

'Stop!' I hear Frank holler from somewhere behind me.

And I do. Not because of him, but because of what I see coming towards me—

Chapter 51

'We're too late.' Father slams and bolts the door in our faces. I do not argue. Do not fight him as he shoves me back inside, but I claw at my hair as if it were on fire. I think I must be going mad because I cannot believe what I saw. It makes no sense. What the hell is going on?

I stare wide-eyed at the door handle, terrified in case it should get turned from the outside. When it doesn't, I sneak a look at my father, wanting reassurance, but he is glaring intently at me, his eyes anything but calming. I know the look well. *Be brave. Don't cry. Sit up straight. Be tough. Like a boy. Frank's Law, remember.*

But I am scared and want my mother.

Barring my way, as if he thinks I am crazy enough to step foot outside, he leans heavily against the door and buries his head in his hands. He is so close, I can smell his breath on my face, and for a moment I think he is about to cry, but instead he barks out a sarcastic laugh that startles me. Not for the first time, I question which one of us is insane.

'What do they want?' I plead, digging my fingernails as hard as I can into my wrist.

Grabbing hold of the offending hand, Father tugs me, first into the kitchen, to pick up the gun and to lock the back door, then marches me into the living room. I do not know if I am his prisoner or not, but I am too stunned to do anything other than obey. What I saw out there has me beat. My father too, only he doesn't realise it yet. He is still going through the motions, reloading his rifle, turning off the lights, hiding in the shadows— as if we stand a chance. *As if we stand a chance.*

'What do they want?' I ask again, peering through a gap in the curtains, making sure what I saw was real, that I didn't imagine it.

They are still out there. The villagers. People we have known all our lives. Men and women. Old and young. Most of them are on foot but others have arrived in vans or pickup trucks. Those on foot carry torches but it is the car headlights trained on the house that dazzle and hurt my eyes. A few of the men are armed with shotguns, some with spades. The spades worry me more than the guns. When you are shot you either die straight away or bleed to death like Jed could do if I don't soon get him to a hospital, but being hit repeatedly with the dull edge of a spade would be unimaginable.

I recognise many of them, but their expressions are new to me, riddled as they are with anger, fear, and something else I can't immediately put a name to—excitement. The missing word pops out of nowhere, like a bad omen. These people are my own, yet they terrify me. A small part of me admits that this has always been the case.

It comes as no shock to see that Bob Black and Daniel are the ringleaders of this unruly mob. Bob sits behind the wheel of Daniel's pickup truck, while Daniel and the lanky ginger-haired youth stand in the open cargo area at the back, drumming up a rising hatred. I do not know how Daniel managed to get out of the truck alive or what happened to the dog, but when I recall the pitiful whining I heard earlier, I feel myself shudder.

When my father unexpectedly wraps me in his arms, I stiffen automatically. *Is this a trick? Is he part of this?* I have never known my father voluntarily pull me into an embrace before. He hugs me so tightly, I think I am about to be crushed.

'Why did you have to come back?' he mumbles into my hair. 'Why did you have to remember anything?' He goes on in a different voice to the one I am accustomed to hearing. 'Sixteen years I've been trying to protect you.'

'From them?' I pull my head away from the sweaty crease in his neck. I must look into his eyes when I say this— 'Because of Mother?'

He takes my face in his hands and I watch his already-swollen eyes well up.

'I wanted no part in it,' he whispers, wagging a silencing finger at me, as if afraid I might scream and bring even more trouble down on us, as if *that* were possible.

'Told 'em so right from the start. That's when they took her.'

Unable to continue, he breaks down and sobs into my hair. Impatiently, I push him away. As much as I've always wanted my father to love me, I need answers, not hugs.

'No part in what, Father? Tell me—'

Outside, the roar of the mob can be heard above our own voices. They are coming for us. In my mind, I see them shouting, gesturing, and shaking their fists in the air. I don't have to explain my fear to my father. I can see the same terror reflected in his eyes.

'Turned up with torches. A night like this one. Threatened to burn us down, don't you remember?'

Screwing up my eyes in concentration, I blink several times as I try to think back to when I was a child. Conjuring up lost memories is never easy, especially when you have been warned against it all your life. Dr Moses was fond of saying that the past was just that, the past, and going back to it was dangerous for someone like me.

Just as I am about to give up, I do remember—

Her smile was all for me that night. Although she must have been as terrified as I am now, she stayed brave for my sake. When I saw her walking with her head held high towards the crowd, I tried to run after her, but my father would not let go of my hand.

'Mummy! Mummy!' I remember screaming. Unlike now, I had no idea what that night was all about or why the villagers had turned up at our door demanding that my mother be sent out to them. The mob might have changed, although I seem to think Bob Black was there

that night too, but the outcome was the same. My mother disappeared into the night as surely as if she had flung herself off that cliff edge.

'It was because of me, wasn't it?' I whimper. 'Something I saw?'

Before he has chance to reply, we hear thumping on the walls. Father grabs hold of me again and pulls me close. When he gestures for me to move away from the wall, I obey without question.

'You made them nervous,' he acknowledges with a proud smirk. 'Always poking your nose in where it wasn't wanted. Your mother and I wanted to send you away from Little Downey, but they wouldn't allow it. Too frightened you would talk. I had no choice but to send you to Dr Moses. It was the only way of keeping you safe. It was either that, or—'

I try to ignore the tremor in his voice that reveals he is as afraid I am. I need him to be brave, like my mother.

'It was human meat I saw, wasn't it? You used to make me deliver it on my bicycle,' I whisper. 'I think I have always known.'

My father's eyes soften momentarily, and I see myself in them, as a child, cycling past him while he stood in front of the butcher's shop, a butcher's saw dangling in his hand. I remember that he used to watch me go and I could never understand why he seemed so angry. At last, I understand, it was them he was angry with, not me.

'They've been eating it since before the war. Generation to generation has kept the craving going. To keep you and Viv safe, I had to become involved, as my father did before me. They threatened to kill her, and you too, if I didn't do what they said.'

'You kill people?'

Fear of my father returns. I cannot bear to be the daughter of a murderer.

'No. Not me.' He is quick to reassure me, but his next words chill me. 'I just... look after the meat.'

His confession sickens me, but I feel my heart hammer again. I hadn't even realised it had paused. *Be grateful for small mercies,* I tell myself. Anything is better than him being a cold-blooded killer. It's too soon to think about whether Dr Moses is somehow embroiled in all this. Another disappointment would surely finish me off.

'And Merry?' I must know.

Father fixes me with such a cold disinterested stare, that I realise he is just as capable of hiding the truth from himself as I am. 'Being locked up so long has driven your mother insane,' he finally admits. 'She was mentally unstable before you went away but after you left, they let her come back, but it was too late by then. She's like them now, addicted and capable of just about anything. They made her that way. Force-fed her like a dog. The bastards. We were lucky they didn't make her walk off the cliff edge like they did so many others, but her madness made them nervous. It was the only thing that kept her safe. The villagers agreed she could stay in the cellar, provided she was not allowed to roam.'

'Oh, my God.' I take a step back in horror and almost collapse to my knees. *Can this be true? My poor gentle mother, who wouldn't have hurt a fly – a cold-blooded killer.*

When my father picks up his gun and goes to the window, I pull at his arm to stop him.

'You can't fight them,' I declare, terrified in case he should open fire on the crowd outside. Not that they don't deserve it, but surely then we would have no chance. 'There are too many.'

In response, an authoritative voice in the crowd rings out. It's a voice I recognise—

'We know you're in there, Frank!' Daniel yells in a deceptively friendly tone. 'Come on out. Nobody else need get hurt.'

Again, I tug at my father's arm. I want him as far away from the window as possible. It's too dangerous. But when my father turns weary eyes on me and shakes his head, I know he has made up his mind to do something foolish.

'Promise me,' he pleads, with his voice cracking, 'whatever happens, whatever they do to me, you'll leave here. Take the baby with you, she's—'

'My sister, yes I know,' I say quickly, hoping for some acknowledgement of his relationship to Merry but once again he dodges the subject, unwilling or unable to accept his part in her demise. My mother might have killed Merry in one of her jealous rages, but my father took her body apart, bit by bit, turning her into a slab of meat, in order to cover up this terrible crime. I must not think about this now, I realise. It won't do any of us any good, least of all Merry.

Convinced there is still time to get my father to change his mind about going out there, I try desperately to come up with a different solution. One that won't involve getting him killed. That hope dies when he presses the gun into my chest.

'It's me they're after now. But just in case.'

'Father, no,' I cry.

He moves as if to hug me, then changes his mind. I sense an argument going on inside his head. *Be brave. Be strong*, he'll be telling himself.

'They won't do anything to you. I've seen to that.'

'You made a deal?' I gasp.

'That's why Daniel's determined on you for a wife. I'd rather you use that gun on yourself than let him get his way. Promise me, you'll do it.'

He gives me a harsh shake. His face is a blur. I cannot see for the tears running down my face. Gingerly, I take the gun from him and nod tearfully.

'Promise. Frank's Law remember?'

'Frank's Law,' I repeat obediently.

Chapter 52

Somewhere in the house a window breaks and glass shatters into hundreds of jagged pieces on the floor. As I follow the shrunken shoulders of my father towards the front door, I imagine I can feel every splintered shard piercing my skin. The desire to punish myself has never been stronger, *all this is my fault, if only I'd stayed away like my father and Dr Moses wanted,* but I will not give in to it. I must stay strong for my father's sake. And Jed's. The villagers will not think of looking for him in the whitewashed building, but my mother is a different matter. As soon as this is over, I have promised myself I will go and find him. Until then I can only pray that he remains safe.

The shouts from outside have grown more persistent yet they sound duller to my ears, until I think that I have grown accustomed to their onslaught. *How is that even possible? How is any of this possible?* I want time to stand still but it races on ahead, like my father, who has managed to get the door open without any trouble. It does not put up a struggle as it did for me earlier. It gives in as easily as my father is doing. I long to make eye contact with him one last time but I can tell, by the stubborn set of his jaw, that he does not want this. Instinctively, I know there will be no final look over his shoulder when he disappears into the crowd. We have said our goodbyes.

When he steps onto the porch, he is greeted with an unhealthy silence that, I for one, find more terrifying that the jeering. I have promised to close the door on him the second he is gone and I will not break my word but I am determined to first capture this moment, leaving nothing out. Before this terrible night is over, I will have imprinted every guilty face on my mind.

Through a crack in the door, I see a field of blue irises and crooked smiles looking back at me; interspersed with flashes of decaying yellow teeth. The villagers' gaunt faces appear sunken with hunger, greed and excitement. *There's that awful word again.* Sickeningly, I realise they are relishing what they are about to do. Every single one of them. I do not see a hint of regret, fear or indecisiveness among them.

Be brave. Be strong. Sit up straight. And no crying. My father remains stoically silent as he walks towards them but I can hear his voice in my head. As if they have but one mind, the villagers shuffle apart, allowing him to move among them.

Just before closing the door on my father's departing back, I tell myself, hard-heartedly, that I will remember this night for the rest of my life. What it smelt like. What it tasted like. What it felt like—the chattering of insects going about their everyday lives as if something horrific was not about to happen. The smell of sweat; the look of fear in my father's eyes; the taste of sea salt; a ghostly mist heading our way, threatening to envelop us in its grasp.

***

Resting my cheek against the glass of the living room window, I watch my father being circled by the bloodthirsty mob. Not like vultures, I think ironically, more like an inquisitive herd of cows. Part of me wants to tear my eyes away, close the curtains and collapse in a disbelieving heap on the floor, but this is not what I have been brought up to do.

My father's head bobs up and down, as if he is pleading for leniency, but he keeps his back straight and his chin up. He has gone out there with a dignity that I feel seeping into my own bones. Holding my breath, until it hurts, I watch Daniel and Bob Black walk up to my father, exchange words, and then push him to his knees. *Oh God, please keep him safe,* I pray, knowing full well that God abandoned me the night he took my mother from me.

Don't let this happen. Don't let this happen. The mantra builds inside my head until I cannot stand the sound of my own inner voice. Instead, I draw a protective heart around my father's silhouette in the misted windowpane, as if that will keep him safe. *I am with you. I am here. I swear I will not look away. Not even at the last minute. I love you, Dad.*

I do not scream, not out loud anyway, when Bob Black aims a massive bolt gun at my father's forehead, and I remain dry eyed when, with a flick of his hand, he tugs my father's head higher, until they are eye to eye. I know enough of this evil man to understand that he wants my father to know it is his hand that will bring about his death.

Before he has chance to pull the trigger, Daniel tries to yank something out of my father's hand, *Merry's charm necklace,* but my father will not let go—not even when Daniel punches him full in the face, knocking him sideways onto the grass. I feel nothing but pride, *the desire for revenge will come later,* when my father claws himself back up and takes his place, as if it was his rightful one, on his knees, both arms behind his back; one hand clinging onto the so-called lucky charm that has never brought us a moment's good luck. Sticking out his bloodied chin in defiance, my father's body language lets the crowd know, in no uncertain terms, that they can do their worst, but they will not break him.

He goes down on the first resounding crack of the bolt gun, *it would kill him to know that they brought him down so easily,* and everyone pauses, as if unsure of themselves. but a rumble of applauding thunder has them on the move again, clapping and whooping, as if a higher power had vindicated their evil actions. Then, goaded on by Daniel, they aim brutal kicks at my father's prostrate body which I occasionally glimpse through their thrashing legs. Stopping only when Bob Black falls to his knees on the ground beside my father, it soon becomes clear that he is not issuing a prayer, nor yet checking for a heartbeat—he is jabbing a knife, right up to the hilt, behind his former friend's ear; ripping through the carotid artery and expertly severing it. He has seen too many beasts recover from the shot of a bolt gun to take any chances with someone as unforgiving as my father.

Chapter 53

Little Downey Beach

The sun beats mercilessly down on our heads, making us sweaty and irritable, even with each other. The baby, swaddled in my arms, makes me hotter still, but she cries whenever I put her down, so I take her everywhere with me; comforting myself with the knowledge that this is what Merry and my father would have wanted. I cannot think of either of them without experiencing a wave of accompanying hatred for those responsible for what happened to them. Rightly or wrongly, I do not hold my mother accountable for her part in Merry's death. As far as I am concerned, she is as blameless as the child in my arms.

It is strange that Darkly should prefer me over her own uncle, but I no longer question things the way I used to. I have, *we have*—I correct myself, momentarily forgetting that I am part of a "We" now—come a long way in the last few days. I might look the same, but I feel so much older and wiser. I never expected to experience such a sudden and overwhelming maternal love for my half-sister, which seems to overshadow everything else, Jed included. The change in him is more obvious. Almost overnight his jet-black hair turned grey and dark circles appeared under his eyes. The laughter has gone from his mismatched eyes. Whenever our eyes meet up now, all we do is exchange pained meaningful looks.

Today, the beach feels enormous, stretching as far as my eyes can see. It occurs to me that anyone looking down on us from the cliff would assume we were a young family enjoying a day out in the sunshine. Nothing could be further from the truth. Jed's shirt is stained with blood, which means his wound is bleeding through the bandages again and I can tell by the way he is wincing that the soreness is also returning. The painkillers he took earlier must have worn off. I know that he will not speak of his own pain, not when his sister suffered the way she did; but with no means of getting him to a hospital, the thought of his wound becoming infected is a constant worry. Even if we did try to make it on foot together, the villagers would never allow me to leave. We are left with only one choice.

He must go while I remain. At least for now, until we figure things out. Jed insists that I have an obligation to go to the police but as I pointed out, who would believe me and what would happen to Darkly if I did? He cannot take her with him. He may not make it as far as the hospital and I cannot run the risk of having her taken from me. They will say I am too unstable to raise a child. If I get caught, I also run the risk of being sent back to Thornhaugh, where they will try once again to make me forget everything I know. If I whisper so much as a word about what has been happening in Little Downey, I might be forced off the cliff edge myself. I cannot bear the thought of what they would do to my body afterwards.

Jed at least gets a second chance. Luckily for him, I was able to cleanly dig out the bullet and stitch down a two-inch-flap of torn skin while he was still unconscious. Although extremely painful, he is on the mend, and, barring infection, I expect him to fully recover. We might not speak of it, but we are both aware of how much worse it could have been. We only have to look at the burnt-out gypsy camp to know this.

Nothing remains of Jed's former home except for the blackened carcass of the car and caravan and a lingering smell of burnt rubber that I do not think will ever fade. The cave in the background has its enormous mouth open as if preparing to swallow the debris whole.

'This is just a warning. If they catch you…' I say, gesturing to the blackened shell.

'What about you?' Jed's anger, like mine, is never far away, but he is not eaten up by it in the same way that I am. He is still optimistic about the future and believes in justice.

I shake my head at him, as if I do not matter, and perhaps I don't, I think, glancing down at the baby, whose eyes are glued to mine. *She* is all that matters now.

'It's too soon,' I say, more decisively than I feel. 'They are watching me all the time. But, as soon as I can, I'll come and find you.'

'*Then* we'll go to the police together.'

I gaze at the sand and idly scuff a pebble with the side of my sandal, but Jed sees through my unwillingness to touch on this subject and, cupping my chin with his hand, he tilts my head so that I am forced to look at him. Childishly, I resent him exerting this power over me.

'We'll get your mother into a proper place where she'll receive all the help she needs.'

'A mental institution?' I say scathingly, snapping my head away from his touch.

'She may never live a normal life again, Natalie. You've got to accept that.'

Chapter 54

The Whitewashed Building – Vivian

It is dusk. The sun is low in the sky, casting a sleepy orange glow over the house by the sea, giving it a warmth that it lacks during the day. The house itself is in darkness, but its adjacent buildings stir with activity. Insects are warming up to provide their usual evening chorus and birds of prey ruffle their feathers in preparation for their first flight of the night.

At the back of the whitewashed building, there is an old grill buried in the dusty ground, which provides ventilation to the underground cellar. Forgotten about for years, overgrown grass grows through its rusty metal bars, which are a good ten inches apart.

When a hand unexpectedly shoots up through one of these bars and a ghostly curl of white breath appears, a wary barn owl, caught unawares, screeches in alarm, before taking to the sky. Unlike the laboured breathing that can be heard below ground, the owl's wings are as silent as a whisper as its creamy underbelly disappears into the night.

***

A tantalising glimpse of that setting sun is also visible through the bars on the metal grill, but it does little to alleviate the dark and depressing conditions of the underground cellar. The stooped figure of Vivian, wearing the same red dress that Natalie wore on her date with Daniel, gazes out of the grill to stare longingly at the sky. Her hands are wrapped like the claws of a dying wisteria around the metal bars. The stench is overwhelming. Blood. Stale urine. Human excrement. Death. But all that goes unnoticed by the woman in the cellar, whose yellowing bloodshot eyes are full of hatred. And something else perhaps—a steely determination that lends her super human strength.

As if to prove this, she slips her right side between the two metal bars of the grill and grimaces, before deliberately dislocating her shoulder in a quick torturous jerking movement, resulting in the sickening snap of bone. Although her eyes glaze over in agony, she is no amateur. Escaping her prison cell is something she has done many times before. As thin as she is, even she cannot pass through the narrow gap yet. Taking in a quick succession of deep breaths, she braces herself, before biting down on her dirt-streaked hand. Then, crying out in pain, she expertly dislocates the other shoulder.

The pain is indescribable, but she is at last able to slide her emaciated body through the gap in the bars to claw her way out of the cellar, grasping at clumps of soil and grass for leverage. Once on firm ground, she collapses in a dishevelled heap but does not waste time relishing the feel of clean air on her ravaged skin. Instead, she trains her eyes on the house by the sea.

Pulling herself into a sitting position, she glances down at her arms, which dangle uselessly by her side. Baring what loose, rotten teeth she has left she relocates first her right shoulder, then her left, never making a sound, before passing out.

Chapter 55

The House By The Sea – Natalie

The creak of the rocking chair on the porch decking reminds me of old bones. I do not dwell on whether I will make old bones. *Why should I live when the others have died?* But I do not stop rocking either. The movement is comforting. This must be what it is like for Darkly when I rock her in my arms. Having finally lost the battle to stay awake, she is asleep in the Moses basket at the side of my bed. I want to keep her with me always, but she will not sleep soundly anywhere else. I am missing her warm little body already.

I desperately miss my father and Merry too, but I cannot think of the latter without being reminded of the birthmark or what happened to her. *My God, as long as I live, I will never forget what I saw. They turned her into a slab of meat.*

It dawns on me that I am in the same boat as my mother and father were all those years ago. If I leave here, or if I talk, someone will get hurt. The thought of the villagers taking Darkly from me fills me with dread. I want more than anything to flee this vile, unspeakable place but she keeps me here. If I betray them, as my father did, I will be killed, as he was. If I do nothing, I am safe. I can stay. But I do not know what conditions will be attached to my safety, nor what plans they have for my mother. No doubt I will find out.

I am not blind to the fact that I started off with the rocking chair turned the other way, facing the direction of the cliff edge, but that it has somehow turned full circle; because I am now staring at the whitewashed building where my mother is kept. But I am not ready to face her yet.

Instead, I think about the way Jed and I parted earlier today. Although we kissed at the last moment, as if to pretend our argument was forgotten, it was a kiss that lacked passion or conviction. Having said our goodbyes, I watched him set off dejectedly along the coastal path, carrying a holdall packed with some of my father's clothes, wondering why I didn't feel sorrow at his going. I still do not understand why I should feel so differently towards him. It's not as if he is to blame for my father's death and God knows, Jed has suffered too.

I suspect my indifference is down to the words he voiced about my mother. I do not share his belief that a mental institution is the right place for her, but as for his assumption that I still believe her capable of leading a normal life—he has no idea how wrong he is.

***

I must have drifted off to sleep in the rocking chair, because when my eyes flicker open, I become aware of two things at once—it is much darker than it was and something is wrong. When I hear the crackly sound of Nina Simone's *I Put A Spell On You* coming from inside the house, I know I am right.

Warily, I get to my feet, and approach the house. Because I am barefoot, I tread lightly, without making so much as a creaking noise on the porch decking, but the mesh door gives me away with an unearthly screech. Once inside, I glance around, but nothing appears amiss. The house is exactly as I left it. Except for the music.

Following the haunting vocals of Nina Simone, I listen to the words of my mother's favourite song as if I am hearing them for the first time, turning them over in my mind as if they are the key to everything that has happened. Peering into the darkened living room, I see the record turning around on the player, and a cold chill runs down my spine.

'Mother?' I squeak, having momentarily lost my voice.

Terrified, in case she should jump out at me, to attack me the same way she did Merry, my eyes dart this way and that, but a quick sweep of the room convinces me she is not hiding in here, so I take a few cautious steps inside. That she was here earlier, I am in no doubt. The record is proof of that. Nobody but my mother would have chosen that song. Marching over to the record player, I rip away its arm, causing the needle to scratch on vinyl. As soon as the music ends, an uneasy silence takes its place. Sighing, because I do not think I could have listened to those words a second longer, it hits me that my fear is as much of a pretender as I am, because the truth is I am no longer afraid of my mother.

Rather than feel relief, this revelation puts me even more on edge. *Why am I not afraid? I know my mother to be a killer, so what does that make me if I am not afraid? Mad—that's what some people would say.*

But that thing is not my mother, I remind myself bitterly, and now I know who, and what, she has become, I can separate myself from her; knowing my real mother died the night they took her from us, or as good as. What is left is a relic, a shadow of the past that wants putting out of its misery, like a wounded animal. Instantly, I am reminded of a baby rabbit I once saw captured by a large rook. The rabbit was unable to escape because the rook had it pinned down with its huge talon. I begged my father to save the rabbit, but he said it was "too far gone", and ordered me not to interfere. I did not disobey, but I stayed and watched the rabbit die an agonising death, to make sure its suffering did eventually end.

Sensing a shadowy figure is lurking menacingly behind me, I experience the same feeling of dread and fascination I felt watching the poor rabbit being eaten alive. Spinning around, I expect to see my mother tearing towards me in a hate filled rage, but there is no one there. Nothing except perhaps for a waft of stale urine and body odour. Creeping into the hallway, I see that the front door is ajar. Moving quickly, I slam it shut and lock it, unable to keep at bay the flashing images of my father exiting it the night he was butchered. *Did that only happen three nights ago?* Sometimes, it feels as if he has been gone forever, other times I forget he is no longer with us. Whatever other grisly thoughts are about to pop into my head, they are forgotten about the moment I hear the baby crying.

'Darkly!' I exclaim in alarm, frightened that my mother may have done something to hurt her. Blaming myself for forgetting about her until now, I run towards the stairs.

***

Rocking the crying baby in my arms, I am aware that I am holding her more tightly than I should so I relax my hold and concentrate on the beautiful blue eyes staring up at me. I am relieved to find she is unharmed but I am still frightened for her. I cannot be certain that my mother knows she is here but her crying is a dead giveaway. Downstairs, I convinced myself that I am no longer afraid of my mother but I *am* afraid of what she might do to Darkly.

'Shush, little one. It's okay. I'm here...' I cajole, in what is meant to be a reassuring tone, but my heart is pounding against my chest and my hands shake uncontrollably. 'I am not going to let anyone hurt you.'

Jiggling her up and down, as she likes me to, I walk over to the window and tug the curtains together, leaving a small gap for me to peer out of. My old childhood bedroom is in darkness. If my mother *is* watching the house, she won't be able to see me standing here.

The night is as it should be; hot, humid, and alive with wildlife. The distant bark of a dog fox is soon followed by the call of a bird of prey. The swoop of a bat circles the house and if I squint my eyes and look closely enough, I can just about make out the tip of a rat's tail scurrying through the long grass. These are the things I grew up observing. Without my father's knowledge, many of these outdoor creatures, the injured ones that is, found their way inside. I used to hide them under my bed and would let them go when they got better. *If they got better.* Snow White, I wasn't, because I was a tortured child, especially after my mother died, hence the cutting, but I did the best I could, given the circumstances.

What isn't natural, what doesn't belong here—is the woman I can see moving furtively towards the whitewashed building. There is something awful about the jerking, snapping movements her bones make; as if she has suffered breaks and fractures that have never healed. As if she knows she is being watched, she turns to look back at the house and I feel my blood run cold. The creature, that I no longer think of as my mother, is wearing the red silk dress which I've long admired but never had the confidence to wear. Yet, even as I acknowledge this fact, I recall the feel of its cool silk fabric against my skin accompanied by a glow of candlelight on my face. Try as I might, I cannot remember anything else about the dress, except that it used to hang in my mother's wardrobe and was a favourite of hers. What I do know is that tonight isn't the first time she has been inside the house. During the last day or two, or even before that if I am honest, I've noticed that things have gone missing. Stupidly, I never thought anything of it at the time, except perhaps that I was mistaken. It wouldn't be the first time.

Knowing she can come and go as she pleases, that tonight isn't a one-off, makes her even more dangerous than I thought. It also means she must already be aware that Darkly is living with me. Glancing down at the baby, whose sobs have died away, I feel an overpowering urge to protect her. *Thank God, she hasn't harmed her*, is all I can think. *Yet*.

When my eyes swing back to the whitewashed building, I see that the woman who used to be my mother is still there. Although she cannot possibly see me, I sense that her hate-filled eyes are all over my face and that her hands, dangling awkwardly by her sides, would claw me to death if they could—like the rook did the rabbit.

'Too far gone,' is what she is, I decide unforgivingly.

***

Even with the gun lying next to me on the bed and two chairs stacked against the door, I cannot sleep. I have been tossing and turning for hours, endlessly checking on Darkly, who is as restless as I am. Often, when I get up to look at her, I find her eyes are open too. Although her gaze follows me around the room, she does not make a sound, preferring to nibble on a plump toe instead. When I talk to her and tell her that she needn't be afraid, that I am here to protect her, she frowns at me, as if to imply she doesn't need looking after. This reminds me so much of Merry that I want to cry.

The window is wide open and a breeze, too warm to bring any comfort, trickles in. I would like to blame our unrest on the oppressive heat but it is fear of my mother returning that keeps me awake. Every noise I hear has me sitting bolt upright, on edge until I can identify where it came from—the creaking of a floorboard reacting to the heat, a woody stem of rosemary tapping on a downstairs window. Each time the crickets outside pause in their chirruping, I hold my breath too, in case they know something I don't.

I look at the clock for the umpteenth time. It is almost 3am. Deep down, I know that it is not just fear of what my mother might do to Darkly that is keeping me awake. Soon I will have to make the dreaded trip into the village, to find out how I am to be received. Only then will I know what lies in store for me. Truthfully, I am surprised I have been left alone this long. Every day I expect a visit, but so far, no one has ventured out here. Before Jed left, he told me I should be thankful for this, because it means they are keeping their end of the bargain they made with my father, but I do not trust them. *Thankful indeed.*

Chapter 56

I must have fallen asleep after all, because a noise different to any I heard earlier rouses me. I am slow to react but when my eyes eventually flicker open, they are immediately drawn to the figure sitting on the edge of my bed. I want to scream. I want to move. But I do neither. Frozen with fear, my eyes swing down to the Moses basket where I can see Darkly. *Thank God she is okay.* Like mine, her eyes are following the hypnotic movement of the silver-plated hairbrush that is being pulled through my mother's matted balding hair.

Wearing the same red dress as before, she has her back turned on me, exposing bruising and scarring worse than my own. As if she were still a beauty, she stares at her toothless reflection in the matching hand mirror and grins manically. She must already have been into her old room to reclaim the set from the dressing table where it is kept. Although she seems oblivious to my presence, I sense that the slightest movement from me could send her into one of her wild rages. I have first-hand experience of how fast she can move when that happens. But when Darkly holds up a chubby hand, as if demanding to hold the brush, I know I must distract her. Mother is close enough to hurt Darkly and I cannot let that happen.

'What are you doing in here, Mother?' I whisper.

Our matching eyes meet in the mirror, but fear of losing myself in those black empty cavities means mine are the first to drop away. When I hear the creaking of bones, I know that she is on her feet. When I smell her stinking breath on my face, I know that she is standing over me. When her long greasy hair dangles down to touch my face, I whimper like a child and draw my knees right up to my chin, as if that will protect me.

'My things. Mine!' she screams, slamming the brush down on my head.

***

There is a dull throbbing in my head as I come to, and a distant memory that won't form properly. Somebody was here, I remember with a start, sitting up too quickly. The room is in darkness and I can't see anything, at least not yet. I listen out for the slightest noise, convinced something is wrong, but soon relax against my pillow again, certain I have woken from a bad dream, nothing more.

Bits of that dream slowly come back to me. They seem real, yet I know them to be false. I couldn't possibly have fallen asleep in the rocking chair, staring in a trance-like state at the whitewashed building, could I? And it is crazy to think that I heard my mother's favourite song being played in the darkened living room that still mourns for my poor father.

I know that all is well, because Darkly is asleep in the Moses basket by the side of my bed. I can make out the huddle of her body in the darkness. There is something hard and unbending next to me, and I stiffen against it—but then I remember that I took my father's gun to bed. I feel safe, knowing it is still there. Feeling dehydrated, I decide to go down for a glass of water.

Switching on the nightlight next to my bed, I gasp in disbelief when I see that the two chairs stacked against the bedroom door have been pushed aside. Almost simultaneously, I realise that Darkly is missing from the Moses basket; that somebody has mimicked the shape of her small body using a bunched-up blanket.

In my desperation to find her, I swing my legs too quickly out of the bed and collapse in a useless heap on the floor, hit by a sudden wave of nausea that immobilises me. The room around me sways, as if I am on a boat, and then blurs. Everything, including my own delayed reactions, seems to occur in slow motion. When my hand comes away from my sticky scalp, I gasp in horror when I see congealed blood on my fingers.

***

I am not surprised to see a circle of candles and oil lamps lighting up the ground near the whitewashed building. I have sensed that the creature, the mad woman from the cellar, my mother, *I have so many names for her,* has been leading up to something like this for days. When the sickly smell of burning wax reaches my nostrils and the fumes from the lamps start to make my eyes smart, I lift my father's rifle closer to my chest. Truthfully, I am not sure how to hold it, let alone use it, but when the baby's indignant cries rise out of the smoke, I manage to cock it all by myself.

I do not see Darkly yet. She is hidden behind the wall of flames, but hearing her outraged cries fills me with hope. She cannot be hurt to cry like that. But I do see a pair of demonic red eyes lurking in the circle and it dawns on me then that Mother is expecting me. I suspect she has been waiting for this moment ever since I came back to Little Downey.

A few steps more and I can see the baby. She lies naked on the ground, her fat little legs kicking out angrily at the open air. I hold my breath. She is okay. But I dare not go to her. Not yet. Right then, she turns her head in my direction and I watch her brow furrow in confusion. As soon as she recognises me, she starts crying again, louder this time. I try to shush her, but this only makes her worse. Like her mother, she is not one to be put aside.

'Oh my God, Darkly,' I whisper tearfully, my eyes darting this way and that, travelling at speed in a circular motion, covering what ground they can, until they come to rest on the ravaged creature who finally steps out of the shadows to confront me.

I cannot take my eyes off the knife in her hand. It is from my father's collection, taken from the butcher's block in the whitewashed building. I now know there was always a good reason for my being afraid of that building and those tools.

Whenever she takes a slow deliberate step towards Darkly, I match her, step-by-step, until we are no more than a dozen feet apart, but she still remains closer to the baby than I am, giving her the upper hand. Her bloodshot eyes light up with something like triumph when she sees my fingers nervously hover over the trigger of the gun.

'Is that really you, Natalie?'

Her voice is as I remember—fun and carefree, musical even. It does not suit the deranged person standing before me.

'I won't let you hurt her, Mother,' I say in a voice far stronger than I feel.

At that, she laughs, a demonic crazy sound, yet I can still see traces of my mother on her ravaged face. Something in the eyes, the toss of her head, which remind me of the old photographs I kept of her—the ones I have treasured for most of my lifetime.

'Mother, please put down the knife,' I plead, risking a quick glance in the baby's direction.

'I gave up my life for you,' Mother rages, making a slicing motion with the knife. A gesture that stops my heart and leaves my mouth dry.

'I know. I'm sorry,' I say, holding up a hand as if that will stop her—as if anything could.

I can't help it. Up close, no matter what she has become, she is still my mother. Because I can no longer deny her existence, hot tears spill down my cheeks. I am a snotty-nosed child again, desperate for her love and approval. This response gets a better reaction. Lowering the knife, she takes a step closer, as if she would comfort me.

'She's nothing to us, Natalie. Nothing.' She gestures to the baby with a flick of the knife.

'She's my sister.'

'Half-sister. Gypsy blood at that,' Mother sneers, resuming her guarding expression over Darkly.

'You used to like the gypsy way of life.' I stall for time, anything to take her mind off the baby. 'Don't you remember how you used to romanticise their nomadic lifestyle?'

It works. She forgets the baby and focuses her attention on me, her face taking on a childlike expression as she tries to work out if what I have told her is true. I am not lying, but I still feel as if I am betraying her. This makes it difficult for me to meet the intensity of her stare and when her eyes flicker with something like sanity, I feel myself weaken. Sensing this, she holds out her arms, as if she would wrap me in them.

'You were such a beautiful baby,' she croons, pulling a sad face. 'It killed me giving you up. Did you ever think of me?'

I think my heart is close to breaking and I wonder what sort of daughter I am, to be stood here pointing a gun at my sick mother.

'Every second. Every day,' I admit, lowering the gun. The temptation to lie it down on the ground and step into my mother's outstretched arms is overwhelming.

'Don't be afraid, child,' she says, the knife disappearing behind her back. 'I would never hurt you.'

I want to believe her. Of course, I do. But when I glance down at the dried blood on my hand, which matches the spattered blood on her chest and arms, I am reminded of how dangerous she is. *This is not my mother*, I tell myself angrily. *This is an imposter.*

I feel my face turn to concrete as I cock the gun once more and jut out my chin in a defiant Powers kind of way. Sensing the change in me, her eyes narrow, and a ferocious anger that was not there before burns in her eyes.

'I would die for you, Natalie,' she says, keeping up the pretence, but this time I am not fooled. Just in time, I see the flash of gleaming metal as she raises the blade above her head and lunges at me.

'Prove it!' I yell.

The gun goes off and a look of utter disbelief appears on her face as she falls to the ground, clawing at the blood spurting out of her stomach. It is over surprisingly quickly. Just a few drawn-out breaths, a trail of black blood spilling from her mouth, it opening and closing as if she wants to say something. Then, nothing. I find it strange that she should look more human in death than she did when she was alive.

Dropping the gun as if it were as diseased and rotten as my mother, I stumble without its reassuring weight. Looking up at the night sky, I howl like a baby, before falling to my knees on the ground. Pulling my mother's stinking body into my lap, I sob unrestrainedly and rock her in my arms, as she once did me. *She's gone,* I tell myself. *It's over.* But I have no idea who pulled the trigger. It couldn't have been me, could it? I am just a child who loves and misses her mother. I am not a killer. It couldn't have been me.

It couldn't have been me.

***

Drip. Splat. Drip.

The sky is grey and cloudy. The air eerily still. Rain bounces off the porch roof and disappears into the overgrown garden, either dissolving into patches of sand or settling on blades of grass that twinkle like a field of lost diamonds. Unlike most people, I have never liked the smell of rain. Its fresh earthy fragrance evokes memories of days spent alone in my bedroom at Thornhaugh, staring out of the long grey window and dreaming of home.

At some point during the early hours of this morning, I collapsed into the rocking chair on the porch with the baby in my arms. I haven't stirred from it since. The sun came up an hour ago, arriving with the rain. My bare arms and legs are numb with cold and my skin is crawling with goosebumps. The heat from Darkly's body is the only thing keeping me warm. Her little fist is wrapped in my tangled hair, and the thumb in her other hand is wedged tightly in her mouth. Although asleep, she continues to suck on it.

My nightdress is stained with mine and my mother's blood but the smell lingering on my body is all her own—a terrible mix of death, stale urine and rotting flesh. In the future, whenever I think of her, I will always associate this smell with her. Gone forever is the memory of the delicate floral perfume she used to wear.

I glare at the whitewashed building as if it were a living breathing enemy. Although I feel nothing, *absolutely nothing—as if I am dead inside*, my fingers claw at the skin on the top of my thigh, creating an angry web of fine red lines. The desire to feel something, if only more pain, has never been stronger. I hear my mother's favourite song playing again, but this time I do not turn around in my chair to find out where the sound is coming from. This time, I suspect the voice, so different to Nina Simone's, is my own, humming the words that I know off by heart.

When the pickup truck hurtles down the track, slipping on wet sand, the rain stops, and the sun comes out. I find myself grinning at the absurdity of that, and keep on grinning, even when Bob Black and Daniel get out of the vehicle and walk towards me. I do not wonder at the look of confusion on their faces. Nothing surprises me anymore.

Chapter 57

Thornhaugh

Sunlight bursts through a pair of stained-glass windows to light up an unfamiliar octagonal-shaped room. On the floor, there is a grape-coloured rug, fraying at the corners, and old-fashioned oak furniture, so tall it almost touches the ceiling, shines with beeswax. A crystal vase heaves with stems of stocks and delphiniums and the curtains, featuring an elegant peacock print, graze the floor. They match the bedcover I am tucked up in. Outside, I can hear the hum of a ride-on lawnmower and the smell of cut grass together with the scent of the flowers, makes me feel I never want to leave this new world I find myself in.

I change my mind when I hear the purposeful march of footsteps approaching my door, followed by the sound of a key being turned in the lock. *Who's there?* I want to shout, but fear prevents me. *Why am I locked in? Where am I?* I shrink down in the bed, wanting to disappear in the folds of the bedspread, and I flinch when the door is thrown open.

Her face is almost as orange as the sun and she is just as energetic. My heart sinks when I see the flash of badge and thick white shoes. She might not be dressed in standard NHS uniform, but I know a psychiatric nurse when I see one.

'Not feeling hungry, Natalie?' she enquires, exposing brilliant white teeth and pointing to a tray by the side of my bed.

I shake my head and allow her to take my temperature. I am as placid as a doll as she bends me first one way then the other, inspecting my arms for the telltale signs of self-harming. She also gazes into my eyes and peers down my throat, looking for other, more obvious signs of ill health.

'You still look peaky.' She tuts, as if this is a direct reflection of her nursing skills. Then, sitting down on the edge of my bed, she shakes her head at me as if trying to work me out. 'Haunted. That's the word I'm looking for,' she adds, sounding pleased with her diagnosis.

She moves faster than anybody I've ever met before. Like a dervish. One minute she's there, on the end of the bed, the next she's gone and retrieved the tray and put it in front of me, is back on the bed in no time at all. Her liveliness has the opposite effect on me. It makes me feel giddy.

'You must eat,' she prompts kindly.

The realisation that I am back in an institution fills me with a growing sense of desperation, but I resist the urge to throw the tray of food on the floor.

'You'll need to keep your strength up, for your visitors' sake if nothing else,' she admonishes, removing the lid from the covered plate of food on my lap.

I am about to ask her, *what visitors?* when she walks abruptly out of the room. As I listen to the echo of her heels clip-clopping away, as fast as any horse, I gaze down at the plate of overcooked sausages, lumpy mashed potatoes and peas, and fight back the urge to vomit.

'There you are, Natalie.'

I glance up to see Dr Moses, *everyone's favourite father figure*, standing there with a big smile on his face. Pulling up a chair, as if we are still the best of friends, he sits down next to me and nods at the plate of unappetising food as if it is worthy of a Michelin star.

'Looks good. Aren't you going to eat it?'

'I guess,' I say, unable to maintain eye contact with him, in case I should give away my real feelings.

Picking up a plastic knife and fork, I chase the peas around on my plate, giving up too easily when I prove incapable of stabbing any one of them. Instead, I slice a burnt end off one of the sausages and pop it in my mouth.

'Good girl.' He sounds more impressed than he should be.

I want to tell him, *It's nothing to get excited about*, but think better of it. There are so many things I need to ask him, like *Where am I?* This is not the Thornhaugh I know. Here, in this room, which is different to any I have come across in this building, I am treated with kindness and respect; as if I were an adult. *Have they given my old room to someone else?* If so, I am not sure how I feel, given that it has been mine for so long. *Is Dr Moses involved with all that went on in Little Downey?* That is another question I would like to throw at him. But I dare not. At least, not yet. One thing I do know, is that I do not like the way he is looking at me. I also recognise that this is something new as I don't recall ever feeling this way before. The trouble is, I don't know who I can trust anymore. If a girl can't trust her own mother, then who?

'How does it feel, knowing you are going home tomorrow?'

I do not have to act surprised by this news, because I truly am. 'I am?' I can think of nothing else to say.

'Now, Natalie,' he warns, with a slight shake of his head. 'We've talked about this.'

I put down the knife and fork and grab hold of the bedspread again, wringing it in my hands. I bite back the first words that spring to mind, *Have we?* But I keep shtum. My whole life has been about staying quiet and keeping things to myself.

'I don't know if I am ready. What if I start—?'

He is looking at me expectantly, willing me to go on, *move on*. All my life, he has wanted me to move on, whereas I have wanted to stay in the same place; never wanting to leave my childhood behind, because that is where my mother is.

'What if I start doing it again?' I ask at last.

'You won't. You've completely recovered from your relapse.' Here, he coughs, and his eyes hit the floor. 'I'm giving you a clean bill of health. You've even got your appetite back.' He points to the plate of cold congealing food that I couldn't be less interested in.

Yet, when I open my mouth to reply, I am surprised to find it full of sausage and potato, which I am forced to chew several times over before I can get a word out.

'I still remember things. Bad things,' I admit between mouthfuls.

I watch his grey eyes flicker with concern and I wonder again if I can trust him. He has always been good to me; better than I deserved. Always there when I needed him. Except, of course, when he wasn't...

I would die for you, Natalie.

You'd better start listening to Frank's Law around here.

You're a mental case. You don't know what you want.

'Subconscious suggestion, that's all it is,' he advises with a tight smile, as if it pains him to hear me voice any doubt.

'But they feel more real than anything else,' I whisper.

'These bogus memories will fade,' he states authoritatively, clapping his knee for extra emphasis. But then his face takes on a mysterious expression and he lowers his voice to a conspiring whisper. 'Hopefully to one day be replaced with happier ones.'

Never taking his eyes off my face, as if keen to record my responses, he gestures to the door, and I do not have to wait long to find out what is going on, because at that precise moment, Daniel's grinning face appears behind it. Before I can react, a small person is bearing down on me. Dr Moses laughs and gets to his feet, making way for them both.

Too much is happening at once. First, Daniel bends down to plant a wet rubbery kiss on my cheek. The smell of him is familiar, although not exactly pleasant. Next, I am swamped in the fat folds of a toddler, who is holding out her arms and demanding to be picked up.

'Mama. Mama.'

Darkly's happy squeals are initially met with laughter and smiles from Daniel and Dr Moses, but when I do not respond to her quickly enough, her bottom lip trembles, and I sense an air of mistrust coming from the two men. Acting instinctively, I scoop

Darkly into my arms and give her a squeeze. 'Hello, baby,' I say, moved to tears. 'Have you missed me?'

This time, my response seems to meet everyone's satisfaction, including my own. As Daniel and Dr Moses share well-meaning glances that somehow exclude me and the child, I find myself staring into the beautiful blue eyes of the baby I once knew. I cannot be sure how long it has been since we were last together, but we re-connect almost instantly. *My God,* I think in utter amazement, *can this chatty energetic little toddler be Darkly?*

'I'll leave you alone with your family now, Natalie. But I'll see you tomorrow before you leave,' Dr Moses instructs.

I want to ask him to stay, tell him that I do not feel safe being left alone with Daniel, but before I can get any words out, Daniel reaches across the bed to possessively close his fingers around my hand. His skin is sweaty and cold at the same time, I notice with irritation, and Dr Moses can't seem to stop nodding and smiling. I want to tell him to stop. That this is not like him at all. Instead, I watch him nod his way out of the room, turning one last time to throw us both an "un-doctor-like" wink before shutting the door.

When Daniel turns to look at me properly for the first time, I mirror his fixed smile, wondering if it hurts his face as much as it is does mine. I don't know how long I can keep this fake expression up, but until I know more, I do not want to expose myself.

'I can't take it in that you're coming home.' He sighs. 'Everyone's so excited. Are you looking forward to it?' He shakes my hand as if his enthusiasm might pass to me, but I hedge my bets.

'Yes and no,' I admit cautiously.

'What's the no part for?'

'Just nervous, I guess.'

Although he looks pained, I am relieved to find that he is exhibiting patience, not anger. This gives me the courage I need to go on.

'Tell me again. Daniel. How long have we been married?'

His laughter, noisy and authentic, not only takes me by surprise but it moves me. Somebody who can laugh like that cannot possibly be a bad person. I sense that there is something inherently good about him, that I have always known this.

'You love hearing about yourself, don't you?' Still chuckling, he presses the end of my nose as if it were a button on a fruit machine and I am not sure if I like this much close contact. It feels too soon. Sensing this, he backs off a little and sighs.

'Three years and nine months. You wore a beautiful white dress, all lace. Your father gave you away. How many more times?'

The way he tells it, as if it were something he'd repeated a dozen times, also feels real.

'And Father? When did he die?' I persevere.

'Must be three years ago now.' Daniel's shoulders sink with the weight of his words and I sense that the memory is painful to him. 'Just after we had Darkly. That's when I took over the business.'

'Business?'

'The butcher's shop.' He looks at me as if he cannot believe I have forgotten such an important part of our history. 'Your father wanted to keep it in the family.'

'Yes of course,' I interrupt quickly. 'Darkly? It's an unusual name, isn't it?'

'That's what we tried telling you at the time. But you wouldn't listen.'

'And we love each other very much?' I want to believe him more than anything else. Of course, I do. But—

'There's not a happier couple in Little Downey,' he says, with a wink.

Chapter 58

It is such a glorious day that even Dr Moses has removed his jacket and loosened his tie. The scent of Thornhaugh roses trickles in through an open window, reminding me of summer afternoons spent playing on the lawn. Not all memories of my time here are bad, I realise sentimentally, feeling suddenly terrified at the thought of leaving.

Dr Moses' office is usually stuffy and masculine but today it is sunny and airy, mainly because the claustrophobic clumps of ivy that normally darkens its walls have been trimmed back. Even the folder with my name printed on it looks shiny and new, as if it came off the typewriter this very morning. Dr Moses sees me looking at it and with a deliberately playful gesture, he stamps the front of the folder with big bold letters—CASE CLOSED. Then, as if he'd drawn a magical rabbit out of a hat, he pushes it across the desk towards me, looking extremely pleased with himself.

'There. See. It's official.'

I cannot think of anything to say straightaway and this earns me a strange blank look. Although my fingers itch to touch the folder, *so I can devour every one of their lies*, I resist.

'Dr Moses, how can I be married and have a child?'

'Natalie. We have talked about this at great length,' Dr Moses complains, sounding deflated.

'But I have no memory of the last few years.'

'Do you remember telling me that you once felt like a ghost, flitting in and out of people's lives, barely there at any one time?'

I nod to acknowledge that I do remember.

'That's exactly what you were for a time, a ghost, but now you're back and for that we're extremely grateful.'

'All that time I was gone?'

'It's true your psychotic imaginings did sometimes get out of hand.' He is gentle with me. 'But there were periods when you were stable enough to go home and live a normal life with Daniel and your family, with his mother's help of course.'

'But at times I wasn't? Is that what you're saying?'

He nods as if it pains him to admit this. 'And we took care of you here, as we've always done.'

How can I be married to someone I only have a vague recollection of? And that I despised him. Surely, I am too young to be someone's mother. None of this makes sense. The memories I have might be blurred and unreliable but what Dr Moses is suggesting feels utterly unreal. My mind hurts from everything I am being told. I have so many questions and too few answers. But I am terrified of saying the wrong thing or challenging this man, who holds such power over me. At Thornhaugh I could be made to disappear forever.

Fighting back tears of frustration, my eyes come to rest on the folder that probably contains all the answers I long for. I am tempted to snatch it off the desk, but it dawns on me that Dr Moses is playing a game. There is no way he is going to let me look inside it.

'It has my maiden name on it,' I point out sullenly.

The folder is back in Dr Moses hands' in no time at all. The frown on his face causes my own to vanish, because I suddenly realise that none of this matters. *Am I not getting out of here today? In which case, I should play the game too. Like they are.*

'I've just remembered.' I laugh self-consciously, as shy as any new bride. 'I don't know what my married surname is. What am I? Mrs… what?'

He spends too long looking at the folder. *Why doesn't he answer?*

'You always do that.' I snort.

'What?'

When he glances up at me, I notice that his eyes are full of confusion. *Aren't I meant to be the one suffering from memory loss?*

'You look at your notes when you don't know what to say.'

My sharp tone snaps him out of his reverie. The folder is back in a drawer before I can think about complaining and he is on his feet, keen to get me out of the door.

'I don't recall your married name for the moment, that's all,' he is curt. 'But I do know your husband is out in reception, waiting to take you home.'

***

A crowd of nurses has gathered in the reception hall to see me off. They are lined up by the grand oak staircase, a giant chandelier picking out strands of grey in their neatly pinned buns. As I make my way through them, shaking hands and trying not to recoil at their unfamiliar smiling faces, I feel out of place in my summer dress, which shows off bare arms and legs. The blue is not a colour I would have chosen myself as it reminds me of Little Downey eyes. Earlier this morning, one of the younger nurses teased curls into my hair and lent me her lip-gloss. At first, I liked what I saw in the mirror, but when Daniel told me I looked sexy, I quickly wiped the sticky stuff off on the back of my hand.

While one of the older nurses hugs me and gives in to noisy tears, *I cannot think who she is*, I watch Dr Moses take Daniel to one side and give him a prescription package.

'She must continue with the medication, Daniel,' Dr Moses advises sternly.

But Daniel is too pleased with himself to take anything seriously. Pumping Dr Moses' hand up and down, he continues to grin like a fool.

'You don't know what it means to me having her back to normal,' Daniel says. And at that moment, both turn to stare at me.

***

We are in a black pickup truck travelling along the coast road, both trying our best to appear natural and relaxed, but I can tell

Daniel is on edge as much as I am. This is what those fixed grins were invented for, I can't help thinking, as I shoot him another fake smile. He is driving faster than I would like but I do not say anything because now that we are away from Thornhaugh, I am more obliged to him than ever. Besides, I don't want to upset him when he is trying so hard. That doesn't stop me wishing he wouldn't insist on holding my hand until it aches, as if he thinks this is what is needed to keep my feet on the ground, because the nearer we get to the cliff edge and the house by the sea, the faster my memories fall on the road in front of us.

I am choking on smoke. Flames appear over the truck's bonnet. I can hear the pitiful cries of a dog and a man screaming to be let out. Fear suffocates me. Then I am running, and falling, and running again, towards my father's house, where a welcoming light seeps out of a downstairs room.

Dr Moses calls these sudden flashbacks "bogus" and promises they will soon fade, to be replaced with happier memories, but they feel real to me. Glancing sneakily at Daniel's profile, I wonder what happy memories I can expect to unearth about him and feel myself blushing. I have no recollection of Daniel and I being together as man and wife.

Neither of us glance to our right when the beach and the relic of the burnt-out gypsy camp comes into view, although I can tell, by our stiff body language, that we are both aware of it. That it means something to each of us.

When we turn off the main road and hit the dirt track, my heart pounds. The house by the sea is up ahead.

As we crawl past the whitewashed building, I realise with a stomach-churning jolt that it has been restored and I don't know whether to feel relieved that the menace of it has finally been obliterated or horrified, for my father's sake. Not only has it been given a fresh coat of paint but the barred windows have been pulled out, like rotten teeth, and replaced with shiny glass windows. Pressing my nose up against the passenger window, I strain my neck to watch it fall away in the distance, ignoring the pressure of Daniel's fingers that seem to want to take my attention away from it.

He is nodding encouragingly at me, and smiling, but I can tell by the way the corners of his eyes crease, that this is not the main surprise of the day. That something even bigger is waiting for us. As we pull up in front of my father's house, I feel my heart sink.

The house by the sea has been painted a white so brilliant, I am at once reminded of the bleached teeth of the smiling nurses at Thornhaugh. Even the broken picket fence has been repaired and stands straight backed and erect, like a child in trouble. A new swing hangs invitingly in the neatly manicured cottage garden and white lace curtains flutter at every window. Not to be outdone, the wooden porch is decorated in bunting and a long picnic table covered in a checked tablecloth heaves with party food. *This is not my home. I do not know this place,* I think, feeling bereft.

When Daniel gestures to the rear of the house, where I can see the cliff edge looming, I spot the "Welcome home" banner for the first time.

***

Almost falling out of the car in shock, I resist the urge to run away. My drained face must give me away though, because Daniel looks as guilty as anything. He must be kicking himself for agreeing to go along with this, and I feel for him, really, I do, but neither of us can do anything about it now.

As we watch people get up from their chairs as if they might wander over and hug us, I am unable to stop myself from backing away. My eyes fill with uncertain tears when I see Bob Black among the crowd, cheerily bouncing Darkly up and down on his lap. This stings in a way I didn't expect it to. I was not permitted to spend time alone with Darkly at Thornhaugh, in case I inadvertently said something that would upset her, yet somebody, Daniel presumably, had deemed Bob Black a suitable guardian. Unable to fight off a rising anger, I turn my attention to the tall ginger-haired youth, who is turning meat on a barbecue. Once again, I am reminded of the orderly at Thornhaugh.

Everybody else is a stranger. Only the obese woman careering unsteadily towards me with a handkerchief pressed to her eye, obviously intent on hugging me to death, seems to know what to do. When Daniel's hand takes control of mine, I lean gratefully against him. Only with his help and support will I get through this day.

Chapter 59

The House By The Sea

B athed in warm sunshine, this room is barely recognisable as my parents' old bedroom. The walls have been painted the same colour as honey, and fresh floral curtains hang at the window. At the bottom of the king size bed, *I wonder which side is mine*, there is a pretty chaise longue that matches the curtains. The creaking floorboards have gone; replaced with a soft carpet that my feet sink into, like wet sand. Daniel tells me that we waited a whole year after my father died before moving in here, but it still feels wrong. My parents' presence is all around me. If I listen hard enough, I imagine I can hear their raised voices arguing through the walls. Worse than that, I sense my mother's eyes are on me. She wouldn't like me in here, touching her things.

Looking at my reflection in the dressing table mirror, I am surprised yet again by how much I resemble her. I'm told I grow more like her every day, yet I think my eyes are blacker than hers ever were. Picking up her silver-plated brush and hand mirror set, which have been polished and shine like new, I brush my hair, thinking it might be time to lay old ghosts to rest, but I am wrong.

My things. Mine.

As soon as I hear the voice—an uneasy memory stirs. Closing my eyes, I recall a vicious blow to the head and the sensation of blood dripping from my ear.

Drip. Splat. Drip.

Imagining I am alone, afraid, and in danger, my eyes flash open and I see my mother's haunted reflection staring back at me. When I drop the brush, her image disappears.

I do not have time to figure out what any of this means because at that moment the door opens, carving a deep groove in the carpet, and Daniel comes in. His cheery whistling and inability to leave me on my own for more than a few minutes grates on my nerves, but I smile anyway, because I do not want to hurt his feelings. Part of me longs to have the creaky old floorboards back so I might know where he is at any given time.

When he comes to stand behind me and runs his hands up and down my bare arms, I try not to flinch, but it is as if a stranger had assaulted me. His eagerness for contact makes me increasingly nervous and I want to shrug him off, but I keep reminding myself that he is my husband. A good one too by all accounts, judging by how patient he has been with me so far. I have no idea what is going on in his mind, but he seems preoccupied with the skin on my arms. They are only faintly scarred.

'Good as new. Smooth as silk,' Daniel mumbles, slipping the strap of my nightdress down on one shoulder, so he can put his lips to the cool white skin there.

I shudder uncontrollably but he seems oblivious to my real feelings. In fact, he goes one step further, circling the top of my thighs through the silky material. As I watch him through the mirror, I see his eyes flare with desire.

'You don't know how long I have waited for this,' he murmurs breathlessly.

When he pulls me to my feet and presses his body against mine, my legs threaten to give way. The terror of this moment has been haunting me since I first arrived home.

'Daniel, I don't think I'm ready,' I say quietly, trying to avoid his hands and mouth.

'You're my wife.' He takes hold of my hand and steers me towards the bed. 'And we've done it a thousand times before.'

***

When I pull back the bed sheets the next morning and expose the blood smears on them, my irritable mood increases. Having woken up with a thumping headache, I feel angry and confused about last night. Daniel must have realised I wasn't ready for what happened, yet he wouldn't take no for an answer. *So much for his being patient and understanding,* I think bitterly. All that went out of the window the moment we were alone.

I may not be experienced in the ways of sex but I am sure he was not as gentle as he could have been, as I am feeling sore and bruised inside. Not only was his lovemaking clumsy, he resisted all my efforts to get him to slow down. At one stage, I even cried out in pain, but he silenced my protests with his mouth. *Should it have hurt that much? Do women grow to like it, as they appear to in movies and books?* The thought of my own parents *doing that* fills me with disgust.

When Daniel comes out of the adjoining en-suite bathroom, which is a new addition to the house, and sees me pointedly looking at the blood, he has the grace to look ashamed.

'It's been a long time. I expect that's why.' He shrugs apologetically, allowing the towel wrapped around his lower half to drop to the floor, where he casually abandons it.

Chapter 60

The sun is already fierce in the sky, causing me to squint, but despite the heat which everyone predicts will reach thirty degrees by the end of today, I have covered up well, to avoid any possibility of burning. With my fair complexion I cannot be too careful. In the last few days I have already witnessed the return of freckles on my nose and cheeks, which I haven't seen since I was a girl. Glancing down at Darkly's olive skin and suntanned hands, I wonder at how different we are.

As always, she holds my hand as if she will never let it go. *Lord help anyone who tries to pry her off me,* I think with a smile. Her hair is matted as usual. No matter how I try to tame it, it bounces right back again, turning her into a feral looking little thing. On that thought, I am reminded of another wild-looking creature, and for some reason my mind wanders over to the whitewashed building. But the memory vanishes quickly, leaving me with nothing to go on, so I turn my attention back to my family.

We have come out to see Daniel off. Every day he insists on this ritual as if it is important, but Darkly and I would much rather be off somewhere by ourselves, making our own memories. If I didn't know better, I would say that Daniel feels excluded by our close mother-daughter relationship and wants us to bond more as a family. Yet the Daniel I have come to know of late is not that sensitive to what other people think and feel.

Patting his trouser pockets, as if making sure he has everything he needs, he hurries over to kiss me sloppily on the forehead. I can tell that his mind is already preoccupied with work. In many ways, he and my father are alike, I realise belatedly.

'Ring me if you need me,' he tells me distractedly.

'Daniel?' I say quickly, before I can change my mind.

'What?'

Although I have his attention, I can tell he wants to get on. Deep down, I suspect his patience with me wore out some time ago, although he does a good job of hiding it.

'What exactly do I do all I day?' I ask. 'I mean, what did I do before?'

He pulls a face, as if unsure how to answer. 'I don't know. Wash. Iron. Cook. Women's stuff, I guess.'

'Women's stuff.' I am scathing, unable to hide my annoyance. He is in too much of a hurry to hold this against me, so he shrugs.

'Don't forget Mam will be popping by later,' he reminds me, pressing a finger to my nose. I am sure he knows this habit of his irritates me, yet he refuses to give it up. I rather suspect he finds my response to it amusing.

'Why?' I fold my arms.

I have met his mother enough times to know that we will never be friends. But I have also learned that Daniel will not tolerate any criticism of her.

'To check up on you two,' he jokes but we both know he is being deadly serious.

Fuming, I watch him get in the truck and drive off. As soon as it is out of sight, I glance down at Darkly, whose bright blue eyes are waiting for mine.

'We don't need checking up on, do we?' I smile mischievously.

***

I mourn this room like no other. Every bit of my mother has been stripped from its walls. The rocking chairs have gone, as has the fireplace—newly plastered walls taking its place. The pine dresser and kitchen table have also disappeared. I have no idea what happened to my mother's willow-patterned bone china and cannot bring myself to ask. I do not know whose idea it was to rid this house of anything that might remind me of my parents or my past, but I suspect Daniel's mother's involvement. *She means well,* I am told, but when I glance around at the new contemporary-style kitchen, I feel I no longer belong. It is Daniel's home now. It has the Harper stamp on it.

Because I don't know where anything is, I have opened most of the cupboard doors in my quest to find what I am looking for. When I first come across the integral dishwasher and digital microwave I am baffled by them. I have no idea how to use such trendy appliances and I suspect I am not the only one because both are pristine and look as if they have never been touched. While I rummage through the cupboards, finding not one single thing I recognise, Darkly plays on the floor, making buzzing sounds. I have to step over her several times, until I have everything I need, including a rolling pin and a packet of meat from the fridge. It's time to face the mess I have created on the island in the middle of the room.

The slate worktop is scattered with flour and broken eggs. I know, without having to look in a mirror, that my face is also dusted with flour. If my father were alive, he would vouch for the fact that I have never been much of a cook. I find the whole process daunting, especially when looking at the recipe book photograph in front of me of a perfect meat pie with golden pastry. I don't know how I will ever be able to successfully replicate it.

I thought I liked keeping house but now I am not so sure. Maybe it's the cooking part that doesn't agree with me. My attention is easily diverted, which is why, instead of rolling out the lumpy pastry, I find myself watching Darkly instead. She has something in her hand which appears to fascinate her and I can tell by the way her shoulders are hunched over it that she doesn't want me to see it. This piques my interest even more.

'What have you got there, Darkly?'

'Busy bee, busy bee,' she chants, reluctantly holding up a bumblebee fridge magnet, which a small part of me instantly recognises. As yet, I don't understand its significance but seeing it bunched up in my daughter's hand makes me feel faint.

'Let me have that,' I demand, storming across the kitchen.

Unused to hearing me speak so sharply and sensing that she is about to have her new toy taken away, Darkly crawls under the breakfast bar and hides, wrapping her chubby little legs around the metal frame of a bar stool, in case I should try to pull her out.

'Mine! Mine!' she screams, as incensed as I am.

Her angry words stop me. This time, I know for sure that I have heard them before. In this very house.

My things. My man. Mine.

Fighting back a wave of nausea, which threatens to knock me off my feet, I want to sit down and rest, but first I must get to the bottom of this.

'I'll swap you for a biscuit,' I whisper deviously, moving towards the biscuit barrel.

Darkly eyes me with suspicion. She is not usually offered sugary treats at this time of the day, so it is natural for her to be mistrustful. Crouching alongside her, underneath the breakfast bar, the exchange gets made when she sees the proffered biscuit in my hand. While she contentedly nibbles the edges of the oatmeal snack, leaving crumbs all around her, I study the bumblebee magnet.

Now you must give me a present.

A woman's voice, young, with a soft Irish accent, echoes around the room. It shocks me to know that another exchange of a different kind took place in this kitchen, although I get the feeling it was the old kitchen, not this new monstrosity. I vaguely remember that this somebody also made me feel like a stranger in my own home. For the briefest of seconds, I see a flash of green eyes and a toss of glossy black hair.

'Natalie! Are you in there?'

As soon as I hear the voice, which is whiny and brash in comparison to the one I heard before, I panic and shoot upwards, hurting my head on the breakfast bar. Glancing quickly around, I wonder if the voice is real this time. My heart sinks when I spot the pink multiple chins of Daniel's mother squashed up against the kitchen window.

Chapter 61

Mother-in-law disapproves of me. I get that. But does she have to make it so obvious? She doesn't even pretend to smile when I come back into the room, just sits there, with a smug look on her face that immediately puts my back up. She doesn't need to tell me that I could do better. It's there on her face, for all to see.

'She's gone down at last,' I sigh, ignoring the way her stubby fingers drum impatiently on the high-gloss kitchen table. *I long to have the old pine table back, the one I carved my young initials into.* Deciding that whatever I do will never be good enough for my mother-in-law, I put on the kettle and find her a slice of cake. That usually cheers her up.

'A bit of a handful, that one, if you ask me. Wilful streak,' she whines, wiping imaginary dust off the edge of the table. 'Daniel was always such a good baby.'

'She's not even three yet,' I utter stiffly. Truthfully, I am not sure how old my daughter is, but I am not going to admit this. The last time I saw her, when I was myself, that is, she was still a baby. When I turn to glare at Daniel's mother, I realise I might as well be talking to myself because she isn't the slightest bit interested. Her whole focus is on the broken eggshells and the floury mess splattered across the island worktop.

'What on earth were you trying to make?' she asks, shaking her head.

'Steak pie.' I sigh, but then I realise I should be feeling proud, not putting myself down. 'It's Daniel's favourite,' I add boastfully. Surely, even she should be happy that I am going out of my way to please her son.

'That's what he says about mine, any road.' She huffs, obviously offended.

When our eyes next meet, neither of us bothers to hide our mutual dislike. I am starting to wonder how long we can continue in such an uncomfortable silence when she puffs out her already ample chest and gets to her feet. Dusting her hands together, as if she means business, she takes an apron out of her bag and slips it on over her floral blouse and stretched-to-the-limit polyester trousers.

'We'd better get started. Houses don't clean themselves, you know,' she bustles.

I am so taken aback, it takes me a few seconds to reply. 'I don't mean to be rude, Mrs Harper...'

'Mrs Harper! Call me Mam. You always used to.'

'Mam,' I declare uncomfortably, 'it's just that... I'd like to get back in the swing of things by myself. If you don't mind.'

As soon as my little speech is over, I glance away, in case she is nursing one of her infamous hurt expressions in the hope I will take back my words. *She is an expert in manipulating people.* I expect her to bite back, but she seems to think better of it.

'Have it your own way.' She shrugs offhandedly. 'You know best, I suppose.'

When I see her stuffing the apron back in her bag, I can hardly believe I got off so lightly. But when she walks dejectedly towards the door, where she pauses for maximum effect, I know I am right to be cynical.

'I'll be seeing you later anyway. Daniel's asked me over for supper.' Her voice is tight with emotion. 'If that's all right with you, Natalie,' she asks pitifully.

She has never needed my permission before and I am not fooled by her display of false humility now, but I go along with it anyway.

'Of course.' I grin, not meaning it.

***

Now that Mother-in-law has been sent packing, I decide to get on and finish the pie, but it isn't going exactly to plan. Keeping one ear out for Darkly, who is still sleeping, I have got as far as stretching the bottom layer of the pastry over the pie dish, but it is full of holes. I may as well give up now, I decide, because it will never live up to Daniel's mother's efforts, but I plough on regardless, hardly knowing why. When I tip the pale pink cuts of flesh into the weighing scales, I fight down a feeling of nausea that isn't new.

Whoever heard of a butcher's daughter not eating meat?
You'd better not let on to folk around here.

Convinced I am about to throw up, I claw my way to the sink and pour myself a glass of water, knocking it back quickly while it is still lukewarm. Although this seems to do the trick, *I no longer feel sick,* I still feel squeamish. Gripping hold of the edge of the sink with one hand, I use my other hand to sweep the hair out of my eyes and feel my whole body stiffen when I see a man standing outside the window.

He is about 150 feet from the house, too far away for me to see his face, but near enough for me to identify he has long scruffy hair and a beard. There is something about the arrogant yet weary way he holds himself that is familiar too, but I cannot place him. This is no casual passer-by, I observe, because he makes no attempt to move away, just continues to stare straight ahead at the house as if he knows I am here, alone.

It enters my head at this point, that, like a lot of other things happening in my life, he might be a figment of my imagination, so I close my eyes tightly and keep them closed for the count of ten, before opening them again.

When I see that he has disappeared, vanished without a trace, I suspect that that this was not the outcome I was hoping for. Strangely, his not being there unnerves me more than his being there.

Chapter 62

The sun is hidden behind partial cloud, but Darkly and I will still be protected from its rays once it comes out again, because we are enjoying the shade of a tree in the garden. For the past five minutes, I have been pushing her on the swing, smiling every time she giggles, which is often. When she stops laughing and points a chubby finger at the house, I think at first that the stranger has come back again, but it is only Daniel.

'Dada. Dada,' Darkly chirps excitedly when his pickup truck comes to a screeching stop outside the house.

When I see him scramble out of the truck and run into the house, leaving both the truck and porch door open, I know something is wrong. Lifting Darkly out of the swing, I make my way over. Hating to be carried, Darkly squirms to be free, so I put her down, but grab her hand to stop her running forward when I see black smoke pouring out of the porch door.

Hanging back, worriedly biting my lip, I wonder what can be happening inside. I don't know whether to be relieved or alarmed when Daniel reappears, wearing oven gloves, to throw what looks like my blackened pie dish onto the sun-bleached grass outside.

'Jesus Christ, Natalie!' he shouts, all the while fanning the smoke away from the house, 'You could have burned the whole place down.'

'Oh God, the pie. I forgot.'

As it dawns on me what I have done, and what the consequences might have been, I gasp and without meaning to, let go of Darkly's hand. Before I know it, she is racing ahead of me; toddling eagerly towards her father.

'Dada. Dada.'

When Daniel furiously brushes past her, intent on throwing water over the smouldering heap on the ground, she falls over and immediately begins to cry.

Feeling angry, I run to scoop her into my arms. 'Daniel,' I hiss reprovingly, wondering how he can be so heartless.

'I haven't got time for this. I'm meant to be at work!' he barks, not once looking our way.

'So why aren't you?' I demand.

'Got a call from Mam.' This time he does look at me, and I am taken aback by the animosity on his face. 'She was upset. Said you practically threw her out of the house.'

So that's what this is all about. I might have known it would be something to do with his precious mother.

'I don't need checking up on, Daniel,' I tell him, defensively folding my arms for the second time today. But I have the grace to blush when I see Daniel glaring pointedly at the black smoke oozing out of the porch door.

'She's been coming here every day for what feels like forever, to cook, clean and look after the baby. Doing your job! And that's how you repay her.'

I have never seen him this angry before. Part of me thinks I ought to back down. After all, a lot of this is my fault. But I can't help myself—

'You resent me for not being here, don't you?' I yell back. 'Why don't you admit it,' I hiss, remembering to lower my voice because I don't want Darkly going through what I did as a child; hearing her parents row all the time.

For a minute, I think he is about to turn his back on us and walk away. The frustration on his face is plain to see, but he stands his ground.

'You're not the only one who suffered, Natalie,' he sighs, all traces of anger gone from his voice. 'I want my wife back that's all. Is that so wrong?'

If I were a better wife, I would see that he is close to tears, but my pride gets in the way.

'I am not going to be watched over in my own home.' My snotty words sound arrogant even to my ears and I immediately wish I could take them back.

'Your home!' Daniel is beside himself with disbelief. 'Frank signed this place over to me years ago. If it weren't for me and Mam, he'd have gone bankrupt. Lost the house, the business, everything.'

'You're lying.' I seethe, not caring that Darkly is tugging at my clothing, trying desperately to get me to stop shouting. All I can think is— *How dare he? How bloody dare he?*

'My father never spent a penny in years. He must have had a small fortune put aside. Is that why you married me, Daniel? So you could take over the business?'

The hurt expression on Daniel's face somehow cuts through my temper and all the fight goes out of me when I hear him say, 'What happened to you, Natalie? Where's the girl I married?'

When he turns and walks back to the pickup truck, I feel guilty as hell. *I went too far, I know I did. Whatever came over me?* Realising I can't let him go like this, I follow—

'Daniel. I'm sorry. Please... I didn't mean it.'

But it's no use. Rather than hear me out, he gets into the truck, hits the accelerator hard and spins away, leaving a cloud of depressing grey dust in his wake.

***

With no hope of resurrecting the steak pie, I manage to rustle up something else for Daniel and his mother, but neither show up for supper, so I have to assume they ate together at her house. *She probably cooked him steak pie on purpose,* I think spitefully, forgetting for the moment that I am meant to be feeling contrite. I have been crying on and off all day, beating myself up over what happened. But it bugs me that Daniel might have confided in her, told her all about our argument and the shameful things I said.

When it grows dark and there is still no sign of Daniel, I trudge wearily up to the bedroom and sit on his empty side of the bed. Too long, I sit staring out of the window hoping to catch a glimpse of the pickup truck's headlights. My mother always swore that the secret to a happy marriage was to never go to bed angry, insisting that couples should stay up and fight instead. All good advice, I am sure, but I cannot argue with Daniel if he isn't here.

Making up my mind to put on the silky nightdress that I know he likes, in case he does decide to return later, I walk over to the matching his and hers wardrobes and pull out items of clothing, not entirely sure where I put the nightdress. I can hardly believe that some of the short revealing dresses in here belong to me. They are nothing like what I would choose. But then I come across something that I am 100% convinced *is* my taste.

Hugged by a smooth layer of cellophane, the simple white lace wedding dress, Bohemian in style, is exactly my size, I am sure of it. Taking it out of the wardrobe, but retaining it on the hanger, I go over to the full-length mirror and hold it up against me.

It has long sleeves and a not too revealing V-back, perfect for a bride who does not want to display too much flesh. And the length is right too. The material feels luxurious against my skin and I long to put it on, to relive one moment of my forgotten life.

How long I stand there, staring dreamily at my reflection, trying my hardest to remember *anything* about my wedding day, and failing, I do not know.

'You were the most beautiful bride Little Downey ever saw.'

Caught unawares, I spin around to see Daniel smiling sadly at me from the doorway. For once, I do not worry about where he came from or how he crept up on me unannounced like that, because he is looking at me with gentle, almost apologetic, eyes.

'You said we were happy.' I hang my head because I wish I could be as beautiful as he seems to think I am. If only I could be more feminine, like my mother, like—

'We are.'

Daniel comes to stand behind me, close enough to touch me, and our eyes meet in the mirror. We smile shyly at each other, but I am the first to glance away.

225

'Was that our first row?' I hug the dress for comfort, in case I do not like his answer.

'We've had a few humdingers before.' He chuckles, putting me at my ease.

'But we always make up, right?' I ask, remembering my mother's advice.

'Right,' he agrees, bending down to kiss my neck.

I know then that I am to be forgiven and I feel the luckiest girl alive but I can't help feeling I haven't done enough to deserve it.

'I'm sorry, Daniel,' I say too quickly. 'I'll try to be a better wife. It was selfish of me, getting sick like that…'

'I couldn't bear to go through it again,' he admits, with a catch to his voice.

'I'm going to put it on. To see what I look like,' I mumble excitedly, taking another look at my reflection in the mirror.

'Later,' he insists, slowly turning me around to face him. The desire on his face is enough to make anyone blush but when the wedding dress falls forgotten to the floor at our feet and he covers my mouth with his own, I do not mind it quite so much as I once did.

Chapter 63

A month has passed since our row and every day with Daniel now feels like a honeymoon. Laughing and holding hands, we explode onto the porch like runaway teenagers unable to stop touching and kissing each other. I am still in my nightdress, but for once I don't care who might see me, because for the first time in my life I feel loved. These last few weeks have been a real eye-opener. At last, I feel normal. For Daniel's sake, I've even made my peace with his mother.

'You won't forget about Mam coming over,' Daniel says at last, when it seems as if we must part for the day after all.

'I'll be extra nice to her, I promise.' I laugh, deliberately crossing my fingers.

We both pause to glance at the liveried post van bouncing along the drive towards us and when we turn back to each other, we smile, as if to acknowledge that we have missed each other in the short time our attentions were elsewhere.

'I wish I didn't have to go to work,' Daniel grumbles, leaning in for one last kiss. Just as I start to think it will never end, he straightens up and presses his finger against my nose, a habit I now find rather endearing. What a difference a few weeks can make!

'See you later,' Daniel calls, acknowledging the postman with a passing nod as he climbs into the pickup truck. I blow him one last kiss and watch him drive off, before I ever get around to signing for the parcel the uncomplaining postman has under his arm.

'You two must be honeymooners behaving like that.' The postman's eyes are lit up with laughter; and something else—a touch of jealousy perhaps.

'It just feels like it.' I laugh. 'We've actually been married three and a half years.'

'Get away,' he jokes. 'My wife hasn't kissed me like that in months and we've only been married a year.'

As I watch him stroll back to his van, a feeling of uncertainty settles on me, depriving me of some of the confidence I felt earlier. *Could there be an element of truth to his words?*

***

While I unwrap the parcel, which I have only got around to thinking about after a busy morning spent chasing around a full-of-beans toddler, I keep one eye on Darkly, who sits in a booster chair at the table, dribbling milk from a plastic cup onto her jam-smeared soldiers.

'Look, Darkly. A present,' I say, sliding out a hard-backed reference book and a sheet of paper, which instructs me to: "Read page 205. Paragraph 62." I poke inside for a letter or any other clue as to who might have sent it but find nothing. Wondering if the medical encyclopaedia is really intended for me, I check the brown paper wrapping again, but it has my name and address on it, so there can be no mistake.

'I wonder who it's from,' I say, flipping through the book until I find the correct page and paragraph. The chapter heading, HUMAN CANNIBALISM, is enough to make me immediately want to put the book aside, but I keep on reading—

Forty-two cases discovered worldwide between 1911 and 2017. Clinically proven to be extremely addictive. Long-term side effects have been known to cause dramatic chemical instability of the brain.

Angrily, I get up from my seat to pace the room. *This has got be a sick joke. Who in their right mind would send such a thing, and why?*

Then, I realise that Darkly is watching me. Her blue eyes have narrowed to dark slits and the frown on her face perfectly mirrors my own. Extremely sensitive to my moods, a behaviour caused, no doubt, by separation anxiety, I know that if I remain angry, this will distress her for the rest of the day. So, I snap the book shut and slide it between some cookery books on a shelf.

'We won't tell Dada about this,' I whisper conspiratorially, forcing myself to smile.

***

The dress looks as I imagined it would. *Even better on,* I think, twirling around in front of the full-length mirror, so I can capture the way it falls from every angle. I haven't been able to stop thinking about the dress all morning, so eventually I gave up on my chores and raced up here, with Darkly on my hip, to try it on. Deciding it doesn't look right with my hair down I rummage in a drawer for a hair clip and put it up. *Much better,* I reflect, admiring the cut of the dress from the back. I try not to feel sad that I missed one of the most important days of my life; that I have no recollection of my wedding day and probably never will. At least I have the dress. *That's something,* I tell myself.

Darkly sits on the bed watching me. She is as enraptured with the wedding dress as I am, never taking her eyes off it. Unlike me, I suspect she is going to be a girly-girl who loves makeup and dresses, because her eyes are sparkling with envy.

'Pretty mama. Pretty,' she coos.

'You're the true princess.' I laugh, scooping her into my arms and tickling her until she giggles uncontrollably. This is a truly happy moment, I can't help thinking, one to cherish.

'You there, Natalie?'

As soon as the shrill voice calls up the stairs, the happy mood is broken. Daniel's mother has the same effect on both of us, I realise flatly. In fact, now that I come to think of it, I realise Darkly never goes near her grandmother at all if she can help it. Being her only grandchild, one she claims to adore, I'm surprised Daniel's mother isn't more affectionate. It bugs me when she overlooks Darkly but so far, I have kept quiet, not wanting to cause too much upset at once.

'Just coming, Mam!' I call, scrambling up from the bed. Hurriedly, I unzip the dress and slip it off my shoulders.

When I step out of the silky folds of material and bend down to pick it up, I notice something inside the lining that I can't remember seeing before—a price tag attached to the dress. Even after I have found a pair of scissors and snipped it off, my fingers do not stop shaking. Belatedly, it occurs to me that the dress looks new, as if it has never been worn. *But it could have been dry-cleaned,* I reason. That would make sense. What doesn't make sense is how I could have missed the price tag. First time around, I mean, on my actual wedding day. Wouldn't it have scratched my skin having to wear it all day? *What if you didn't, Natalie? What if you never wore the dress at all? What if there wasn't any wedding?*

***

I should be grateful. Daniel's mother has spent hours cleaning the house. The table is set for dinner and there is something delicious in the oven, judging by the wonderful smell emanating from the kitchen. Having expertly rolled pastry right in front of me for the fourth time in so many weeks, *I will never forgive her for that,* she is now tackling the ironing.

'A walk will do you good. Everything's done. Darkly's having her nap.'

Realising she wants me out of the house, *her house,* I am tempted to refuse, to spite her, but then I decide she could be right. A walk will probably do me some good.

Chapter 64

Little Downey Beach

The ocean is wild and at odds with itself today, which perfectly matches my mood. Every so often it rears up, like an angry horse, before crashing down on the rocks that jut out from the cliff edge. I am sitting here on my rock, witnessing all this, thinking how lucky I am to have this view to myself. Scooting a small pebble into the water, and hearing it land with a satisfying plop, I feel as if I am the only person alive. I guess that's what the untameable Welsh coastline does—gives us a sense of how small and insignificant we all are.

Perhaps that is why it takes me longer than usual to register the sound of a dog barking. The beaches here are normally empty, no matter the time of year, so I do not expect to be interrupted. But when I glance over my shoulder, I see a scruffy-looking dog, no more than a puppy really, tearing about on the beach, tongue foolishly lolling out and ears pricked. Realising I am in no danger of being savaged, *I have an aversion to dogs that I think is relatively new,* I am about to whistle it over, when I spot the dog's owner.

The man and the dog stop when they see me. Selfishly, I do not want to share this part of the beach with anyone else, so I hope they will turn and walk away again, in the opposite direction. But oh no, they decide to head straight towards me. *How annoying,* I think, getting to my feet. *If they think I am going to stand here and make small talk, they've got another thing coming.*

As they draw closer, it dawns on me that this is the same man I saw outside the window. He has the same long scruffy hair and beard. The same arrogant stance. Standing there, alone on the beach, with no other people around, I feel afraid. There is something about him that unsettles me. I feel it now, as I did the first time I saw him all those weeks ago. Yet a part of me longs to know who the stranger is and why he has this effect on me.

Every painstakingly slow step he takes towards me reveals more of his face and features and I find I cannot move. Trembling from head to toe, I can shake my head in denial all I like, but beneath the beard and long hair, I recognise him. His eyes. *Oh my God his eyes.*

'You're not real!' I shout, not wanting him to come any closer. 'You don't exist.'

He halts in front of me, seeming to understand that I need some space, but the dog is not so polite. It launches itself playfully at me, almost unbalancing me.

'I suppose he's not real either,' I hear him say. Same old sarcastic voice.

He approaches me then, and my eyes dart constantly between him and the house by the sea, whose shadow falls on the beach in front of us. When he is close enough to put a hand on my arm, my trembling increases and I want to cry. *Oh God I want to cry.*

'If I'm not real, how come I can touch you?' he states matter-of-factly.

One blue eye. One brown eye.

Are you my boyfriend?

I was hoping to be.

'I'm imagining this,' I tell myself, refusing to look at him. 'I must have forgotten to take my medication. That's all.'

'I waited. I waited a long time for you, Natalie.'

'You're not real!' I scream, backing away from him. 'You're not real.'

'What's my name?' he demands, refusing to let go of my arm.

'I'm not going back there… to the institution. You can't make me,' I snap, managing to shrug him off at last, but then the tears come. 'Dr Moses said I made a complete recovery.'

'What's my name?' he barks again.

'Jed,' I sob. 'It's Jed.'

***

We are in the mouth of a cave on a secluded part of the beach, hidden from view. It is dark and damp inside, but Jed has managed to get a small fire going and is making tea, *as if that will make everything okay.* Seawater dribbles in through rock pools, where the dog tries to catch crabs, and water splashes onto our heads through cracks in the rock ceiling.

I watch him as if I have spent my whole life watching him. The tattooed ladies on his arms, evidence of a past that excludes me, come to life as he stirs the tea. My eyes jealously shift away from them and travel over his body. Images of us kissing goodbye and him walking dejectedly away come back to me. But when I see the pink strawberry mark on his bare back, which is just like Darkly's, I close my eyes and blank everything out.

Not quite everything.

The baby has one too. See.

Glancing down at the charm necklace in my hand, which he thinks will help unlock my past, means nothing to me so far; but one mystery I have managed to solve all by myself.

'You sent me that book, didn't you?'

Jed turns to look at me. 'I thought it might prompt you into remembering something,' he admits. 'But I got tired of waiting.'

'I have a home. A husband.' I am as angry with myself as I am him, but all I see on his face is pity. When he reaches out for my hand and I ignore it, he shakes his head sadly.

'What you have is a lie, Natalie.'

Childishly, I place both hands over my ears and move away from him. 'I don't want to know anything, even if it is the truth.'

'You're living on the illusions they're feeding you. Daniel, Dr Moses, the villagers. None of it is true, Natalie. You know it isn't.'

He pauses as if unsure whether to go on, then continues in a less harsh tone, 'You remember what they did to Merry?'

Merry's birthmark. I'd know it anywhere.

'That was a bad dream. It didn't happen.'

'They cut her up. Turned her into a piece of meat,' he persists angrily.

'No.' I won't have it. I don't care what he says. It can't be true.

'And slaughtered your father too. Or was that also a dream?'

I get to my feet, angrier even than Jed is now. 'My father was a drinker. He died of liver disease,' I insist.

He gets to his feet too, grabs my arm and shakes me. I get the feeling he thinks this will be enough to jolt my memory. If only it were that easy.

'That's what they want you to believe. Think, Natalie, think. You can remember if you try hard enough.'

When he shakes me again, harder this time, I slap him across the face. His anger is no match for mine.

'You're as bad as they are. Always trying to get me to forget or remember.'

He turns away to hide the tears that appear in his eyes. 'A bride never forgets the best day of her life,' he groans wretchedly. 'Can you honestly remember anything about your wedding day?'

'There were pink freesias and linen tablecloths,' I reply robotically. 'My father wore a blue suit with a pink buttonhole and I wore a beautiful lace dress. It hangs in my wardrobe.'

Remembering my own doubts from this morning, I do not feel so certain of anything anymore. *Could Jed be right?*

'It's still got the price tag on,' I admit dejectedly. I have never got over this fact, I realise with sudden perception.

'And the wedding photos?' he prompts gently. 'Where are they? Are there *any* pictures in your house?'

I shake my head. One of the first things I noticed on returning home was the lack of photographs. *If he's right about that, could he be right about everything else?*

'We don't behave like an old married couple,' I point out, remembering the postman's comments from this morning.

Needing to sit, before I fall, I flop on the wet sand and look out to sea, longing to go back in time to this morning, when everything was different. Where did that happy moment with Darkly on the bed go? As for the laughter I shared with Daniel—

When I feel Jed kneel beside me and take both my hands in his, I turn to look at him.

'I'm not somebody's wife? Somebody's mother?'

Chapter 65

The House By The Sea

I must look like a wild thing as I stumble into the kitchen. My hair is knotted and windswept and it feels as if my eyes are all over the place, a sure sign that I am late taking my medication. Seated at the table, in the middle of eating their meal, Daniel and his mother pause, with their cutlery in the air, to stare at me as if I were an intruder. *And perhaps I am.*

'Where have you been?' Daniel asks. 'We were getting worried. Are you all right?'

'I'm fine. Sorry. I lost track of time, that's all.'

I rest my hands on the back of a chair and tell myself to calm down. My heart is beating so loud I am surprised they cannot hear it. Daniel goes on eating, but I can tell by the set of his jaw that he is annoyed with me. His mother simply stares. When I notice the joint of rare beef in the middle of the table and see meat juices running down her triple chins, I retch, convinced more than ever that I do not belong among these people. Mistaking my unsteady appearance for signs of hunger and fatigue, Daniel's mother gets to her feet.

'We kept it hot for you,' she says, busying herself with plates and saucepans. 'Come and sit down.'

'I'm not hungry. Where's Darkly?' I ask impatiently.

Mother and son share a guarded look, sensing something odd about my behaviour.

'She's been in bed this last half an hour or so,' Daniel's mother explains in a voice she would use to a child.

'I want to see her,' I snap, walking towards the door, but Daniel gets there before me. With a deceptive smile on his face, he turns me around and guides me back to the table.

'Eat first,' he hisses in my ear, his fingers nipping at my skin. 'Mam's cooked it special. Gone to a lot of trouble.'

So, I sit down. I have little choice really. Even so, I inch away from the pan of sizzling meat. Just looking at it makes me feel queasy. *How could I have ever gone back to eating it again? Did they force me? Was that always the plan? To make me like them.* I will never forgive either of them for this month-long deception. How could they be so cruel? When Daniel's mother puts a heaped plateful of potatoes and cabbage in front of me and carves a slice from the end of the joint, I run to the sink and bring up a mouthful of vomit.

'What on earth has got into her?' Daniel's mother shrieks.

'Where did you go today, Natalie? Who did you talk to?' Daniel asks suspiciously.

'He's becoming quite the jealous husband, your son,' I joke, trying out a laugh on Daniel's mother, which seems to do the trick, as she sits back down again. They even resume eating. Joining them at the table, *I must try to appear normal,* I butter some bread, to steady my shaking fingers more than anything, and when I next glance at Daniel, it's obvious he knows something is up. He looks to his mother for guidance, but she is as baffled as he is.

'Word is,' Daniel talks with his mouth full, 'there's some tramp hanging around again. Long hair with a beard. Did you see anyone like that on your walk?'

He observes me warily and I remind myself that he doesn't know anything, or we wouldn't be having this conversation. *He's trying to trick me.* Shaking my head, I concentrate on eating my bread and butter, but even that is difficult to get down.

'Yeah… well,' he takes another enormous mouthful of food, barely pausing to chew before he swallows, 'he won't be around much longer. Once we find him—'

Although I am not supposed to, I see the warning glance pass from mother to son and acting on it, he shuts up. On her feet again, as if she can't bear to be idle for long, Daniel's mother slides a large slice of meat onto my plate and waits expectantly.

'Tuck in,' she says, elbowing me none too gently.

I push the plate away. I will not look at it a second longer.

They turned her into a piece of meat.

'I can't face it.' I feel sick all over again.

'That's nice,' Daniel's mother huffs. 'It only took me hours to prepare while you were out gallivanting.'

'Eat it,' Daniel commands from across the table.

'No,' I snap, but hang my head, not wanting to battle with Daniel's icy blue eyes. I am afraid. But there is nothing he can say or do that will make me eat it.

'I never heard of a butcher's wife turning her nose up at a good joint of meat before.' Daniel scrapes back his chair and starts to remove his belt.

Is he insane? Does he really mean to whip me? Do people still behave like that? Little Downey may be old fashioned, but this is something else. I look at his mother in alarm. Surely, even she wouldn't countenance something like that. But judging by the look of shame on her face, I get the feeling this isn't the first time Daniel has abused me.

'There's no call for that, son. She'll eat it when she's good and ready,' she urges him.

'No, I won't,' I declare, surprising all of us, including myself.

Although I am grateful to Daniel's mother for sticking up for me, she is no friend of mine. I only have to look at the way she has been pushing me around since I came home to know this. Not one gentle word have I had from her. As for my so-called husband, who continues to glare at me, even though he's sat back down in his chair, I think the Daniel with the gentle eyes never existed, except in my imagination. If I was unsure before, I am convinced now that he is not a man I would ever marry.

'Something's got into you. Somebody got to you, didn't they?' he declares at last, placing the belt on the table; a reminder of what he is capable of.

I say nothing, but I stare right back at him, refusing to be intimidated. *I am a Powers,* I remind myself. But when his fist crashes down on the table, I jump to my feet.

'Something did get into me, Daniel!' I yell. 'I'm expecting a baby.'

Mouths wide open, they stare at me in astonishment, unable to process this news. Daniel is the first to break the silence.

'Isn't it too soon to know that?'

'A woman has a sixth sense about these things.' I glance nervously at Daniel's mother, hoping for more of the support she showed earlier. 'Isn't that right, Mam?'

Pulling many different faces, she thinks long and hard about this. A lot seems to depend on her answer, because Daniel's eyes are on her, not me.

'Can't argue with that. I knew I was carrying you,' she glances fondly at Daniel, 'after a couple of weeks. This *is* wonderful news. No wonder she's gone off her food.'

Looking stunned, Daniel flops into his chair. 'I'm going to be a father.'

'Don't sound so surprised, Daniel,' I hiss sarcastically. 'Anyone would think we'd never had a baby before.'

***

Darkly is asleep in her big-girl cot in my old bedroom, which, like the rest of the house, has undergone a dramatic change. Painted fairy-tale pink, the room has everything a real-life princess could want, including a doll's house, rocking horse and army of dolls and soft toys. When I first saw this room, I couldn't help thinking the decoration was too old for a toddler. It felt as if Darkly's personality had already been decided upon; denying her the chance to become her own version of her. I do not like her sleeping in here on her own and would much rather have her in with us, but Daniel won't allow it. Men do like their rules, I find. When he goes on like that, he reminds me of my father.

Gently, so as not to wake Darkly, I tuck the pink Disney duvet around her, knowing it will soon get kicked off again. She is one of those children who would run around naked all day long if she could; hating to be restricted in any way. She is much more of an outdoor girl than I ever was, and I suppose this is why she is as brown as she is. But then I remind myself that the sun isn't solely responsible for her olive colouring. If everything Jed told me is true, and I have no reason to disbelieve him, then Darkly is my sister, not my daughter.

Half-sister. Gypsy blood at that.

I will always love her as my own of course. The new life growing inside me will not change that. I was not lying when I informed Daniel and my mother-in-law that I am expecting. Nor do I need to see a doctor to know that I am with child, *that's not how things are done in Little Downey.* I have a natural intuition for such things, as I am sure my own mother did before me. I still struggle to believe that she is gone. Memories of her fill my head.

***

Pausing over a photo of my mother, I am sitting cross-legged on the bedroom floor, like the girl I used to be, surrounded by boxes of old photographs, when Daniel comes in. This time, his presence does not surprise me. Rather, I have been waiting for him to make an appearance. Seeing the photographs, he looks perplexed.

'Looking for something?' he asks quietly.

'The wedding album,' I reply matter-of-factly.

'What wedding album?'

'Ours, silly.' I dart him a deceitful smile, which confuses him further. I begin to think my husband is not as intelligent as I once thought. 'There must be one,' I insist. 'Where is it?'

When his blue eyes go off to the left and afterwards blink in rapid succession I know that he is ruffled. No doubt his mind is busy at work trying to come up with the perfect lie.

'Over at Mam's,' he says eventually. 'We thought looking at it might upset you.'

'It was the best day of my life, Daniel,' I reply convincingly, without a hint of sarcasm. 'I want to remember it for a *long* time to come.'

Chapter 66

I like today already, I decide, because this is the first morning Daniel hasn't insisted on us going down to see him off. I rather think the sun is on my side too, because it sits shyly behind a cloud and refuses to come out. This behaviour reminds me of Darkly, who does the same thing whenever Daniel is in a bad mood, which is increasingly often. However, she has no need to hide from him today, even if he is in a right grump, because I have her safely wrapped in my arms. I only hope she doesn't sense what dark thoughts are on *my* mind.

We watch from Darkly's bedroom window, as Daniel storms, blond hair bobbing, towards the pickup truck, hands on the hunt for the keys in his pockets. He doesn't glance up at the window as he gets inside the vehicle, but he will—

As soon as he finds the charm necklace wrapped around the steering wheel, he is out of the truck in an instant. From his body language, I can tell he is shaken by the discovery.

Now who's seeing things, I think smugly.

As if he knows he is being watched, he darts a suspicious glance up at the window, *see. I knew I was right,* and his accusing eyes settle on us.

Waving enthusiastically, I prompt Darkly to wave too, and she responds energetically.

'We are the perfect wife and daughter, aren't we?' I chuckle, delighted by how innocent we must appear, yet another part of me suspects that my laughter borders on the manic.

'Perfic,' Darkly agrees, trying out the new word for the first time and finding it funny.

We are still laughing when Daniel rips the charm necklace from the steering wheel and tosses it into the long grass. Getting back into the truck, he slams the door shut and speeds away, kicking up a cloud of vengeful dust behind him.

As soon as he is gone, I feel my face settling into a scowl. Luckily, Darkly does not notice. She goes on waving.

'That's it. Wave goodbye to your father, Darkly,' I tell her ominously.

***

Swirls of black smoke spur me into action. Once again, I have been sitting at the kitchen table staring into space, unaware of what is going on around me. When I finally realise the toast is burning, I rescue it from the toaster and singe my fingers in the process.

'Damn it,' I exclaim, annoyed with myself for having drifted away. *I have a child and one on the way*, I remind myself, *I need to start acting responsibly. That's partly why I stopped taking my medication again. They can't be good for me, let alone the baby.*

At this point, my eyes swing to Darkly, who is sitting in her booster seat at the opposite end of the table. I remember leaving her munching on cereal; using her chubby little fingers to scoop out the honeyed loops from the milk. But, looking at her now, I see that her expression has changed to one of anger, and something else that I can't quite put a name to. Not yet anyway.

I think she is about to cry angry tears but she surprises me by swiping the plastic bowl of cereal to the floor, milk splattering everywhere. Like blood from a deep cut.

Drip. Splat. Drip.

'What's the matter?' I implore.

'No like. Want sausages,' she demands, petulantly pointing to the fridge.

'You can't have sausages for breakfast, sweetheart,' I tell her. 'Mama will do you some nice new toast.'

'Want sausages.' Darkly confronts me as another adult might.

Noticing at last that there is an icy blueness to Darkly's eyes that wasn't there before, I feel a dreadful sense of foreboding. Every day, I have been hoping to see a hint of darkness creep into her eyes, which would make her more like me, or even a flash of green, inherited from Merry, but I realise, with a sickening dread, that this is never going to happen. I have seen enough pairs of Little Downey eyes not to know them for what they are.

I fly into action when Darkly screams. Banging her fists on the table, and flinging her head about, her eyes never leave my face as she watches me take out a packet of sausages from the fridge. Under pressure to speed up, I take out a frying pan and move towards the hob, but this only makes her cry louder. By now, her face is red and ugly, with angry tears spilling down her cheeks. I have never seen her like this before. In this moment, she reminds me of my mother-in-law.

'What's wrong? I thought you wanted sausages.'

As soon as I am close enough, her chubby little fists grab for the sausages. This urge for meat terrifies me. Knowing that this is no ordinary tantrum, I obediently hand over the uncooked sausages and watch, sickened, as my little girl ravenously sinks her teeth into the raw flesh, ripping through the packaging in her haste to get at it. I cannot bear to see the look of pure pleasure that passes over her face when she swallows her first mouthful.

Chapter 67

Dr Moses once assured me that the desire to get one's own back on those who hurt us is a natural emotion. He was referring to how I felt about my mother and father, and my abandonment issues, but nothing about the way I feel now could ever be described as natural. I want to lash out at every person in Little Downey for what they have done to Darkly.

She might not be my biological daughter, but she is mine in every way that matters. I would do anything for her. The desire for revenge is taking me over, filling me with a cold and ruthless determination that I didn't know I was capable of. Now that my old memories have also come flooding back, I remember promising myself that I would one day take my revenge for what the villagers did to my parents. That time is now. The slaughterhouse and Bob Black might be where my story began but I decide how it ends.

As soon as the van pulls up outside, I am out of the house with a seductive smile painted on my face, ready to greet Bob Black. He is in as much of a hurry as I am, I can tell, because in our rush, our bodies almost collide on the porch. I make sure this is where he stays. If I have anything to do with it, he will never step foot inside my father's house again. I cannot believe how easy he is making everything for me. He does not suspect me at all. The clues are there but he chooses not to see them. *Don't say I didn't warn you.*

'I came as soon as I could, Natalie,' he says breathlessly. 'Where's the tramp?'

'He ran in there.' I point towards the whitewashed building. 'I caught him looking at me through the window,' I add, feigning a timidity that I do not feel.

This admission immediately gets his attention. It takes a voyeur to know one, I suppose. I watch him standing there, red-faced, and sweaty, with his hands on his hips, *hands that have mercilessly slaughtered many living things, including my own father*, looking at me the way he has always looked at me—since I was a little girl. He used to look at my mother the same way, I remember. *Like a piece of meat.* A habit of his that got my father's back up.

Having deliberately changed into cut-off shorts and a tight T-shirt, his eyes unapologetically roam my body. Boldly, I stare back, saying nothing, which he seems to take as an invitation to keep on gawping. *This is fine with me, for now,* I decide. *Let him look.* I almost laugh when his glasses fog up and slip further down his sweltering nose.

'Did you manage to get hold of Daniel?' Bob drags his eyes away from my crotch to glance over at what used to be my father's workshop; not a trace of remorse evident on his face.

'He's not answering his mobile.' I shrug. 'I'm guessing he's out on a delivery.'

'You stay inside and lock the door,' Bob insists. 'If there is anybody about still. They won't get past me.'

'Oh, thank you,' I gush. Then, with a hint of sarcasm that I cannot keep from my voice— 'I hope you brought your gun.'

As soon as the words are out of my mouth, I picture this horrible little man aiming a bolt gun at my father's head. How I manage to keep on smiling, I do not know, but the horror of that night must show on my face, because he is frowning at me, as if he suspects me of something. Acting quickly, *Merry would be proud of me,* I stretch provocatively and push my thumbs into the belt loops of my shorts, tugging them further down and exposing more flesh. I am no longer a girl, I realise. I am a woman who can use her body to get what she wants. I have had sex and experienced desire for a man, so I know how to do this. When I see what impact this has on him, I know he is putty in my hands.

'Don't need no gun to scare off a tramp,' he boasts, puffing out his own chest.

*****

The inside of my father's old workshop has had a fresh coat of paint and the ever-present stink of rotting meat has disappeared; gone forever, I hope. Sunlight leaks in through the new glass windows to light up the building but this deception does not fool me. For me, this will always be a dark savage place—the home of my childhood nightmares. Even now, relics of the past remain. Meat hooks sway above my head, clanging ominously like church bells and the butcher's block and the cutting tools are still here, although I notice straight away that one piece is missing from the set. *Who could have taken it?*

Bob doesn't hear me come in. He's too busy congratulating himself on spotting the dust scrapes on the floor where the butcher's block has been moved.

'So that's where you've been hiding.' He harrumphs, staring at the secret trap door.

He has no idea I am standing behind him. I watch him tug a packet of Silk Cut out of his pocket and stick a crumpled cigarette into his mouth. Lighting it, he takes a long drawn-out drag, relishing the hit of tobacco. I have never smoked but I know what it is like to battle with addiction and I envy him his relief. He puffs a few smoke rings in the air before deciding to tackle the heavy trap door. The creak of it being lifted sends a chill up my spine.

Don't expect too much, Natalie. The years haven't been kind to her.

'Can you see anything?' I enquire innocently.

Dropping the trap door, Bob Black swings around to face me, a look of panic in his eyes.

'Jesus. You gave me a scare. I thought I told you to stay indoors. It's not safe for you to be out here. Not with a lunatic about.' As if realising what he has said, he grimaces and runs a hand through his dishevelled hair. 'No offence, Natalie,' he apologises awkwardly.

If I didn't know better, I'd think he meant it.

'None taken.' I shrug.

'It wasn't a dig at you,' he assures me, turning his back on me once again, to concentrate on who or what might be down in the cellar. 'I mean, you're one of us.'

He lifts open the trap door again, and I advance on him, slowly. There is no hurry. I have waited a long time for this moment. Images of my father going down on the first resounding crack of the bolt gun and Darkly gnawing on raw meat flood my mind. Strangely, I feel the same excitement building in me that I sensed in the villagers on the night they butchered my father.

'Aren't I just,' I mumble, bringing out the missing butcher's saw from behind my back.

Chapter 68

The House By The Sea – Daniel

The kitchen is in darkness. The lack of any welcome and absence of cooking smells puts Daniel in an even worse mood than he was in before. When he switches on the light, to reveal a messy kitchen, an angry scowl spreads across his face.

'Natalie?' he calls menacingly.

When his foot knocks against something on the floor, he bends down to investigate a plastic cereal bowl, which smells of sour milk, before hurling it across the room.

'Natalie?' he shouts, his frustration building.

Altogether, it's been a long day. He's hot, thirsty, tired, and hungry; in exactly that order. And to top it off, Natalie decides to do a runner. Today of all days. Shrugging, he walks over to the fridge and opens it. Taking out a carton of orange juice, he drinks straight from it, not bothering with a glass. Once he's slaked his thirst, his mind turns to food. Peering into the fridge, he grabs the remaining half of a pork pie and shoves it in his mouth. It won't satisfy his hunger for long, but it will do for now. He's about to shut the fridge door and go in search of Natalie when he spots something odd.

On the lower shelf of the fridge there is a large tongue resting on a folded-up piece of kitchen towel which has turned pink from absorbing blood. At first, he thinks it must be a pig's tongue, but wonders where Natalie could have got hold of one. She certainly hasn't asked him to bring one home. Taking it out of the fridge, he balances it on one hand, clearly puzzled by it. On closer inspection, he decides it is too small to have come from any pig. Besides, most pig tongues are covered in grey fat. This one is made up almost entirely of lean meat and is bright pink in comparison.

When the strong smell of tobacco reaches his nostrils, he drops the tongue on the floor and spits out his last mouthful of pork pie.

'Natalie!' he screams, heading for the stairs.

Having checked all the upstairs rooms for signs of Natalie and finding none, Daniel comes hurtling back down the stairs again, this time too fast for his own legs to keep up. When he catches sight of a woman in a red dress with wild hair and bloodied limbs disappearing into the kitchen, he loses his balance and concentration.

'What the fuck.'

Daniel trips and tumbles down the last few steps. On landing, his head meets up with the stone floor. The last thing he sees before passing out is a woman's face bending over him, her long black hair dangling down to tickle his face.

Chapter 69

The House By The Sea – Natalie

Like a good wife, I dutifully tidy the kitchen, returning it to its usual order. *The look on Daniel's face when he saw the tongue was priceless. If only he could have seen himself. I don't think I've ever laughed so hard.* Yet, knowing how dangerous my husband can be, I keep one eye on him through the doorway, where he is sprawled at the bottom of the stairs, a streak of crimson dripping from his forehead onto the floor.

Drip. Splat. Drip.

He shows no sign of recovery yet. No matter. I can wait. Picking up Bob Black's tongue from the kitchen floor, I look at it, all shrivelled up in my fingers and count my blessings. It will never come out to poke lustfully at any other young girl.

Returning to the hallway, I bend down and balance the tongue on Daniel's chest, terrified he will regain consciousness and catch me. If that should happen, there is no telling what he might do. He is much stronger than I am, at least physically. I would be lucky if I survived this night at all. The best I could hope for would be a permanent return to Thornhaugh.

Even with one leg awkwardly tucked up under him, he looks peaceful lying there. When his cold blue eyes are not visible, like now, his blond hair and youthful features lend him an air of innocence. It's a shame he couldn't have been a better man. Better father. Better husband. Had he have been any of those things, I could have forgiven him a lot.

Placing a silent kiss on his forehead, right on top of his wound, I taste his blood for the first time and leave it there on my lip as a gruesome reminder of our fake marriage and all the lies that have been spun. Knowing he hates his fringe getting in his eyes, I even stroke away a few strands of hair, so it won't bother him.

'When you wake up, you know where to find me,' I whisper in his ear.

Chapter 70

The House By The Sea – Daniel

The shadowy figure moves away, leaving Daniel unsure as to whether he wants it to return or not. Vaguely, he remembers someone caressing his forehead and whispering in his ear. As yet, he doesn't remember what happened or why he is lying at the bottom of the stairs. Did he fall? Pass out? All he knows is, his head hurts like fuck. When he reaches up to touch it and his hand comes away covered in blood, he sits up in shock. But that makes everything worse. Feeling as if he might pass out again, Daniel is about to flop back down on the floor when he sees the bloody tongue resting in his lap.

'Jesus Christ!' he shrieks, flipping the tongue off him and scrambling to his feet.

Staggering from the hallway into the kitchen, he remains dazed and confused, but bits of what happened quickly come back to him. Coming home. Natalie missing. The fridge. The human tongue. A smoker's tongue, he corrects himself. Who does he know that smokes?

'Natalie, where are you?' he calls desperately.

This time, when he flicks the light switch, the lights in the kitchen do not come on. So, he lurches back into the hall and tries the lights in here. The same happens. Nothing works. Guessing that the electricity supply has deliberately been disconnected, he groans aloud and stumbles towards the door. Once he is outside in the fresh air, he feels a little better; less nauseous. When he sees the woman in the red dress running through a pathway of lit candles towards the whitewashed building, he lashes out at the air around him.

'What the hell's going on?' he yells in disbelief.

When he sees a light come on in the building, instinct tells him to follow.

When you wake up, you know where to find me.

***

The first thing Daniel sees when he swings open the door to the whitewashed building is a large rat sitting on the butcher's block. It appears to be nibbling on something and doesn't show any fear of him, not even when it turns its small black eyes in his direction. Knowing this to be an unnatural reaction, Daniel shudders. Grabbing a cleaver from the other end of the butcher's block, he creeps up on the rat and, taking it by surprise, whacks it, sends it flying across the room. He hears the rat falling to the floor, followed by an angry hiss and the scurrying of clawed feet as it runs for cover. For one terrifying moment, Daniel thinks it is going to come back and attack him, but thankfully it does not.

As his eyes adapt to the dimly lit room, he feels safer in his surroundings. But then he reminds himself that he is not alone. He saw her come in here. Where can she be hiding? Surely not down in the cellar? She'd have to be crazy to do something like that. But then again, he mustn't forget that she *is* and always has been crazy.

Swatting away flies, the place is full of them, he sees the telltale scrapes on the floor where the butcher's block has been moved. He knows that the trap door has recently been opened because it is clear of cobwebs and dust. Not so the butcher's block, which is covered in some sort of sticky substance. Deciding that this must be what the rat was feasting on, Daniel scoops some out with his finger, noticing that it has sharp bits in it that prick his skin. Grabbing the oil lantern from the windowsill, he holds it over the butcher's block and stumbles backwards when he realises he is looking at a mass of splintered bone, fragments of ventricle and cerebral fluid; the kind found in the human brain.

Before Daniel can open his mouth to scream, something drips onto his face. Blinking madly, he glances up to see a thick coil of red, green and purple tubular intestines, dangling from a meat hook above his head. The stench is horrendous. The blood and liquid seeping onto his face even more so.

In Daniel's haste to flee, he accidentally knocks the lantern against the meat hook, and the intestines drop down to coil around his shoulders.

'Get them off me,' he screams, momentarily paralysed with fear.

Realising no one is coming to help him. Not now. Not ever. He claws madly at the intestines. When his fingernails fill with their soft meaty goo, he retches and brings up a foul-smelling liquid from the pit of his stomach. Angrily kicking his way free of the entrails, he crouches down low, wiser to what is going on. Only when he is certain there is nothing immediately above his head does he dare swing the lantern around the rest of the room.

'Jesus Christ.' He gasps in horror.

Attached to every meat hook is a human part of some kind or other. A slice of chest, an arm, part of a hand with a gold ring on its wedding finger. Backing further away, until his spine comes into contact with the wall, Daniel senses there is something even more horrible waiting for him in the darkness. Filled with a terrible foreboding, he slowly turns his head and his heart stops when he sees a pair of glassy, bloodshot eyes staring back at him through a pair of cracked spectacles. The look of surprise on the dead man's face matches his own but Daniel immediately recognises the owner of the decapitated head.

Bob Black's head swaying from side to side brings Daniel out in a cold sweat. The metal hook has been driven straight through his face, exiting through the hole that was once his mouth. Only part of the face remains, but both eyes, eerily turned on Daniel, survive.

'Fuck this.'

Making up his mind to get the hell out of there, while he still can, Daniel is about to make a dash for the door when he hears muffled cries coming from the cellar below. Knowing somebody is down there changes everything.

It could be Natalie. The soon-to-be mother of his child.

***

The flickering flame of the oil lantern goes out when Daniel is only halfway down the ladder. Closing his eyes, he holds his breath. The luck he's been having, he should have guessed this would happen. The murmurings that led him down here have stopped but he continues down the ladder anyway, certain that somebody *is* down here. There is no going back, he tells himself, no matter what happens.

As soon as his feet hit the cellar floor, he fumbles with the oil lantern, panicking when he cannot relight it. That's when he hears a scraping sliding noise coming from a far corner. He likens it to the sound of a corpse being dragged along the floor. This spurs him on to have another go at the lantern and after discarding several dud matches, which all go out the second they are lit, he finds one that works long enough to get it alight.

When the glow of the lantern falls on a bare foot, Daniel freezes. But just as quickly, the foot is whipped away again, retreating into the shadows. Daniel's heart is racing so fast he thinks he might have a heart attack. The thought of dying down here sobers him.

'Who's there?' Daniel calls softly, afraid of his own voice.

There it is again, the same muffled cry he heard earlier. Stumbling forward, he holds the lantern out in front of him in the hope that it will act as a barrier to whatever he meets.

At last he sees her. Trussed up like an animal—gagged, bound and huddled in the corner, her knees drawn up to her chest. At least she is alive, he consoles himself, fighting back angry tears. Her eyes, so familiar they are heartbreaking to see, roll around in her head as if they cannot take in what they are seeing; but they appeal for help at the same time.

'Mam. Oh my God. Mam.'

Hurrying towards her, he pulls madly at the ropes, hoping to free her, but they are bound tightly and she flinches whenever he touches her. Clearly, she is in an excruciating amount of pain. He doesn't want to think about how long she might have been left like this but the smell of stale urine on her clothing indicates she has been down here some time. He rips away the gaffer tape from her mouth, knowing that this will also cause pain.

'Who did this to you?' he demands as soon as her mouth is free.

Before she can reply, they hear the creaking hinges of the trap door being lowered and they turn at the same time to see who is there. Just before the trap door closes on them, Daniel catches a glimpse of the woman's straggly long hair and black eyes. He also gets to see her cold unforgiving face for the first time.

'My God, Natalie. Why?' he screams.

Chapter 71

The Whitewashed Building – Natalie

It is done. They can harm us no more. Not Daniel, who will never again threaten me with his belt, nor his bullying mother who, in the later stages of her confinement, reminded me of the pig who frantically tried to scrabble its way out of the slaughterhouse. As for Bob Black, he had to be dead before I would go anywhere near him.

Ignoring the muffled cries coming from the cellar, I slide the butcher's block back over the trap door. It is heavy, and I am feeling weak, exhausted even, but I drum up the strength from somewhere to get the job finished. The banging on the trap door takes me back once again to the night my father was slaughtered like an animal on his own property. If I shut my eyes, I can hear the villagers thumping on the walls of our house, demanding first that my mother be sent out to them, and then years later, my father too.

I peer curiously at the ground beneath my feet, wondering what is going on down there, but my interest is a passing one, mild at that. Noisily hacking up a mouthful of phlegm, I take great pleasure in spitting it out on the floor, right where I imagine their heads to be. Not a very ladylike gesture, I admit, but it feels fitting for the occasion. If my father were here, I know he would applaud my action.

'Put two rats together and starve them,' I declare, dusting my hands together in a triumphant gesture, 'they end up eating each other. That's Frank's Law.'

Chapter 72

Little Downey

Spring is over. Summer is on its way. I hope it will not be a scorcher again, like last year. The yellow time of year has passed. The daffodils, primroses, and dandelions are all gone. I will miss the bleating of the newborn lambs but look forward to the red, white, and blue month of May, which we are now entering. Every day I spot something different in the hedgerow— an early red orchid or white cow parsley. I am not so keen on the bluebells in the woods. They remind me of my mother-in-law's eyes. I can't picture those small blue eyes without thinking of the pig in the slaughterhouse scrambling to be free.

Putting that memory to one side, I cycle down the hill past The Black Bull public house, but I do not look inside its darkened windows to find out if I am being watched. I know that all eyes will be on me. Even the lone fisherman preparing to launch his boat in the bay does a double take when he sees me. Despite feeling anxious about what today will bring, I find the constant clicking of the wheels on the road reassuring. I might be in charge but my mother's old shopper seems to have a life of its own, as if it knows where it is going.

The lingering smell of beer coming from the pub makes me think of my father. I can't help wishing he were here to enjoy a warm frothy bitter. He wouldn't consider eight o'clock in the morning too early for a pint. I miss him every day, my mother less so. Memories of her are spoiled, tainted forever. Sometimes I think it would have been better for everyone if she really had gone over the cliff edge that day.

This is my new life, I keep reminding myself. Those who would hurt us are gone and there is nothing to fear anymore. Nobody can touch me now, unless… but that is unlikely to happen as Jed no longer exists in my world. This new world of mine is not exactly what I wanted it to be, but for my family's sake I must embrace it. There is nowhere else for us to go. Little Downey is *us* or *we are* Little Downey—whichever way you look at it, the result is the same. *We belong here as much as anybody else,* I think defiantly, attacking the pedals with renewed vigour. So far, we have kept our distance from the villagers, but today that changes. I need them to fall under my spell as Jed and Merry once did. As Bob Black did; more fool him. If we are to survive here, we must fit in.

Perhaps because of this, I begin to see beauty in Little Downey for the first time. I have always loved the surrounding coastal countryside, but until now, the village has only ever symbolised ugliness and evil to me. Picking up speed, as the road takes another dip, I free-wheel past a row of pretty cottages that nudge their way onto the street, as if they crave attention from passers-by. Painted pastel shades of blue, yellow and pink, they have walled gardens in the same-coloured stone. At this time of the morning, the village is usually silent, but today it is alive with activity; as if it knows change is on its way. There is a twitch at every net curtain as I continue my journey. The sun, high in the sky behind me, acts like a giant hand, propelling me forward, in case I chicken out.

There is a small huddle of villagers up ahead. Obviously, word of what is about to happen has got around already, which was my intention after all. At first, I fear that they will bar my way but as soon as I ring the bell on my bike, they move aside. Relieved to discover they are no threat to me, my courage soars.

'Hello, Mrs Blackwell. How are you?' I enquire chirpily, taking the tall woman by surprise. I can guess what she is thinking, *the bloody audacity of her.*

'Mr Edwards. Lovely morning, isn't it?'

I cannot resist tormenting them. It is not as if they do not deserve it. It is worth it, to see them staring at me in open-mouthed amazement. They know my story. They are aware of what I have done but because of who and what I am, they must tolerate me as best they can. If they are to carry on as they have always done, they need me, as they needed my father before me, especially now Daniel is no longer around. Little Downey has always been good at covering up deaths. There was no inquest after my father died, nor was there one when Daniel and his mother disappeared. A tragic accident, I believe they called it.

'You're looking well, Mrs Gibbs.' I nod at one of Daniel's most loyal customers.

Instantly, she becomes like a statue; afraid of being singled out. She needn't bother. I have only one thing on my mind. There it is, looking exactly as I imagined it would—

It is over nine months since I last saw it. During that time, I have meticulously planned and organised its refurbishment, but this is the first time I have ventured into the village to see it for myself. The absence of a butcher's shop in the village must have driven the villagers crazy, but the wait is over.

Braking sharply, I come to a stop in the street, feeling unexpectedly tearful and emotional. I have worked so hard and it looks, well... beautiful.

The green paintwork suits its surroundings and the candy-striped canopy, which makes me think of my father's favourite boiled sweets, gives it a picture postcard feel. You could argue that it looks more like a florist than a butcher's shop, but I tell myself this is not a bad thing. The new sign is up; right above the shop door where the old one used to hang. "Frank Powers and Daughter" it says.

***

As I tie an apron around my waist, I glance around the shop with pride. Everything sparkles like new—the glass counter, the seaside rock-striped walls and the shutters which let in glimpses of natural sunlight even when they are closed. In one corner, where the rusty old freezer used to stand, there is a sofa, where customers can help themselves to a coffee and a homemade sausage roll. My eyes do not linger on the cuts of meat on display, which bear the familiar "Slaughtered in Little Downey" stamp, but the dried herbs that dangle down from the ceiling to replace those awful meat hooks, do get my approval.

Timidly, as if fearful of annoying anyone, a man steps out of an internal door marked "Private. Staff only" and jumps in alarm when he sees me. Sam is a small, nervous man, prone to bouts of depression. He doesn't say much but he is always extremely polite and well mannered. Unassuming, he is calming to be around and more importantly, he is no gossip. Perhaps because of this, I trust him in a way I never expected to.

'Hello, Sam,' I say shyly.

'Mrs Har...Har..per. Miss Pow...ers.' Sam has a stutter, which comes and goes, according to his mood. 'I don't know what to call you,' he admits finally, with no trouble at all.

'Natalie will do just fine,' I tell him, knowing that he will never address me as such. He would see this as taking liberties.

Peering out of one of the gaps in the shuttered windows, I see a crowd has gathered outside. The way they squawk amongst themselves reminds me of a wake of vultures. Fearing I might lose my nerve, I turn to Sam for reassurance, but he offers none, just stands up a bit taller, which kind of has the same effect. Releasing the wooden louver blind with a nervous ping, I turn the sign on the door to open and take my place behind the counter. There is little I can do about my trembling hands, which show me up as the imposter I am.

First to enter is the pub landlady, who has the aura of a faded movie star about her. I watch her bosom-barge her way past the other middle-aged ladies, who suck in their breaths in an insulted fashion, but nevertheless fall obediently in line behind her.

Little Downey eyes, all of them.

I cannot remember her name, but I do know that she always had a soft spot for my father, so I am hoping she will be kind to me.

'Mrs Owen,' I squeak, suddenly remembering her surname.
'Natalie.' She gives nothing away.

As I wait for her to place an order, I find myself staring at the large gold earrings which jangle against her solid neck. When I see that they also have Sam's attention, I smile inwardly. This is exactly the sort of thing to put his fragile nerves on edge.

'What will it be?' Sam barks impatiently, as if we are taking up far too much of his time. His authority takes us all by surprise.

'I'll have a pound of sausages, please,' the landlady cowers at Sam's strict tone but her eyes seek out mine, insistent upon me personally serving her.

Rising to the challenge, I slip on a pair of gloves and weigh and wrap up the sausages without making too much of a hash of it. But when I eventually hand the packet over, I become aware that everyone's critical eyes are on me.

'Will that be all?' I gulp.

'And four slices of that smoked bacon.' Defiantly, she points to the glass counter.

She raises an over-plucked eyebrow when I deliberately add an extra rasher of bacon to her order. Knowing that this will get tongues wagging, I ring up the purchase on the till. It is a long time since I helped my father in the shop but I remember everything he taught me.

'I was sorry to hear about your husband and mother-in-law,' the pub landlady says, her blunt face softening a fraction. 'Some sort of accident, wasn't it?'

I smile as if I am in agreement with her but refuse to be drawn on the subject.

'I have a little something special out back,' I offer cautiously, carefully choosing my words. 'If you're interested, that is.'

It feels to me as if the whole shop— me, Sam and the landlady included, all share the same meaningful look. When she nods enthusiastically, I slide my eyes in Sam's direction, hardly daring to believe we could have won them over this easily.

'Sam?'

Dragging his feet in an unhurried way, as if he doesn't want to miss anything, Sam disappears into the back room, quietly closing the door behind him.

'You're your father's daughter all right, Natalie,' the pub landlady squeals excitedly, her shopping bag open at the ready. As if she had always been on my side, she nods importantly to those queuing behind her.

When Sam comes back through with the parcel of meat, I hand it to her without looking at it. Without so much as a thank you, it disappears into her bag. She rummages around in her handbag, for what seems like forever, before eventually taking out her purse.

'Why don't I put that on your account.' I wave the purse away.

'Thank you very much.'

I watch her almost blush with pleasure as the purse speedily finds its way back into the crammed handbag. Gesturing to the shopping bag dangling by her side, I cough deliberately, to draw attention to what I am about to say.

'You will find nothing has changed since my father's day,' I declare loudly.

Chapter 73

The House By The Sea

Having been born angry, the baby never stops crying. The only time he settles is when I drive the thirteen miles to the next village where the child minder lives. Once there, he is as good as gold. *Is it my fault?* I ask myself for the hundredth time. I am seriously starting to believe that babies can be born hating their parents. No matter what I try to do with him, like change his nappy or bottle feed him, he fights me at every opportunity. I can't think why my father ever longed for a boy. They are horrid, I decide.

Because I have insisted on changing his nappy, he is bawling his head off. I pace the kitchen, doing all the things I am supposed to do, like patting him on the back to bring up wind and removing his Babygro so he is free to kick his legs, but all to no avail.

Darkly plays with her toys on the floor but sometimes frowns at me, as if she thinks I am deliberately making her little brother cry. In these moments, she is so like Merry, I have to catch my breath. When did the child get to be so grown up? In my mind, she is not yet four, but she appears older; could easily be mistaken for a five-year-old.

Turning my attention back to my squawking son, I ask myself if he is like this because I couldn't breastfeed him. There was a good reason for that, but it's not something I like to think about. Not then. Not now. Darkly was such a good baby. Easy in comparison. Although they are different, they do share similarities—they each have the same strawberry-pink birthmark on their back.

When the frying pan on the hob bubbles and splatters, I put the baby down in his bouncy chair and he immediately stops crying. I want to call him names, but that would not be nice. He is just a baby, after all. Stepping over Darkly's toys, I go over to the range and take the frying pan off the heat, keeping one eye on the baby, who is contentedly dribbling on his fingers and staring wide eyed around the room.

Turning my attention back to the frying pan, just in time as it happens, a blob of burning hot oil splatters out of the pan onto my hand.

'Shit.' I remember, in time, to say this under my breath so Darkly does not pick me up on it. She sees and hears everything, that child.

I suck my hand to cool it. *I don't know why I don't go straight to the tap and run cold water over it, but I do not.* Instead, I watch fascinated as the oil continues to sizzle and splat out of the pan onto the range, leaving angry little fat balls everywhere.

Drip. Splat. Drip.

When I next glance up, there is a man standing in the open doorway. The first thing I notice about him is that he looks at home leaning against the doorpost. About the same height as me, he has grey shoulder-length hair tied in a ponytail.

'Jed,' I exclaim.

I cannot say for sure if I am pleased to see him or not. The last time we met, he was bearded and scruffy but he is now back to his good-looking clean-shaven self. How could I have forgotten his mismatched eyes? One blue. One brown. Why haven't I missed waking up to them every morning? Then, I look at my children, Darkly in particular, and I know why.

'You don't seem surprised,' he declares in the familiar singsong Irish accent I never thought to hear again.

It is true. Now that I come to think of it, I am not the least bit surprised. What does flummox me though, is the fact I cannot seem to get any words out. We have a million and one things to say to each other, yet we stand there gawping stupidly at one another.

Eventually, he tears his eyes away from mine long enough to glance down at Darkly, who stares back at him with Merry's eyes.

'She gets more like her every day.'

'She calls *me* Mummy now.'

My critical tone surprises him. Truth is I don't know where it came from myself.

'And so, you are.' He gestures to the baby. 'What did you have?'

'A boy,' I reply tersely, wondering what has gotten into me. This is Jed. My Jed. And he is back. 'We call him Frank.' I find a smile for him at last, but I think it arrives too late. Jed doubts me now. I can see it in his face.

'I hear you've re-opened the shop,' he states, without any trace of disapproval.

'Well, I *am* a butcher's daughter.'

Except perhaps not in the way you imagine, I secretly think.

'I don't know how to be anything else.' I laugh off any embarrassment I might feel.

Darkly tugs at my hand, her eyes darting nervously between me and Jed. 'Who that man?'

'Go and play on the swing,' I order coldly. 'I'll call you when dinner is ready.'

Jed and I remain silent as Darkly clatters outside in a pair of high-heel shoes that are way too big for her. I have no idea where she got them from. They are certainly not mine. I would never wear anything so fashionable or uncomfortable.

For something to do, I lay the table. These days my mother's willow-patterned china service comes out at every meal. I hate to see it go to waste.

'Sit down. Stay for some dinner,' I say in a friendlier tone.

'Thanks,' he says, coming in proper.

Not wanting to assume anything, I turn to him and say, 'I take it you *are* planning on staying a while?' In a way, it would be unbearable if this were not his intention.

He throws me a casual nod, not wanting to give away too much, then sits down at the table. I swear that his eyes never once leave my face. My skin burns because of this.

'You're looking well,' he observes.

'After two babies,' *there's that stupid nervous laugh again,* 'I'll take that as a compliment.'

'Just one baby, Natalie.'

It is my turn to be surprised. I would never have thought Jed would pick me up on such a thing. He is right of course but the reminder was unnecessary and, in my opinion, cruel. Trying to hide my feelings from him, I go over to the frying pan and turn the joint of meat over so that the other side will brown.

'There was a time you couldn't look at it without wanting to throw up,' he observes.

He is doing too much observing for my liking, I decide, so I am relieved when he flicks through a large reference book lying open on the table. As soon as his back is turned, I peel off a thin strip of barely cooked meat and pop it in my mouth. It is a childish gesture, I know, but I want to get back at him for what he said.

'Just thinking about what they did makes me sick to my stomach,' he pulls a face, then continues flipping through the pages of the book. 'There's a lot to talk about. Merry for one thing. And the police.'

'You haven't said anything.' Fear makes me grip onto the handle of the frying pan. Sensing panic in my voice, he twists in his chair to look at me. It is his turn to feel hurt.

'I wouldn't put you or Darkly in any danger. You know that. But once we're away from here…'

His words make my heart sink. Today started out so promising but now it is filled with a bittersweet menace. Although Jed does not know it, his very existence threatens ours. Our whole way of life depends on his silence. Darkly can never leave Little Downey. It would be the death of her. Send her mad even.

'After dinner, Jed.' I play for more time. 'When the children are in bed. We'll talk then.'

Seeming reassured, Jed turns his attention back to the book. I have no idea where it came from. I am certain it was not there before.

'Is this the book I sent you?' he asks.

I want to tell him that I don't know, that I thought he had brought it with him. But I say nothing. Luckily, he doesn't require an answer.

'I never read it properly before. Never got the chance,' he admits.

When the tone of his voice changes, I know that he is reading from the book.

'Human cannibalism.' He grimaces. 'Forty-two cases discovered worldwide between 1911 and 2017. Clinically proven to be…' he begins.

I know for certain that the book and the subject matter have nothing to do with me, because I would never leave such a thing out for Darkly to find. Yet, while he pauses, and I wait and wait and wait, I find myself holding my breath, till it hurts.

'Extremely addictive.'

Aware that the grease from the fatty piece of lamb is trickling down my chin, I remove the pan from the hob and stare at the back of Jed's head.

What if I start…

What if I start doing it again?

A numbness creeps over me as I hear myself repeatedly asking Dr Moses the same question. But Jed's voice droning on in the background brings me back to the present. *Oh God, he is such a stupidly slow reader*, I think spitefully, wondering when he will ever shut up. But then it hits me that I already know the answer to that question.

'Long-term side effects have been known to cause dramatic instability…'

There is a catch to his voice as he pauses. Here it comes—

'Of the brain.'

At last he turns to face me, a startled look of fear and comprehension dawning in his different-coloured eyes.

'It's taken you a long time to figure it out, hasn't it, Jed?' I state coldly.

With the force of someone far stronger than myself, I hit him sideways on with the frying pan, catching the top and side of his head. Everything happens in slow motion. Bone splinters. Blood splatters. There is a sickening thud and a stunned silence as he goes down.

Where the joint of meat ends up, I do not know, but the hot meat fat continues to drizzle down Jed's sun-weathered face, and I thank God it is over, that he cannot feel the pain. But then, his eyelids blink open, to stare accusingly at me, and I realise with a heavy heart that he is stunned, not dead. Pulse racing with terror, I imagine that both of his eyes have turned blue, yet I know that to be impossible. Deciding I cannot have him looking at me in such a reproachful way, I am left with no choice but to raise the frying pan again.

Second guessing me, Jed rolls onto his front and desperately tries to crawl towards the door. I am reminded yet again of the pig in the slaughterhouse, frantically trying to get away. Like that pig, Jed is going nowhere. His movements are painfully slow, and a deep head wound leaves behind a trail of blood on the floor.

The baby watches Jed with interest, bouncing up and down in his chair, as if encouraging him to move faster. This is so cute. I manage to find a smile for him, before turning my attention back to my beautiful gypsy lover. Deciding that it would be kinder to put him out of his misery before he reaches the door, I go to stand over him. Sensing that my shadow is looming, he turns to look up at me. His eyes are filled with such sadness, I want to cry. *Don't plead. Don't beg. It will all be over soon.*

Without any hesitation, I bring the frying pan down with such force on his battered head, the cast iron structure splits into two, right down the middle. This time, when his eyes change colour, to a milky white, I know that it is done.

When the baby renews its crying, I drop the remains of the handle, and walk over to pick him up. Straightaway, I rock him.

This always used to do the trick for Darkly, but not so my son, who continues to sob into my shoulder. Ignoring the blood splats on both our faces, I gaze into his perfectly blue eyes and share some perfectly good advice.

'Never trust a man who *isn't* your father. That's Natalie's law.'

Chapter 74

Little Downey Beach – Darkly

It is dusk. Soon, any remaining snippets of daylight will disappear, along with Darkly's tears. On no account must her mother know that she has been crying. In her world, tears are not allowed. Rubbing her reddened eyes, she sways on the swing hanging from the branch of a dying apple tree and scuffs her bare feet in the sandy soil. She doesn't smile, as other children do, but nobody ever notices or comments on this peculiarity.

She does not take her eyes off the house by the sea, hoping that the door will eventually open and her mother will come out to welcome her back inside. She knows better than to try to go back in before being asked. Sometimes she can be out here for hours. Once, she spent a whole night outside, alone and forgotten about. Scratching her arm until it reddens, Darkly stops what she is doing as soon as she sees her mother come onto the porch. Ambling over, she pulls down the sleeves on her top to hide the fresh scratches on her arms but doesn't know why she bothers. Nobody ever looks at her that closely.

Her mother is mostly in shadow but Darkly can make out the shape of a butcher's saw in her hand. Blood drips from the saw onto the porch decking.

Drip. Splat. Drip.

Darkly had dared to hope that this time would be different. The man seemed so nice. Not like the others. But the faraway look on her mother's face tells a different story. It is unnerving for Darkly to have her mother stare at her as if she doesn't exist. She has that certain look in her eye again. The one that warns Darkly not to tell the truth, under any circumstances. The truth only makes her mother angry and confused. Usually, her mother's eyes are as black as a raven's but right now they are smoky grey. The colour reminds Darkly of ash left behind after a fire has burnt itself out. At times like this, Darkly knows it is best to avoid her mother, but she wants to find out about the man. For some reason she cannot comprehend, he is important to her.

'Who that man, Mama?' Darkly asks, trying to peer through the open door into the kitchen. She wants to see. She doesn't want to see.

'What man, darling?' Her mother is vague.

Darkly can tell that her mother does not want to come back from the secret recesses of her mind, where she is hiding. But she must. Tugging impatiently on her hand, Darkly watches her mother's beautiful face fill with confusion, quickly followed by anger.

'I don't see any man,' her mother snaps. 'Have you been making things up again?'

Shaking her head in fearful denial, Darkly backs away, but is nowhere near quick enough.

'You must stand up straight. Don't slouch.' With nipping fingers, her mother shakes her hard, until her head wobbles on her shoulders. Biting her lip, Darkly prays that her tears will go unnoticed. But her mother notices everything when it suits her.

'No tears, Darkly.' Her mother tuts, abruptly letting go. 'Mama won't tolerate it.'

Darkly is saddened to see the distant look return to her mother's eyes. At least while she is being shaken and shouted at, she is being shown attention. Now, as if she were in a world of her own, her mother hums a song to herself. This is nothing new. Whenever she gets like this, the same depressing tune shows up, like an unwelcome visitor. Then, unexpectedly, her mother marches back into the house and slams the porch door shut.

Chapter 75

The House By The Sea – Natalie

As I step over Jed's dead body, I amuse myself by wondering if his hand will snake out and grab my ankle. Isn't that what happens in scary movies? But this is no movie, I remind myself, pausing to stare at what is left of him. His chest has been split down the middle, the skin is lying in folds by his side. The intestines and organs have been removed and sit in a bloody pile on an old-fashioned butcher's weighing scales. I have made such a neat job of cutting up Jed's body, I do not think my father could have done better.

Going over to the sink, I drop the butcher's saw in a bowl of soapy water and turning on a tap, I let the cold water rinse away the blood on my hands. I stand there much longer than I should, gazing dreamily out of the window, remembering the day Jed showed up outside. He came back for me, like he said he would. *Poor Jed.* If only things could have been different. But thinking like this will only make me maudlin. The trouble is it is too quiet out here, even for me. The silence is suffocating. The baby, *I must start thinking of him as Frank*, is asleep, *thank goodness,* and Darkly is outside playing on her swing. She never gets tired of being outdoors. Such a happy little thing. We do not get any visitors out here so it's just me and the children most of the time. It can be a lonely life, but it is best this way.

When I sense movement behind me, I don't think anything of it at first. But when I hear the scrape of a shoe being dragged on the floor, I spin around so fast I think something inside my head pops.

It is impossible. There is no way—

Even I am not crazy enough to believe that this could be happening.

'You're dead,' I say accusingly to Jed's corpse, which has somehow pulled itself into a sitting position on the floor, surrounded by a large puddle of his own blood.

I watch in disbelief as Jed tries to stretch the trimmed back skin over the empty cavity of his chest, pulling a sad, confused face when he realises his organs are no longer there. His face is badly burned, almost cooked in parts, and bits of meat stick to his hair. When he stops what he is doing to stare at me, my blood runs cold.

'You're not real. You don't exist,' I hiss, reaching blindly for the butcher's saw. But as my hand settles around the handle, I am hit by a memory so strong and powerful, I drop it.

There is a man standing in the open doorway. The first thing I notice about him is that he looks at home leaning against the doorpost. About the same height as me, he has grey shoulder-length hair tied in a ponytail.

'Jed,' I exclaim.

'Sorry.' He throws me a quizzical look, seems embarrassed even. 'You must have me confused with somebody else. The name's Tom. Tom Banks. I'm looking for my dog. Lost him on the beach. He's old and deaf and I'm worried about him.'

He looks like Jed. Sounds like Jed. But—

When the porch door slams shut of its own accord, the jarring travels the length of my body. I glance fearfully back at the other doorway, but the man calling himself Tom Banks has vanished and Jed's body is as it was – dead and butchered on the kitchen floor.

That's when the music eerily starts to play. Nina Simone's haunting track 'I Put A Spell On You' wraps itself around me, like a protective blanket. The song, once a favourite of my mother's, and now mine too, soothes me as no other can. It lures me into the living room, but my movements are unnaturally slow, as if my body does not belong to me. My eyes feel incredibly heavy and my feet make no sound on the floor. I watch, fascinated, as the heavily scratched record spins around on the old-fashioned player. My first thought, on seeing it, is when did all this old stuff return? Didn't Daniel throw out the record player and my mother's willow-patterned dinner service when I was still in Thornhaugh?

Thornhaugh seems such a long time ago now. A different life almost. As for Daniel, I can barely remember what he looked like, although I will never forget his smell. Who could? Realising that the music has stopped, I lift the needle and gently replace it on the vinyl. As the opening ballad plays once more, I think I hear laughter coming from somewhere inside the house.

'Is that you, Mother?' My voice is a whisper, barely discernible above the music, but it is enough to drive the laughter away.

When my glance settles on a framed photograph turned face down on the mantelpiece, a sense of dread takes hold of me and won't let go. *Where has it come from? Why is it turned face down? Has it been there all along? Have I been ignoring its existence?*

Sweat trickles down the back of my neck as I walk over to the fireplace. My hands shake so much, I have to take a deep breath before I am physically able to pick up the photograph. Even when it is in my hands, I do not turn it over. I keep my eyes closed as more forgotten memories assail me. I feel them crawling over me, like vermin, digging their way in.

'And there's no mad woman in the cellar out to get me?' I hear my own voice, back from the past, intent on tormenting me.

'Nobody is out to get you, Natalie.' Calming reassurance from Dr Moses. *'I have a copy of your mother's death certificate right here if you want to see it.'*

Next thing I know, I am in Little Downey cemetery watching my seven-year-old self at my mother's funeral. *There are a great many people there, villagers mostly, but it pours with rain, and a sea of umbrellas has gone up around the grave. Six men, including a tearful Bob Black, carry her coffin, but only two are needed. Towards the end, my mother barely weighed a thing. She never overcame her battle with anorexia, which the doctors warned would kill her in the end, but it was depression and a sense of desperation that sent her over the cliff edge that day.*

My father holds my hand tightly, until it hurts. The black suit he is wearing looks big on him and his face is gaunt and grey. Today is the first time he's shaved in over a week and his skin is covered in small cuts. He is doing what he warned me not to—sobbing unrestrainedly, while my eyes remain dry. A boy with yellow hair and bright blue eyes edges forward to stand next to me. He surprises me by taking my other hand in his. I like the feel of his hand better than my father's, so I reward him with a smile and right there on the spot I commit myself to a lifelong friendship with him.

Fighting back tears, *I don't yet know why I am crying but I sense that the reason, when it eventually hits me, will knock me off my feet,* I glance down at the photograph in my hands, too terrified to turn it over and look at it.

The voices. Oh my God the voices. They won't go away.

'I want my wife back, that's all.' I hear the voice of the boy I have known all my life, overwrought and filled with emotion. *'What happened to the girl I married?'*

Chapter 76

Unable to stand it any longer, I turn the photograph over and what I see does indeed bring me to my knees. At the same time, the music comes to an abrupt halt, needle scratching on vinyl, and the room fills with ghostly white noise.

The white lace dress. Smiling faces. Confetti in our hair. It is a picture of Daniel and I on our wedding day. We look extremely happy. The red brick walls of Thornhaugh loom menacingly in the background but it makes sense that I would be married from there. Tracing Daniel's face with my finger, my tears spill onto the photograph, blurring both our faces. I cannot wipe them away quickly enough. I think I am about to die from shock, but I clench my eyes together and force myself to go back to that day.

Confetti everywhere, even on our eyelids, but we don't notice or care. We only have eyes, sparkling ones at that, for each other. Daniel's eyes are blue, like my beloved ocean, and I intend to swim in them every day for the rest of my life. He can't take his eyes off me. Knowing this makes me tingle all over. I can't wait for him to unzip me out of my beautiful wedding dress. Rather stupidly, I left the price tag on and it itches like mad.

As we kiss on the grand staircase, a chorus of cheers go up. All our friends and family are here. Not one of them made it through the ceremony with a dry eye. Daniel's mother, wearing a hideous purple number, stands next to Bob Black who fidgets in a shirt and tie. Every time he looks at me, he is reminded of my mother. This is why he acts oddly around me. The poor man always loved her, even after she married my father, but she never looked twice at him. He wasn't the only one. Andrew Muxlow was another of her admirers, but his obsession drove him mad. They say he ended up in Thornhaugh too.

As we come down the staircase, I search the upturned faces of our wedding party, hoping to see my father.

I would recognise the pale blue suit he is wearing anywhere, having helped him choose it. A few hours ago, when I was still Natalie Powers, not Natalie Harper as I am now, I pinned that pink buttonhole to his jacket. As usual, he stands at the back, not wanting to draw attention to himself. But he can't disguise the look of pride on his face.

When Daniel first asked for my hand in marriage, my father cried tears of joy. Having Daniel for a son-in-law means the world to him. Not only does Daniel know the butchery trade inside and out, they get along famously too. My father is more relaxed, knowing I will be taken care of in his absence. I was always such a worry to him. It also pleases him that he has somebody to leave the business to. Back then, there was never much chance of me becoming a butcher. Back then, we did not know that my father wouldn't survive another year.

My legs are curled under me as I sit on the floor, cradling the photograph in my arms as if it were a child. I wish, desperately, that I *was* a child again, without responsibility or any past to speak of. I would give anything to have my father with me. A girl needs her daddy. Rocking myself backwards and forwards, I try not to think of his last days. But the memories keep on coming and there is nothing I can do to stop them.

Surrounded by a labyrinth of tubes and wiring attached to monitors, my father lies in a comatose state in a private hospital room. His condition is weak, critical. Although he has an oxygen mask strapped to his face, his breathing is laboured. I want to loosen the elastic strap around his face, which has left a deep red mark, but we have been told not to interfere. We are only allowed to hold his hand. So, we sit either side of the bed, Daniel, and I, each clinging on to a lifeless hand, hoping for a miracle.

My father's eyes are closed but his mouth is open. I find out for the first time that he has a black filling at the back of his mouth. I do not know why this should fascinate me, but it does. He wears a blue gown with tiny flowers on it and I badly want to slap the nurse who put it on him. I am glad he cannot see it, doesn't know. It would offend his masculinity.

My father's swollen legs gape through the gown. They are yellow and blue. His jaundiced skin is almost the same colour as the vase of daffodils on the bedside table. Whenever a nurse comes into the room to shine a torch in his eyes, I notice that they are yellow too. The blue of Little Downey has already left his body.

'And father? When did he die?' I hear myself asking Daniel.

'Must be three years ago now. Liver disease.'

I remember that Daniel hadn't been able to speak of my father's passing without showing emotion for the man he loved as if he were his own father.

Too hard. Too cruel. Too unforgiving. My father didn't deserve to suffer as he did. *But you do, Natalie.* The thought comes from nowhere, poking me with its destructive finger. Sitting up suddenly, *no slouching, Natalie,* as if a bolt of lightning had passed through me, I finally get to know the person I am. She has been hiding for a very long time.

The cockerel is too plump for its own good. I have seen it strutting around outside, stealing all the corn and bossing the others about. Because he is hopping mad most of the time, we call him Fury. His eyes are blood orange with a small black dot in each of them. The dots are furious with me, I can tell, because until now, nobody has got close enough to handle him. Not my father, nor Daniel either. I am the first to manage it. He clucks wildly and tries to peck me as I swing him upside down by the legs.

Placing him on the wooden block, which is stained dark red from years of use, I press down on his brown and white body, so he does not flap around too much. His head twists this way and that, but as the shadow of the axe looms, he freezes in terror. As if he knows.

Day changes to night and I am kneeling in the roadside. The pickup truck is parked a few feet away and the driver's door swings open. There is no one else around, so I am not sure how I got here. I don't drive, do I? Or do I? I am bent over an injured dog. It is a tall scruffy lurcher type. Looks as if a car has hit it. Its soft brown eyes appeal to me for help but the rest of its body twitches uncontrollably. When I place my hands on the dog's jaw and skull, it whines, as if it thinks it is being petted one last time. Then, with a quick skilful movement, I break its neck—forcing its head up and at an angle, not sideways like in the movies. That doesn't work at all. I know it is done when the dog's head flops into my lap.

'I ain't afraid of nothing or nobody, 'cept you and your madness.' My father bawled those condemning words at me on more than one occasion. Now, I understand why. Glancing down at the photograph, I wonder where all the tears have gone. I see my reflection in the glass, yet I do not recognise myself. White face. Black eyes. Long black tangled hair. I could be my mother. I could be Merry.

'Is this me?' I whimper. 'Is this who I am?'

Dr Moses was right when he said I was like a ghost, flitting in and out of people's lives, barely there at any one time. Mostly, I have been absent, spending long periods at Thornhaugh, constantly reliving the same nightmares until they felt like my reality and growing ever distrustful of my family. Everybody I knew insisted that my mother was dead, but I refused to accept this. By imagining she was still alive, I was able to convince myself that I was not insane—they were. Is that why I stopped taking my medication, to prove a point? Even though I had been warned coming off it could increase my psychotic imaginings. Some things remain true though. The cannibalism for one thing. As my father explained, the village has been dependent on human meat since before the war. Generation to generation has kept this craving going. This dependency contributed to everybody's craziness in Little Downey. We are socially awkward for a reason.

Despite all I have learnt about myself, I feel an overwhelming sense of relief that I did not kill my mother, that my father died surrounded by people he loved, not by a bolt gun on his own property. I thank God too that Merry was not turned into a piece of meat because the brother and sister never existed outside my imagination. Merry was everything I wanted to be. I see that now.

As for Jed, I realise I used him to help fuel my fantasies. He was my partner in crime. But even he betrayed me in the end. 'Yours is the biggest secret of all,' he had warned me. And he was right.

The man in the kitchen is not Jed. Just some poor unfortunate stranger who made the fatal mistake of knocking on our door. Shouldn't the severe gloomy cliff edge have kept him away? Gradually, it dawns on me that everything Daniel ever told me was true. He was never a threat to me or Darkly – I was my own enemy all along.

That must mean that Darkly is mine too. Of course, she is. All that hair. Those dark black eyes, so like my own and my mother's before me. Whatever made me think they were blue? But what about the birthmark? Quickly, I pull down my top, so I can look over my shoulder at the skin there. Sure enough, the same strawberry pink birthmark that both my children have inherited is there for anyone to see. My mother had the same mark too, I remember.

Although I am pleased to discover that Darkly is my own, I do not forget the horrible truth, which is lurking around the corner, waiting to mow me down.

Daniel. Daniel. Daniel.

The love of my life. How could I have known? *How could I have not known?*

'It's not my fault.' I start crying again, uncontrollably this time. Anger is building inside me. Soon it will erupt. 'Not my fault.' I shake my head wildly. 'They have made me like this. Turned me into one of them.'

LIAR.

I look down to see Daniel's face smiling up at me from the picture frame. I close my eyes, not wanting to see, not wanting to know.

COWARD.

At this, my eyes flash open. *I am a Powers and we are not cowards.* Hurling the photograph against the wall, where it shatters, I make up my mind never to look at it again. I feel my face contorting with pain and horror. This level of sickening self-awareness will drive me mad, insane. I will never be able to escape it.

'Oh God, what have I done?'

Somebody is screaming. A raw tormented howl of anguish. I clasp my hands over my ears, unable to bear it. *Shut up. Stop, please.* I drive my thumbnail into one of the blue veins on my wrist, until the pain is excruciating.

Still, the screaming goes on.

'I am somebody's wife. Somebody's mother.'

The person who is screaming is me.

Chapter 77

Little Downey Beach – Darkly

Gulls scream and take to the sky when they see Darkly plodding dejectedly along the beach, dragging her bare feet in the sand. Choosing not to walk in a straight line, she zigzags, leaving behind an unpredictable pattern of child-size footprints. Gazing up at the gulls, as they circle over the house by the sea, she wonders if they know. If they sense anything. But then, turning her attention back to the ocean that she loves, she realises the tide, which has been coming in this last hour, has changed its mind, and is pulling away from the cliff edge as if it knows her family's terrible secrets and cannot bear to go any closer.

The house by the sea, towering above the cliff top, remains in creepy darkness. She is tired, oh so tired, and hungry too. Having already skipped lunch and dinner, her stomach constantly rumbles. As soon as she has eaten, *if she ever gets to eat,* she will go straight to bed and forget this day ever happened. She's getting good at that. She is a natural storyteller. Everyone says so. Everyone except her mother, that is.

As the tide recedes, it leaves behind a trail of bones in the sand. Unsurprised by them, Darkly picks one up and scoots it into the sea. It lands with a silly plop that makes her giggle. Picking up another larger bone, shaped rather like a human arm, she pretends it is a sword and play fights with an imaginary foe. But as soon as she sees a dim light appear in one of the downstairs windows, she drops the bone and races towards home. It is the sign she has been waiting for. Dinnertime at last.

Epilogue

Today

You wake up in a strange place surrounded by strange people. You know they are strange because they all have the same icy blue eyes and blank expressions. You have no idea where you are, or who you are even. But wait, you remember something. Something from before.

Too late. The fleeting memory is gone. Much as you try, you cannot get it back again. So, you focus on what is going on around you instead. There is a scrape of metal. Hiss of plastic. You are surrounded by whispers, faraway at first, then close, then distant again. Your eyes feel heavy, but the stench of stale urine and bleached hallways keeps you awake. Through a crack in the door, you catch a glimpse of an ornate chandelier and a majestic oak staircase.

A cold draught wraps itself around you, like the arms of someone you have never met, and in the distance, you hear the flush of a toilet, the hum of a radio—ordinary sounds that you once took for granted. Somewhere out there, in the real world, beyond the stained-glass windows, mothers are pushing babies in prams, people are jogging, catching a train or sending text messages. A man is helping a woman change a tyre on her car. An affair is going on in a cheap hotel. You wish you were any one of them.

They are talking. Telling you things you're supposed to know, but you don't. Why don't you remember? And why are you strapped to the bed? Is it because you are a danger to yourself or to others? Why is it so important to them that you remember? More importantly, what if you remember and start doing it again?

Drip. Splat. Drip.

You think there must be a tap leaking somewhere, and when you strain your neck as far as it will go, you see water dripping from a faulty drink dispenser. You are so thirsty, you would give anything for a glass of it right now. Why did you not notice how dry your throat was? You then realise there are plenty of other things you haven't noticed until now. A drip attached to your right arm is one of them. Your skin looks wrinkled and old against the needle taped to your hand, as if it doesn't belong to you. Knowing there is nothing you can do to stop it, you obsessively follow the movement of whatever nasty substance is inside the IV bag as it slowly invades your veins.

A flurry of movement sends waves of perfumed air your way. There is a shuffle of sensible shoes. A gleaming of white teeth. You wonder what is going on. But then, in *he* comes, and you realise his appearance is not a surprise. Secretly, you have been expecting this moment. You thought you were so clever guessing the ending, didn't you? It wasn't what you hoped for, but in a way kind of expected. The clues were there all along.

Except for the eyes, he is just as described. Everything you imagined and more. Tall and handsome in a light grey suit, there is a sparkle of cufflink at his slender wrist and the colour of his hair matches his suit. His eyes though are not grey at all. You were misinformed about them. They are as blue as an ocean on the clearest coldest day. There is such a calming quality to them that you begin to fear that you are about to be hypnotised against your will.

'There you are. I suspect you're feeling tired, a little confused even?'

It feels strange having Dr Moses smiling down on you. Before you've even had chance to get over this fact, he's sitting on the edge of your bed, acting as if you and he are the best of friends. A nurse hovers in the background smiling in a way that is meant to reassure. She fails miserably. Busily, she counts out coloured pills in her hand and you wonder if they are for you. Correction. You *know* they are for you.

'You've got to forget everything you think you know. Subconscious suggestion, that's all it is.' Dr Moses removes a lid from a tray on your lap that you didn't even know was there.

'Don't worry.' He pats your hand in a fatherly fashion. You don't want it to stop, but it does, rather too quickly for your liking. 'We'll soon have you on your feet again.'

You almost believe him. You want to believe him. You feel as if you have known him a very long time. His ways are familiar to you. As is this building, now you come to think of it. Realising that something is expected of you, you look down on an unappetising plate of overcooked sausages, lumpy mash and peas, and fight off a feeling of nausea. When you glance back up, at Dr Moses' face, there is a smile waiting there for you and his blue eyes are full of encouragement. *Little Downey eyes.*

'Eat up,' he instructs. 'And then perhaps you'd like to go home.'

The End

Acknowledgements

As always, thank you to my publisher, Bloodhound Books and to the rest of the team who work tirelessly in the background. This was a complex story that required several re-writes. This meant publication was pushed back three times. However, Betsy and I were both in agreement that we wanted it to be the best book it could be. With her help, we managed to achieve this. I couldn't have done it without you Betsy! Huge thanks also to Alexina for initially recognising the book's potential and editor Morgen Bailey for all her hard work. Up until this point in my life I had no idea what onomatopoeic meant.

Special mention goes to a team of talented beta readers who provided support during the book's early stages. The Butcher's Daughter has gone through a lot of changes since then, but David McCaffrey, Sarah Denzil, Ross Greenwood, Darren Richards, Shani Struthers and Sean Turner all took time out of their exceptionally busy schedules to provide me with invaluable feedback —and I just want to say what superstars you all are.

After reading The Butcher's Daughter, you may have guessed that I am a vegetarian (vegan on a good day), but I want you to know that I am not precious about it. I would never preach to meat-eaters about my beliefs or expect them to alter their views. I have even been known to make bacon sandwiches for friends. But it may surprise you to know that I only turned vegetarian during the writing of this book. This came about during the early research phase when I visited local butcher shops and slaughterhouses to get a feel for such places. Although some were better than others, what I saw and heard there changed my mindset forever; my husband's too, after reading the first two chapters of this book.

I appreciate that some of the slaughterhouse scenes in The Butcher's Daughter could be upsetting for some. Several readers have told me that it put them off eating meat. These scenes might even attract poor reviews, but however gruesome and squeamish you find them—all I ask is that you remember these "killing days" are not fictional. Every year in the UK approximately 2.6 million cows, 10 million pigs, 14.5 million sheep and 950 million birds are "humanely slaughtered" for human consumption. I can assure you that vegetable slaughterhouses are a much nicer place to visit!

On that note, if you ever find yourself in New York, why not drop into the aptly-named "The Butcher's Daughter," a plant-based restaurant, juice café and veggie slaughterhouse, where they treat fruit and veg as a butcher would meat. The owner has been kind enough to ask me to drop in any time I am visiting to talk about my book.

Now that the serious part is over, I come to the best bit. This is when I get to thank my lovely readers for all their support, especially my ARC reading group. You know who you are! Your loyalty and friendship mean everything.